Barossa

BOOKS BY JOHN CLIVE:

KG 200 (with J. D. Gilman)
The Last Liberator

Barossa

by John Clive

Delacorte Press / New York

Published by
Delacorte Press
1 Dag Hammarskjold Plaza
New York, N.Y. 10017

"Mulga Bill's Bicycle" published by the Halstead Press, Sydney, Australia.

Manufactured in the United States of America

First printing

Designed by Laura Bernay

Library of Congress Cataloging in Publication Data

Clive, John.
    Barossa.

    I. Title.
PR6053.L53B37   1981   823'.914   80-26429
ISBN 0-440-00433-0

To my wife, Carole, and our two children, Alexander and Hannah, who have shared my joys and disappointments with equal enthusiasm. Also, for the Odeon cinema, North Finchley. Long since gone, but lives in happy memory, full of Errol Flynns and Alan Hales, and *Sea Hawks* on a Warner Bros. Spanish Main. . . .

When the sun shines in that blue suburban sky,
I hear "Penny Lane" and toy planes flyin' high.
I see metal glinting brightly
As they twist and turn above.
And I can hear them chatter,
But they're not the words of love.
Men are dying, men are burning,
Locked inside their fiery shell.
But to us it was a game,
We didn't know or feel their Hell.
We would watch them spiral earthwards,
Coming slowly down to die.
Then we cheered and clapped our hands,
Cos' our side still ruled the sky. . . .

—From "Children of the War,"
a song by John Clive

1. London, 1940

The boy was fascinated. He lay on his stomach in the long grass, not far from the spinney, the evening sun warm on his back. He could see the soldiers were working hard, stripped to the waist, the sweat glistening on them as they passed the sandbags along the human chain, from the lorry to the gun emplacement.

Other soldiers had the back-breaking task of stacking the sandbags around the gun, building a protective wall. But it was the undulating, wobbling dance of the barrage balloon as it slowly filled with gas that drew his eyes like a magnet. Great folds of silver silken material, gradually rolled upright, swelling as gas was pumped in. First the fins emerged. Then the fat, bulbous cigar-shaped body appeared, and it began to look a bit like the pictures he had seen of the airships. Slowly it filled out, assuming its final rounded shape. It was dumpy, silver, and beautiful. As it strained against the steel hawser, trying to fly, the boy was irresistibly reminded of Dumbo.

The golf course was alive with activity. Gun carriers wheeling in more anti-aircraft weapons. The lorries churning up the immaculate green carpet that had for years been the playground for those who could afford to play golf. Now a more deadly game was in prospect.

The boy was about eight years old, with fair hair and gray eyes. He was wearing short trousers and his shirt was torn where he had caught it on the iron railings that bounded the woods behind him. Soon the railings would disappear, consumed by the war effort that demanded every spare scrap of metal. Never before had the war seemed as exciting to the boy than at this moment. He had followed the progress of the battles in the newspaper every day. Trying to understand what was happening by studying the maps with their arrows pointing this way and that. He didn't see them anymore—no more arrows. Just black swastikas all the way up to the English Channel. The battles were lost in Europe. Now this, and for the first time he felt he wanted to go to school, to tell them what was happening on the golf course behind his house.

It was getting late, and he was feeling hungry; he knew he should have been back for his tea ages ago. He'd probably get a clout behind the ear unless he could quickly interest his mother in what was going on.

In the end hunger overcame his curiosity, and he turned and started to crawl back through the grass. The boy stayed close to the ground, the tall grass of the rough, yellowed by the sun, hiding his presence from the soldiers working around the battery. He had just reached the gap in the railings that divided the thin strip of woods from the course when he heard a twig snap. He stopped and laid his head on the ground, straining his ears, listening. He felt the ground vibrate slightly as someone moved through the grass near the railings in front.

He lay still, trying to control his breathing—it sounded like thunder in his ears. He could hear the grass swishing against legs as the muffled footsteps came closer, then the sound of a stick being drawn along the railings. He wanted to leap up and run for it, but the only way out was through the gap. He pressed his face into the grass and lay absolutely still. The sound of the stick on the railings reverberated in his head, then stopped suddenly.

It was quiet, just the distant sounds of the soldiers calling to each other as they worked; then a man's voice, almost on top of him:

"Hello, what are you doing here?"

The boy's heart leaped into his mouth. He buried his head deeper into the grass, hoping he would go away. He felt the man kneel down beside him, and a hand rested on his shoulder.

"Come on, get up—there's nothing to be afraid of."

Slowly the boy raised his head, leaning on his elbow. He saw a uniform, then a brown leather belt and buckles that shone brightly in the sunshine. He sat up, wiping away a piece of grass that had stuck to his forehead. He could see the holster now, hanging from the belt. The black handle of a pistol poked from beneath the loose flap. The officer smiled, aware of the boy's gaze.

"It's alright, I'm not going to shoot you, but you did give me quite a shock."

The boy didn't say anything. He studied the man, shielding his eyes from the sun. He was wearing an army officer's uniform and cap, and from beneath the brim the blue eyes seemed to be laughing at him.

"Come on, young man, speak up—what's your name?"

The boy cleared his throat, pulling himself slightly away from the officer.

"Billy," he said, then added almost inaudibly, "Billy Redston."

The officer sat down cross-legged in front of him. "Billy, eh? Where do you live?"

The boy waved his arm in the general direction of the woods. "Over that way."

The officer glanced toward the railings. "How did you get through those?"

"There's a gap," Billy said sullenly. He didn't want anyone else to know about it.

The officer pushed his cap back on his head and fished out a handkerchief from his pocket, slowly wiping the perspiration from his face, then from the leather hatband inside the cap. Billy watched him, fascinated by the gun still poking from the holster.

"You're not supposed to be here or watching what's going on down there." The officer nodded toward the battery, which was out of sight over the crest of the low hill. "I should report you, you know." The boy looked frightened and the officer waved an arm. "It's alright, I won't, but you will have to show me how you got here." He stood up and leaned down, offering the boy his hand. "Come on—first the gap in these railings." Billy gripped the officer's soft hand and clambered to his feet.

"It's just over here." He pointed toward a bush, then slipped around behind it, pushing it back and exposing a gap of about two feet. Three rungs of the railings were missing.

"Effective camouflage—I'd probably have missed that."

Billy gazed uncertainly at the officer, who slapped the side of his leg with his baton impatiently and said, "Lead on, boy. If I'm to cordon off this area efficiently I have to know how you got here."

Reluctantly Billy crawled through the gap in the railings. He hoped the officer would get stuck. He didn't want him to see his secret place in the woods, but the officer squeezed through without too much trouble and Billy led the way toward the woods. Perhaps he could go back a slightly different way. He stared at the ground in front of him. He'd worn a slight track on his visits to the golf course and he waited until they came to a large bush that barred the way to the spinney; then he veered left. He heard the officer stop behind him and he turned around. The eyes seemed to be smiling at him again. "I think the path goes this way." The officer pointed at the other side of the bush. The boy's face dropped and the officer could see his disappointment. He wondered why the boy had tried to lead him away.

The trees closed over their heads, patches of sunlight slanting through the gaps, the soft hum of insects vibrating within their warmth. The ground was soft, though there had been no rain for nearly a month. They came to a small clearing and the path divided, one trail veering off to the left, the other continuing forward. The boy marched stolidly onward. He heard the officer stop but continued to walk forward, hoping he would follow.

The officer watched the receding figure of the boy, sensing his determination. He called out, "Wait." The boy continued, ignoring him. Again, "Wait," this time more harshly. The boy stopped, not looking around. He seemed poised, almost ready to run.

"You're not going to try to run away, are you?" Then softly, the words echoing curiously in the small gap beneath the trees: "I still have the gun, you know."

Billy turned and looked back at the officer. His hand was resting on the flap of the holster, his eyes dark, obscured beneath the brim of the cap. He felt frightened. Then the officer pushed the cap back and grinned. "Come on, show me what's over here—it looks interesting."

Billy walked slowly in front of him toward the side of the clearing where the ground rose slightly in a bank covered by long grass and heavy undergrowth. A patch of grass had been flattened and the boy stopped in front of some foliage between two trees. He stood there for a moment unmoving, then said quietly, "It's my sanctuary." He didn't turn around. The officer stared intently, then slowly discerned the shape of a hide. The shadows of the overhanging branches and the careful way the boy had allowed the long grass to grow up around it made the hide almost impossible to spot unless one knew of its existence.

"That's marvelous," the officer said. The admiration in his voice lifted the boy's gloom. He turned and looked back at him.

"You like it?" The expression in his eyes uncertain, yet hopeful. The officer stepped closer, examining it.

"Yes, I do—it's very good. I'd never have found it unless you'd shown me." He didn't mention the faint track leading to it—he didn't want to disappoint the boy.

"How do you get inside?"

Billy untied a piece of string hidden behind a branch and pulled. A small hatch lifted slowly and the officer could see that the foliage camouflaging was losing its color.

"What do you do when the leaves on the hatch die?"

Billy tied off the string again, leaving the dark gap of the entrance exposed. "I have to change it every few days." He glanced up at the officer. "Do you want to look inside?" The officer looked dubiously at the darkened interior. "It's all right," Billy said. "I've got a torch in there." He crawled into the hide and pulled the torch from under a blanket that he'd removed from his bed. So far his mother hadn't discovered its loss. He switched on the torch and the officer crawled in beside him after removing his cap.

"May I?" He held out his hand for the torch and Billy gave it to him. He shone the beam around the interior. The boy had dug out a small area of the bank that formed the walls of the hide and built up a roof with young saplings interwoven with thin, pliable branches, which had in turn been covered by clods of grass that he had removed originally from the bank. One or two spiders scuttled around, alarmed by the intrusion, but the boy didn't seem to mind.

"It's terrific," the officer said admiringly. "You did this by yourself?"

Billy nodded. "Yes."

The officer brushed some dirt from his sleeve. "Am I the first one you've shown it to?"

The boy lowered his gaze. "Yes. I wanted it to be a secret." The boy was sitting on the blanket facing him, his legs drawn up in front of him.

The officer put his hand on the boy's knee. "I promise I won't tell anyone. It shall be our secret." Billy glanced at the officer, who was gazing at him intently, the light from the torch casting strange shadows on his face.

"You promise?"

"I promise. No one shall know of this place except you and me, Billy." His soft hand slid slowly up the inside of the boy's leg beneath the short trousers. It felt hot against Billy's flesh. The officer's face was close to him now, and he could see his eyes glittering, reflecting the light from the torch. Billy felt his throat constrict, bile in his mouth, dry with fear.

"I'll let you look at my pistol if you're a good boy." The soft hand was forcing itself higher up inside his trousers. His stomach muscles contracted, shrinking from the officer's hand. He tried to draw back, but the wall of the hide pressed into his spine. His hands clawed at the soft earth, trying to force himself away from the man, but there was nowhere to go; the hide was a prison, he had to get out. His reaction was instinctive, involuntary. He threw dirt into the face and mouth that was inches from his own. The officer fell backward. The soft hand pulled away from inside his short trousers, the man crying out, choking as he spat out the dirt, and trying to rub it frantically from his eyes. Billy leaped past him, out of the narrow entrance, and ran for the edge of the clearing. Suddenly the woods were around him again, his feet pounding into the soft mattress of long dead leaves and undergrowth. Shafts of sunlight flickering in his eyes. At last he reached another set of railings that bordered the edge of the woods from the narrow, rutted road that separated the spinney from the row of terraced houses backing onto it. Billy slipped through them, panting with relief, and ran to the front of his house, collapsing onto the doorstep, trying to regain his breath. The sun had disappeared behind his home and long shadows stretched out in front of him, almost reaching the other side of the road. He was sweating, but suddenly felt cold. He heard the air-raid siren slowly wind up to its mournful cry, dipping and rising like Billy's heartbeat. The Luftwaffe were coming early tonight. He rang the doorbell and waited for his mother to open it.

Billy followed his usual routine, collecting his books and a pillow to take down to their makeshift shelter beneath the stairs. They were late, and he was still in his room trying to decide which books to take when the battery opened up. The noise was deafening; it battered against Billy's eardrums in great waves of sound. His chest felt as though it were vibrating. He rushed to the window and pulled back the curtains. He could see the flashes of the anti-aircraft guns behind the trees of the spinney. But it was the sky that he gazed up at, dumbfounded. Red tracers of flak were spurting upward from the gun emplacements, gradually disappearing into the beams of the searchlights flickering among the clouds, which hung motionless, pale and ghostly. The beams formed white circles of light that would sometimes vanish into the black void between the cumulus.

His mother came rushing into the room and swept the

blackout curtains back across the window. She grabbed his pillow and some blankets and started pushing him down the stairs toward the shelter beneath them. She called to his grandfather, asking him to join them, but he wouldn't come. He complained bitterly about the noise, but no goddamn Germans were going to get him out of his bed.

Billy liked his Granddad. He liked his musky smell of pipe tobacco and crumpled clothing. His fingers, grimy with earth that had accumulated over the years, had worked into the cracks of his horny hand. As far as Billy knew, he'd always been a gardener. Sometimes he would tell him stories about the big houses he had worked for, and the people who lived in them. His Granddad had come to live with them after Billy's father had gone away three or four years before. Billy still shuddered when he remembered the fight between his parents, the shouts and screams, the bellows from his father, the crashes as crockery and saucepans were flung against the wall. Terrified, he had lain in his bed, burying his head beneath the pillow, trying to shut out the noise. Then, when he was about four, his father had gone, and the house seemed strangely quiet and peaceful. Billy was glad, and he would be much older before he began to miss him. . . .

Billy was trying to disentangle the line on his fishing rod when the front doorbell rang the following morning. He ran to the door, ignoring his mother's cry to let her answer it. He flung the door open and it crashed back against the wall. Billy had broken the stop two days before. He looked up and saw two men outlined by the bright sunlight behind them, standing on the porch. One of them spoke. He recognized the voice instantly. "Hello, Billy."

He stepped backward, grabbing the edge of the door,

and was about to slam it shut when his mother arrived.
She stopped him.

"What do you think you are doing?" There was an edge
on her voice and he knew she would have clouted him if
the two men had not been there. He said nothing and
stood quietly behind her as she turned and faced them on
the doorstep, smiling. "Yes?"

The officer touched the peak of his cap deferentially. "I
think Billy was slightly alarmed to see me, Mrs. Redston."

She was puzzled. "You know Billy?"

"Yes." He glanced at the air-raid warden beside him,
including him in the explanation. "I found Billy up on the
golf course yesterday watching our arrival. I told him he
shouldn't have been there, of course, and I was following
him back through the woods when he ran away."

Billy instinctively backed away from his mother into
the hallway before she could grab him.

"Come here," she commanded. Billy didn't move.

The officer interceded, immediately aware that the boy
had said nothing so far, and not wanting to precipitate
any explanations. "I really don't think you can blame the
boy too much, Mrs. Redston. He may well have been
frightened. And he certainly didn't lie to me about his
name." He moved quickly on, anxious to change the subject. "In any case that's not why I called to see you today."

Billy's mother turned around to face him, interested.
"Oh?"

The officer glanced again at the ARP man for support.
He cleared his throat and spoke for the first time.

"No, er . . . Mrs. Redston, we are going around all the
houses that border the golf course, checking the shelter
arrangements. Do you have an Anderson shelter in the
garden?"

Billy was clinging to the back of his mother's skirt. He
felt the officer's eyes upon him while they were talking

and glanced up. He was staring at him. There seemed to be no expression in his eyes; they were empty. Apprehensively he moved behind his mother again. She was calling for his grandfather. "Dad, can you come here a minute?"

He appeared in the kitchen doorway, removed the smelly old pipe that Billy loved from his mouth, and clasped it in his horny hand. He appraised the two men in the doorway as he approached, and nodded.

"Morning," he said tersely. Then turned to Billy's mother. "What is it, Betty?"

The officer interrupted. "May I explain, Mrs. Redston?" he said, somewhat over-politely.

The old man looked at him expressionlessly, waiting. Billy sensed that his grandfather was annoyed, but the officer pressed on.

"We've set up an anti-aircraft unit on the golf course. . . ."

The old man cut in. "I know, the bloody thing kept me awake all night."

The officer was slightly taken aback. "I daresay, but we are there to try and protect you, Mister, er . . ."

"Lindsay," the old man said dryly.

The officer eyed him uncomfortably for a moment, then continued. "Yes, well, the point is, we are trying to find out what your shelter arrangements are."

Billy watched his Granddad closely. He took a puff on the pipe, then said without undue emphasis, "I stay in my bed. The boy here"—he indicated Billy—"and his mother sleep beneath the staircase." He stared contemplatively at the officer through a cloud of tobacco smoke. The officer coughed affectedly, trying to indicate that the smoke was offensive to him. The old man continued to puff contentedly on the pipe.

"I'm afraid that's not good enough, Mr. Lindsay. . . ."

"Oh, yes it is," the old man said, deliberately misunderstanding him. "I specially re-enforced that area myself and nothing'll bring it down except a direct hit. Even in a shelter they wouldn't be safe from that."

Billy's mother could see that the officer was getting annoyed and tried to placate him. "What is it that you want us to do?"

He turned to her with some relief. "Now that the anti-aircraft unit is on the golf course, you are very exposed here, and if you haven't got an Anderson shelter in the garden, then you will have to go to the nearest communal shelter whenever there is an air raid. There is no option," he added shortly.

Billy saw his Granddad's neck get very red at the back and clutched excitedly at his mother's skirt.

"Is that so?" the old man bridled. "Well, I'll tell you somethin'. I haven't got out of my bed once for the bloody Luftwaffe so far, and I ain't gonna get out now just because some wet-behind-the-ears, toffee-nosed officer thinks he can tell me what to do. . . ."

The officer turned to the air-raid warden. "I'm sorry," he said contemptuously, "there's no way of dealing with people like this—they just don't know what's good for them." He couldn't keep the sneer out of his voice, and had no intention of doing so. He half turned, about to leave, but the old man's hand shot out and grabbed him by the lapels of his uniform, almost lifting him clear of the ground with one hand. Billy could see the fear on the officer's face as his cap fell to the floor and his feet scrabbled for a toehold on the porch. The old man held him effortlessly at arm's length. "Listen, I don't want you or your kind to come around to my daughter's house again, trying to bully her into doin' something she doesn't want to." He jabbed the stem of his pipe into the officer's chest to emphasize the point. "I look after them now, and if we want to stay here in our house, that's what we shall do."

The officer's eyes were bulging with his exertions to free

himself, but he hung limply now, not trying to escape from the iron grip the old man had on him. "I was only thinking of their safety," he gasped.

"You look after your safety, I'll look after mine, just as I did in the first war. I had a basinful of officers just like you, waving their little pistols about, always telling us what to do until I didn't have any of my mates left anymore. Well, I'm not in the army now, see, so you can take your bleedin' pistol and your Sam Browne belt and piss off, alright?"

Billy gazed up at his grandfather open-mouthed—he'd never heard him swear before. The old man lowered the officer to the ground and shoved him gently backward. He stumbled and would have fallen if the warden hadn't caught his arm. They both backed away from the front door and the old man picked up the cap and threw it after them.

"Better take it—otherwise no one's gonna salute you."

Billy stood beside his Granddad and watched them leave. Somehow he felt as though they had won something. The feeling lasted as long as it took for his mother to slam the door. Then a flood of abuse poured over his poor Granddad as she accused him of everything from wanting to see them killed to behaving like a common lout in front of an officer. She would go to the communal shelter, and take Billy with her; he could do what he liked. They began to shout angrily at each other, and Billy backed away from the din, slipping out through the kitchen door and into the woods where it was quiet. It was then that he discovered the wall of barbed wire that had been erected around the golf course. No longer would he be able to watch the soldiers. . . .

Billy woke with a start. It was the air-raid siren wailing in the distance. His mother told him to lie still and not make a noise. He looked around the huge communal shelter. It was full, hundreds of people, complete strangers sleeping nose to tail. None of them stirred, so Billy just lay there, listening.

There, he could hear it. The faint but continuous booming sound of the battery as it opened up on the raiders. Suddenly there was a huge explosion nearby, and the shelter seemed to shudder a little. People were sitting up now, some of them gazing anxiously around them. Billy heard the whine of the bombs as they fell. Then a series of explosions that got louder and more violent as they fell nearer. The last one seemed to land on the shelter, and Billy saw the concrete roof actually bulge downward as though it were made of jelly. Several people screamed, and his mother put her arms around him, holding him tightly to her. He wasn't frightened, just curious, and he wanted to see if the roof would fall in, but it didn't. There were two more explosions that caused the shelter to shake. A cloud of white dust descended on them, causing people to cough.

A woman came running into the shelter from outside. Her hair was on fire and she was screaming dreadfully. Billy just stared, fascinated. His mother shouted to him not to move, grabbed a blanket and flung it over the woman, who continued to shriek horribly. Other people rushed forward to try and help. Billy could contain his curiosity no longer. As the crowd gathered around the woman lying on the floor, he made his way quietly through the jostling people to the door of the shelter and looked out. It was an incredible sight. The department store behind the shelter had been hit by high-explosive and petrol bombs. The night sky was lit up as though by a dazzling firework display. Sparks and pieces of blazing wood and material were falling all around the shelter and crashing onto the parked vans in the forecourt. It seemed to the boy as though it were raining fire.

Billy loved it; he must have stood there for ages, excited and thrilled, unaware of the dangers. Fire engines arrived, clanging their way through the crowded forecourt. Firemen leaped from their tenders before they'd stopped, pulling out long hoses; water burst from them, arcing high through the smoke and flames, aimed at the gutted, blackened windows, seeking to blanket and control the inferno inside the building.

Billy heard someone calling his name. It appeared to be coming from outside the shelter. It was a man's voice. He shielded his eyes from the glare and peered out onto the forecourt. He heard it again . . . "Billy." It was his grandfather's voice. Then he saw him, lying under one of the parked moving vans, sheltered from the rain of sparks and flame falling all around him. Billy waved.

"Where's your mother, Billy? Is she alright?"

"She's inside," Billy called back, "looking after a lady, but we're okay. Are you coming in?"

His grandfather shifted uncomfortably from one elbow to the next. "No, I'm going back home if you're alright. You get back inside with your mum." Billy watched him crawl back under the vans until he was clear of the sparks, then he went back inside to look for his mother.

The rear gunner of the Heinkel bomber leaned forward, peering into the black night sky, laced with flak tracer, the cumulus below him glowing slightly, suffused with an eerie light from the fires in the city below. He thought he had seen something, a dark shadow drifting between the cloud cover behind the bomber. It was cold in the tiny steel compartment, but the young gunner's hands were sweating inside the gloves as he gripped the twin handles of the machine gun. A circle of light traced a pattern across the cumulus beneath him, looking like a giant white slug sliding slowly across a cotton-wool floor. Then the searchlight found a gap in the clouds immediately behind them, bursting through, exposing the night fighter in a brilliant white light as it was poised to attack the Heinkel.

The gunner screamed a warning to his pilot, who pushed the stick forward, seeking the cover of the clouds below. The Heinkel, a well-armed medium bomber, could not compete with the night fighter for maneuverability or firepower, and the Luftwaffe pilot knew it. The rear gunner's voice was screaming in his ears, warning him that the night fighter was on his tail.

The pilot's back tensed, waiting for the impact of the cannon. The cloud below was rushing up to engulf them, but this moment of extreme danger seemed to be stretching endlessly, standing still, poised between life and death. Then the first tendrils of cloud whipped past the diving wings of the bomber as they plunged into the dark mass of the cloud. The pilot straightened the Heinkel out, banking to the left. They were safe, at least for the moment, but he was taking no more chances.

He ordered the bomb aimer to dump their deadly cargo. The Heinkel leaped, momentarily released from the weight as the long stick of high explosives dropped from the belly of the bomber. The pilot adjusted his controls, checked their position, and headed back toward the coast and Occupied Europe.

As the bombs sliced through the clouds toward the empty dark spaces of North London, the guns of the ack-ack battery on the golf course continued to spit their flak up into the night sky. Most of it burst uselessly, falling as shrapnel on the city and later collected by the children and swapped in the schoolyards. The thick, deadly, high-explosive bombs, dropped in fear, aimed at nothing, fell silently through the flak-filled sky toward the suburban streets below.

The first bomb landed in a park, shattering a tree and killing only a bird. The others began to kill in earnest, falling unerringly on houses, missing the empty streets between, bursting the homes apart, tracing a line directly toward the department store and the shelter beside it. One fell among the moving vans where Billy's grandfather had been sheltering moments before, turning them over, ripping them apart like toys in the hands of a destructive child. Two scored direct hits on the shelter, and the last plunged into the inferno of the store, exploding the walls outward, engulfing the already disintegrating structure of the shelter beside it.

Billy stopped as he heard the crunch of the exploding bombs, each one drawing nearer than the last. Suddenly he was frightened. He looked for his mother as people around him began to scream.

He saw her emerging from the crowd gathered around the woman whose hair had been alight. He called out, "Mummy, mummy." She turned toward him and smiled with relief; then the first bomb hit the shelter behind her. She screamed his name and ran toward him, her arms extended. He began to run toward her. Then the shelter collapsed. There was a dreadful pain in his ears as the pressure from the second exploding bomb hit him. Then darkness, more pain. Then nothing.

Billy's grandfather never left the site of the shelter for more than an hour in the three days that followed. The army and rescue services worked frantically round the clock, burrowing beneath the rubble to find survivors from the two hundred or more people who had been in the shelter when it was hit. They began to find the pathetic remains at first light next morning. Slowly the death toll started to mount. None were found alive on the first or second day. The grim procession of bodies was carried tenderly down the line of men, who worked stubbornly on, hoping to find at least one alive. They found Billy's mother on the third day, her arms still outstretched, reaching for her son. Billy's grandfather walked dry-eyed and numb beside the stretcher that carried the body of his daughter. He could not cry—there was still Billy. If they saw his grief, they would not let him stay. He watched them push the stretcher into the ambulance. There were three others inside, and now it was full. They closed the doors quietly and carefully drove the ambulance from the mound of rubble, past the burnt-out moving vans and out of his sight.

He stood there unmoving, gazing sightlessly at the corner where the ambulance had disappeared, oblivious of the activity around him. A woman from the Women's Voluntary Service touched his arm and asked him if he wanted some tea; he did not hear her. His thoughts were on the huge mound of rubble behind him and what it might contain. He heard someone cry out; the ritual was already horribly familiar—another body had been found. He turned and walked slowly back. The woman from the WVS gazed anxiously after him but did not follow. She too was becoming used to the horror.

He wasn't sure whether he was alive or dead. Several times he had regained consciousness in the tiny alcove of concrete that had protected him, preventing the huge mass of weight above from crushing him. He did not know how long he had been there. He had tried to cry out, but dust had descended, choking him. In the cold black darkness he could not tell what effect it had, so he stopped and lay still. The pain in his head was bearable, but it was the cold, the inability to move, and the dreadful thirst that were the hardest to bear.

He wanted his mother and whimpered in the dark, too frightened to cry out for her. It never occurred to him that she might be dead. It wasn't real—it hadn't happened. It was like a dreadful dream and soon he would wake up in his bed, the sun streaming through the window as his mother pulled open the blackout curtains. . .

He was so thirsty. He tried licking his lips, but that just seemed to make it worse. He was cold, unable to move, the sharp edges of the concrete digging into his flesh, hurting him. "Oh, mother, please come soon, bring me some water. . . ." He could hear something, faint, distant. He listened carefully, uncertain of what it was, or whether he could hear it at all. Again he heard a noise, and this time he felt the broken concrete around him vibrate slightly. Perhaps someone was trying to find him— he hoped they wouldn't go away. "Please don't go away. . . ." He relapsed mercifully into unconsciousness again.

The ferrous concrete was no more than six inches from his face. Dimly he could see the huge crack about two inches wide, extending from left to right, within which a cobweb, shining silver gray, swayed slowly in an air current. He blinked. Was he awake or asleep? He *could* see it. He blew softly and the cobweb swayed dangerously. Some dust drifted down onto his face, getting in his eyes. He clenched them shut, moving his eyes around. When they seemed to be clear, he opened them again. He could still see it: the cobweb remained. Light was filtering into his alcove for the first time. He raised his head slightly. It seemed to be coming from somewhere down by his feet. He could actually see them now, the toes of his shoes poking out above the lump of concrete that prevented his legs from moving.

The weight of the slab was supported on either side by broken pieces of concrete, and he was lucky that it had been impossible to move them. If he had tried, he would have dislodged the heavy slab, and crushed his legs beneath it. He listened again intently: the noises did seem to be getting louder. A lump of concrete, about the size of a brick, was lying between his legs. Slowly he reached for it, making sure nothing would be dislodged. It did not seem to be supporting anything. Gingerly he lifted it clear. Nothing happened. He put both hands around it, shut his eyes tightly, and struck the concrete above him three times. Small pieces of loose concrete and rubble came sliding down through the crack. He averted his face, but the dust and dirt filled his ears and nostrils, causing him to sneeze. He waited. The noises above him had stopped. Again he raised the lump of concrete and struck the roof of the alcove three times. Moments later he heard three loud knocks from above. He risked opening his eyes. The light seemed brighter—they'd heard him. For the first time Billy began to cry, the tears rolling slowly down the sides of his white, dust-covered face. . . .

He didn't remember much after that, just the voices getting louder, nearer. Then he was blinking in the daylight, and strange faces were peering down at him, asking him questions. He couldn't talk: his mouth was dry and seemed full of dirt. Someone gave him some water. He choked, spitting out the dirt, then swallowing some of it. Nothing had ever tasted so good. He heard someone calling his name and then he saw his grandfather. He was smiling and crying at the same time. Billy reached up to touch him. Suddenly his legs were free and his grandfather lifted him easily, with great strength yet infinite care.

Several soldiers tried to help him put the boy on a stretcher, but he drew back, his eyes glaring at them, refusing to let them touch Billy. He began to move slowly down the side of the bomb site, carrying the boy tenderly. Once he tripped and nearly fell. A soldier tried to support him. The old man stopped dead, swaying exhaustedly. "Leave him," he snarled. The soldier stared, shocked by the bitterness, the hatred in his voice: "If you stupid bastards hadn't forced them into this death trap, none of this would have happened."

The soldier glanced at his sergeant, who was standing quietly behind the old man. He shook his head and the soldier stepped back. Slowly he resumed his climb down the mountain of rubble. The soldiers, the rescue workers, all had stopped and were watching him carry the boy toward the waiting ambulance. No sound broke the silence, just the old man's boots and the occasional tiny avalanche that they dislodged as he made his way to the bottom.

He reached the ambulance and stood waiting patiently for someone to open the door. The WVS lady did so and he didn't object when she helped him up the step.

He put Billy on a stretcher and wiped some of the dust from the boy's face. Billy opened his eyes and looked at him, searching for his gnarled and horny hand. The doors banged shut and Billy felt the ambulance begin to move.

2. Barossa Valley, Australia, 1942

The Austin Seven bounced heavily as it crossed the railway line for the second time since leaving Tanunda. The boy couldn't remember being this way before and he was puzzled.

"Why do we keep crossing the railway line, mummy?"

Gerda, his mother, was concentrating on the driving and she had only half heard his question. She found it difficult to turn her thoughts away from what awaited her at the end of this journey. She glanced at her son.

"I'm sorry, Erich, what did you say?"

"The railway line . . . why do we keep crossing it all the time?"

"It's the road, darling. It twists and turns while the railway tries to stay in a straight line, and since they are both going in the same direction, they cross each other."

"Oh," he said, and sat quietly thinking about that for a while.

It was hot in the tiny car, and the sun bounced off the narrow bitumen road ahead, shimmering slightly in the distance. There was seldom a lot of traffic on the road, though it was the main route through from Adelaide into the Barossa Valley, but the war and petrol rationing had reduced what few vehicles there were down to a trickle.

Gerda Spengler had saved every drop she could get in the hope that she would be able to make this journey and begin to visit her husband on a regular basis.

The verdant valley stretched out on either side of the road, which wound between the vineyards, the only real industry in the area. Neat rows of vines spread out in symmetrical lines toward the rounded hills bordering the cultivated region to the east, separating it from the barren tundra that descended toward the Murray River beyond. Sometimes, startlingly beautiful patches of purple weed known as "Salvation Jane" would dot the valley floor, of no practical value. Salvation only to the legendary Jane, whose sheep, it was said, had once been saved from starvation when the drought of some long lost summer had removed all the grass. It was certainly useless to the practical, hardworking German community that had first settled the Barossa in the middle of the nineteenth century; but they tolerated the weed since it grew in such profusion and was almost impossible to remove permanently.

The old Austin toiled up the rise, then eased itself down the other side as they entered Lyndoch—a few single-storied houses, one shop, and some palm trees. Gerda turned left toward Williamstown, crossed the railway line yet again, and then they were out of Lyndoch, closer to the husband she had not seen for the last two years.

"How much further, mummy?"

It was as if Erich had read her mind. She turned and smiled at him. He looked so like his father. Blue eyes, fair hair, and a funny way of scratching the top of his eyebrow when he was puzzled, exactly the same as Gunther.

The boy was four now, and his father would notice how much he had changed. She felt the tears stinging the back of her eyes and bit hard on her lip, trying not to let her son see her distress.

"Not long, darling," she said. "We'll soon be there."

She wondered how much Gunther had changed, and glanced at herself in the rearview mirror. She was wearing hardly any make-up—she knew he didn't like it—and although there were signs of strain around her eyes, her skin was brown from the sun and the pink-flowered summer dress showed it off to its best advantage.

They had now left what was regarded by the German community as Barossa Valley. Although the countryside had not altered, there were fewer vineyards. Certainly the people of Williamstown were not of German descent.

Williamstown, like Lyndoch, had only one main street, though it did have a bakery and a fish-and-chip shop defiantly proclaiming its British stock.

Gerda didn't stop—she knew where she was going. She had tried to gain entrance to the internment camp once before without permission and had been quickly turned away. She took the right fork south of Williamstown and slowly closed up behind an old Morris Eight van on the road in front of her. Gerda knew the Austin had little or no acceleration, so she did not try to overtake it. As they neared the turnoff to the right she was surprised to see that the van intended to do the same. A brown arm and hand extended to give her a clear indication. Both vehicles turned off the main road and began to bump over the dirt track, fording a shallow creek that had Erich leaning excitedly out of the window, trying to see if there were any fish.

Gerda shouted at him, nervously aware of the danger of his falling out since they were bumping about so much. The van was making slow progress up the hill, but the driver seemed to know where he was going. Gerda wound up the window and told Erich to do the same as the van was throwing up clouds of dust behind it. Down the steep side of the hill to her left she caught a glimpse of the South Para River before it was obscured once again by the dust. Erich tugged at her arm and shouted something, but she couldn't hear him because the engine was making too much noise, but when he pointed, she saw a small brown kangaroo leaping, startled, away from them between the black wattle trees to her right.

Slowly the two vehicles crawled up the dirt track until they finally crested the ridge at the top. The ground here had been cleared, and away off the track to her left, on a flat stretch of ground, was the camp.

There were about ten long, low wooden huts, raised slightly off the ground on concrete blocks. They were arranged roughly into a square, completely surrounded on all sides by a high wire fence. The only entrance was a solid wooden gate facing the track. In front of the gate was a shack with a tin roof and a low porch. The van pulled over to the right, stopping beside the track, while Gerda brought the Austin Seven to a halt in front of the gate. A cloud of dust surrounded the car, and as it subsided she could see small groups of men inside the compound staring curiously at her, but no sign of her husband.

Erich was already out of the car and looking through the fence. Gerda climbed stiffly from the driver's seat, and as she did so a man emerged from the shack. He was of medium height and had a sallow face, unshaven, and wore a bush shirt and dark, shabby trousers, stained around the crotch. A rifle rested in the crook of his arm and already the flies were settling on the sweat-stained hatband of his battered trilby. He stepped down off the porch and eyed her speculatively. He was about twenty-seven, but looked older.

Gerda pulled the envelope from her handbag. "My

name is Gerda Spengler," she said, trying not to sound as nervous as she felt. "My husband is here." She pointed toward the camp. "Interned."

The man glanced toward the compound and jerked his thumb at the boy. "No one's allowed near the wire. Didn't you see the sign on the track?"

Gerda called Erich back and apologized. "No, I'm sorry. There was so much dust I didn't see it."

Gerda waved an arm at the flies, but the man seemed unaffected by them, even when they landed on his face. Perhaps that's why he didn't shave, she thought. He shifted the rifle from one arm to the next. "What do you want?"

"I've come to see my husband. I've got papers." She handed him the letter she had received the day before, authorizing a visit once a month. He took it from her but didn't look at it. His eyes moved slowly down from her face to her brown neck, then her firm breasts, pausing for a moment, then lowered to her stomach. The dress had stuck tight to her because of the heat and Gerda pulled it down, loosening it from her body. She felt as though she were being undressed. His eyes flicked back to her face again and she lowered her gaze quickly. Silently he read for what seemed like an eternity. Erich, happy to be released from the car, ran over to the van where the driver was unloading trays of bread.

The man glanced up from beneath the dirty brim of the trilby. "This is okay, it seems to be in order."

Gerda sighed with relief and held out her hand for the letter. "Good."

The man pulled the letter away from her. "There's just one thing. . . ." He stopped. He seemed to be grinning at her. Suddenly she was apprehensive again.

"What is it, what's wrong?"

He tapped the letter on his thumb. "There's nothing wrong—it's just that no one's allowed in here without a search." He glanced over the track. "Not even the baker." He gazed at her unblinkingly. "I've never searched a woman before." Gerda looked toward the compound, looking vainly for Gunther. Some of the internees were gathering near the gate, watching silently.

"He won't do you any good, lady," the guard leered, "least, not until I've let you in."

Gerda felt sick inside. "Isn't there a woman?"

The guard glanced at the men crowding the fence. "What do you think?" He leaned the rifle against the porch. "Now, are you going in, or going home?"

Gerda swallowed down the fear welling up inside her throat. "Could you do the search inside. I don't want . . ." She looked at the men standing inside the wire, then turned back to the guard. "I don't want my son to see."

The guard glanced at Erich, who was helping the baker unload. "He's not interested. Besides I can't take you inside, they"—he nodded toward the compound—"might think something else was happening, then I could lose my job."

Gerda knew she had no option. "I am going to see my husband."

"Sure, lady, sure. Just as soon as I am satisfied." He grinned again obscenely. He stepped toward her and Gerda tried not to shrink from him. He smelled; he probably hadn't bathed in a year. He reached out toward her.

"You lay one hand on her and I'll kill you, Dyker." Gerda turned quickly. He was standing near the gate, gripping the wires with both hands, his knuckles white with tension. He looked older, his hair thinning slightly at the front, unkempt. His clothes hung loosely around him, but it was unmistakably her husband.

The guard laughed. "I'm glad you turned up, Spengler." His voice hardened. "I thought you might be the only one to miss it." He glanced at the other internees. "Now you'll all be able to see how conscientiously I do my job." He put his hands behind Gerda's neck and felt up inside her hair. His face was only inches from hers, his breath foul. He said quietly, so that only she could hear, "You'd be surprised at how many places a woman can hide things."

Spengler gripped the wire in his fists, shaking it as though he would tear it from the ground, screaming abuse at Dyker. The guard stared at Gerda. "You'd better tell him to stop, lady. Otherwise you'll never get to see him, I promise."

She bit her lip, trying to control herself, then turned her head toward her husband. His hands were torn, the blood dripping unheeded into the dust at his feet. Their eyes met, his tortured, desperate, hers pleading. She shook her head and mouthed silently, "Please." She forced herself round to face the guard again. "Get it over with."

He looked contemptuously at her husband. "Anything to oblige, lady." His hands slid slowly over her shoulders, then down, lingering, suggestively, on her breasts. One of the men in the compound cried out softly, "Jesus."

Gunther turned and leaped upon him frenziedly. He was torn away by half a dozen others, who pressed him face down into the dust, sitting on him until he ceased to struggle. Gerda closed her eyes and felt the tears rolling down her face. The guard's hands slid down her sides, then across her stomach, pushing her dress in between her legs, his fingers pressing into her, feeling. He took her hand and pressed it against his crotch. She could feel his erection, hard inside his trousers. His mouth close to her ear, he whispered, "Is that big enough for you, lady?"

Gerda had her eyes shut tight, trying to blot out every sight and touch from her mind. She didn't hear the horseman arrive, nor did Dyker. His voice was the first thing that penetrated her violation.

"Turn round, Dyker. I want to see your face before I kill you."

She felt the guard freeze against her and opened her eyes. The horse was tall and black, sweating slightly. The man astride it wore a wide-brimmed hat, a short, gray jacket, and a wide gunbelt fastened around his waist. The gun in his hand pointed unerringly at the guard's back. The guard stepped away from her but didn't turn around.

"It's alright, Barney, the woman's got a pass to go in." His voice shook slightly, betraying his fear. "I was just searching her, that's all."

Gerda watched the horseman dismount, his gun never wavering for an instant. He moved slowly until he was standing directly behind the guard. "Dyker, turn around."

The guard licked his lips nervously. "Come off it, Barney, you've got a gun on me."

The horseman slipped the gun back into the holster. "Not any more, Dyker. I promise you it's in my holster."

Slowly the guard turned, his erection still bulging inside his trousers. Barney jerked his knee up savagely into Dyker's crotch. The guard screamed with pain and fell to the ground, rolling around in agony, the dust clouding up as his knees were pulled convulsively into his stomach.

Erich broke away from the baker, who had been holding him, and ran over to his mother, crying, clasping her around the waist, clinging to her. The horseman stepped over the thrashing figure, ignoring him. He removed his hat. "I'm sorry, ma'am—is there anything I can do for you?" He turned the hat in his hands awkwardly. "Maybe you and the boy would like to come inside and clean up a little."

Gerda put her arms around Erich's head, pressing him to her stomach. "That's kind of you, but please, may I just see my husband?"

The man nodded and walked over to the heavy wooden gates, unlocking a huge padlock and pulling back some bolts. He stepped inside the compound and the crowd of men around Spengler fell back. He was still lying face down in the dust, unconscious. Barney reached down and pulled him to his feet, slipping one of his arms around his shoulders. Gerda grabbed the other one and between them they dragged him toward one of the huts, Erich running in front and opening the door. They negotiated the three rough wooden steps. Inside it was cooler, and they laid him down tenderly on one of the beds.

Gerda knelt beside him and brushed the hair back from his eyes, then Barney returned with a tin mug of cold water, which she forced between her husband's lips. She wiped the blood from his lacerated hands and tore some strips from a sheet, wrapping them tightly around them. His eyes flicked open, and for an instant he didn't seem to recognize her. Then he pulled her savagely down on top of him, tears blinding his eyes.

Barney waited a moment until they had composed themselves, then he touched Gerda's elbow. "I'll make sure no one comes inside, Mrs. Spengler." He crushed the hat between his two hands and glanced at Erich. "If you and Mr. Spengler would like to be alone for a little while later . . . well, I can always give the boy a ride on my horse."

Erich's eyes lit up and Gerda stood, holding out her hand. "Thank you," she said simply. He touched it briefly, crammed his hat back on his head, and left the hut.

Erich was standing by the foot of the bed, looking at his father, who pulled himself upright and swung his legs onto the floor of the hut. Gerda held up her hand. "Don't get up, Gunther," she said, glancing at Erich, who was still standing uncertainly, waiting. "This is Daddy, Erich."

She knelt down beside her husband. "He's been waiting to see you for such a long time, Gunther."

The man held out his arms and the boy flew into them. Gunther crushed him to his chest, burying his head in the boy's hair, holding out his bandaged hand for Gerda, who wrapped her arms around them both. After a moment the boy disentangled himself from them, almost smothered by the warmth of their embrace. He looked first at his father, then at his mother, seeing the wetness on their cheeks. "Why are you both crying? Aren't you happy to be together?"

They glanced at each other, suddenly aware of the impenetrable logic of the child's question. They laughed, breaking the tension. Gunther stood up, sweeping the boy into his arms and placing him on the bed. He stepped back a pace, studying his appearance.

"Now then"—he grasped Gerda's hand tightly, holding her beside him—"let me have a look at you." The boy's eyes dropped under his scrutiny and he held out his arms to his mother, who picked him up, then sat on the bed, pulling her husband down too, the boy on her knee. Erich gazed at his father shyly and turned to his mother as though unsure as to whom he should address his question. "Mummy?"

She smiled at her husband and kissed his hand. "Yes, darling," she said to the boy. The child squirmed his way to the floor and glanced at the door of the hut.

"Can I go and ride on the man's horse, please?"

Gunther looked at his wife, puzzled. "What man?" he said quietly. "What's he talking about?" She put her hand on his face tenderly. "The guard that helped me bring you in here—Barney, I think his name is. He said that Erich could have a ride on his horse . . . I think he is trying to be helpful."

He looked at her, stunned. "Helpful?" He took her hand

between both of his. "Gerda, don't you realize what they have done to us? The way that animal treated you out there, turning you into a public display?"

She turned her head away sharply. "Don't! Gunther, please."

He sat silent for a moment, dejected. Then, speaking almost to himself, "Gerda, I am a printer; I used to make newspapers. I have sat up here on this barren hillside for nearly two years now, doing nothing. There is nothing for me to do. I think . . ." He stopped for a moment, rubbing his forehead with his fingers. "I think I am beginning to go mad. I cannot even escape. Where would I escape to? To Germany?" His anger was suppressed, but frightening in its lack of passion. "I am not a German. I have always lived here. Yet they say I am an *alien*." Disbelief, tinged with anguish, emphasized the last word. "The Review Committee deemed me to be unfriendly to the inhabitants of Australia"—he paused, his eyes glittering with hatred—"yet you say this man wants to be helpful." He gestured toward the door, then gazed down at his feet and said tonelessly, "I hate him."

Erich tugged at his trousers, not understanding his father's words. "Daddy, please, can I have a ride on the horse?"

Gunther leaped to his feet, knocking the boy sideways to the floor. He stood with his back to her, his shoulders shaking with rage. Erich started to cry and the man turned swiftly, picking him up and holding the boy at arm's length, face to face, staring at him with a quiet intensity that sent a quiver of fear through his mother. He spoke slowly, deliberately, holding the boy tightly by the arms. "Listen to me, Erich. You will not ride on that man's horse, and for as long as you live you will accept nothing from people like him. Do you understand?" The words were spat out, incensed. The boy nodded dumbly, terrified. Gunther paused, swallowing hard, trying to control himself. "I have been locked away in here from you, from your mother—only because *my* mother and father came from Germany. And because your father worked for a newspaper that had a German name. I have done nothing." He shook his head. "Nothing that is wrong." The boy looked at Gerda, his eyes wide with fear, but she just sat very still, waiting for him to finish, aware that if she tried to snatch the boy from him in his present state, it could be dangerous—he might do anything.

The man shook his son gently. "Look at me, Erich. I want you always to remember what I am saying. You must never let these people do to you what they have done to me. Owe them nothing, give them nothing, do not trust them or they will surely take you, as well, away from those that you love. Do you promise to remember that, Erich?" He shook the boy again to make him speak. "Promise me." The child could not feel his hands and arms any longer—they were numb from the grip his father had on his upper arms.

He didn't dare cry; he knew that instinctively, and the terror he felt at this moment would never completely leave him. "Yes, father," he whispered, "I promise."

It was a promise that he would always keep.

3. Germany, December 24, 1944

He woke with a start, unsure for a moment of where he was. He tried to sit up, but it was difficult. The soldier's body was sprawled half across him, pinning him into the corner of the compartment.

It was dark, but he could just see the vague shapes of the people asleep on the seat opposite. Four of them, all men, cramped together, their heads lolling to one side or resting on each other, their bodies moving slightly to the motion of the train.

His neck was stiff and ached abominably. Slowly he tried to move the inert heavy figure without waking him, but it was impossible. The soldier groaned, flinging out an arm that caught Bruno across the side of his face. Angrily he pushed the soldier from him. The soldier sat up, gazed at him blankly for a moment, then slumped the other way, leaning against his companion, asleep instantly.

They were both infantrymen, very young. Probably on their way to the western front where Patton's Third Army was reeling back toward Bastogne after the surprise German offensive through the Ardennes.

Bruno Heissler pitied them; he did not believe the

offensive could last long. He knew how desperately difficult it was to get fuel and supplies even at Peenemunde,
which had top priority. And the journey from Peenemunde had not been reassuring.

He had been held up in Berlin for nearly twenty-four
hours, waiting for a connection to Frankfurt, and he had
been shocked to see the devastation that the Allied air
bombardment had wrought on the city.

Whole streets flattened, hardly a building undamaged.
Much of it no longer recognizable. Row after row of
gaunt, empty skeletons pointing up to the omniscient sky.
So different from a few years before when he and many
other proud young men had been presented to Hitler in
the Chancellory. They had introduced him as one of the
young scientists who would make rockets for the Führer
that would ascend to the stars.

Had he really believed that? He'd certainly wanted to.
Since childhood he had been fascinated by the stars and
thoughts of space travel. He'd worked with brilliant en-
gineers, they'd perfected rockets that would climb into
the stratosphere, it was only one step on to break the
gravitational pull of the earth and reach into space. True,
the V-2 was an offensive weapon of war, but had his ef-
forts been any different from those of similar status working for the Allies? He did not think so. He knew that they
also were engaged on a nuclear fission program and what
kind of weapon would that be? Whole cities destroyed,
hundreds of thousands killed, whichever side perfected it
first.

He pushed the depressing thought from his mind and
rubbed some of the condensation from the window with
the palm of his hand. It was just beginning to get light
and he glanced quickly at his watch . . . just before seven.
They had passed through Wiesbaden during the night
and they should be running parallel to the Rhine now. He

peered intently out of the little space he had cleared in the window again. The long train emerged slowly from the woods and off to his left, gleaming dully through the early morning mist, he caught a glimpse of the river.

The depression lifted and he felt a small glow of excitement and anticipation. Soon he would be back home in Koblenz and his long journey from the rocket site at Peenemunde would be over. He did not intend to go back and he wondered if Vaas would be at the rendezvous.

Koblenz was only half the city he remembered. The devastation he had seen all the way from Peenemunde extended to even this quiet spa town. Perhaps it was not as extensive as some he had passed through, but the areas around the station were badly hit. Deep bomb craters pockmarking what were left of the streets. Few people about on this frosty morning before Christmas. Those that were seemed apathetic, dazed from the air raid of the previous night.

Bruno lugged his heavy suitcase, picking his way through the rubble, heading in the general direction of the river and the university to the east. The bomb damage grew less severe, and high above the hill on the far bank of the Rhine he could see the outline of the medieval castle. It appeared to be undamaged, the towering granite walls of the structure etched clearly against the blue wintry sky. The sun rose red through the cold December mist, casting long shadows across the river.

The ancient hotel opposite the university was just as he remembered it structurally. But it was not the bright lively place of his student days. No welcoming smell of freshly brewed coffee wafting in from the restaurant near the entrance. The building was unheated; a vague damp, musky smell pervaded his nostrils as he carried his bag in through the main double doors. Behind the walnut reception desk he could just see the back of an old man bent over a simple oil stove, his white straggly hair falling over the woolen scarf he had wrapped around his neck. Bruno recognized him at once. He stopped and quietly put the heavy bag down onto the faded carpet, then silently crossed to the desk. He leaned over and said, "Albert, I want the long room next to the cellar downstairs tonight . . . there is going to be a reunion." The old man who had been warming his hands over the stove turned and gazed at him incredulously.

"Bruno," he smiled hugely, recognizing him, and he stood up. "Bruno Heissler!" His hair was whiter than Bruno remembered it, but the smile was the same, spreading right across his old lined face, happy to see him. He lifted up the flap in the counter, emerged from behind the desk, and they embraced, pleased to see each other undamaged and alive after such a long time. They held each other at arm's length for a moment, smiling. Then Albert raised a finger. "Wait, I have an idea. Leave your bag here and come with me." He led the way downstairs to the beer cellar. It hadn't changed. Long wooden tables, benches. A few, more private alcoves where they used to play cards and thump the table in turn. Albert went behind the bar and from beneath it lifted, with considerable pride, a full bottle of whisky.

"Not scotch perhaps—but good whisky nevertheless." He poured out two large measures, putting a little water into his own. He handed the other glass to Bruno. "Straight, as I recall." The grin beamed across his face again. Bruno raised his glass and clicked it against Albert's.

"Good friends," he said quietly, looking intently at the old man. Albert raised his glass as well. "Good friends," he repeated, then threw back his head and emptied the glass in one experienced swallow.

The rendezvous was arranged for early that evening, hopefully before the bombers could join them for Christmas Eve. Bruno waited in the long room adjoining the cellar. Albert had set the table beautifully. The silver gleamed, and the best crockery shone, heightened by the wood fire Albert had lit for the first time in a year. Just a few pieces of holly hung around the paintings on the wall, but it sufficed. Christmas would not go uncelebrated. He raised his glass, gazing into the flames of the fire, wondering why his former colleague from the university had asked him to come here.

He had seen him only once since 1940. Two years ago, when Vaas had returned from the heavy water plant at Verwork in Norway. Heinrich Vaas, like himself, had been recruited directly into the war effort from the university, where he had worked steadily and brilliantly on nuclear physics. He was an enigma, tall, slightly older than Bruno; he had alternately attracted and repelled the younger man. His work on nuclear physics and the effects of radiation was stunning; his intellectual grasp of the possibilities of nuclear fission demanded respect. But in a sense it was this concentration on the potential for destruction that seemed, to Bruno, at least, unhealthy.

Nuclear energy had enormous potential for mankind, not the least of which was the possibility of its providing the breakthrough for space exploration. That was what interested Bruno. They had made incredible progress at the Peenemunde Research Establishment since the war began, and he did not doubt that they now led the world in rocket technology. As early as October 1942 they had successfully launched a V-2 rocket. Subsequently the program had been delayed by the massive raid of Bomber

Command on the night of August 17 and 18, 1943, which had killed Dr. Thiel, one of the leading designers. As a result of that raid the rocket trials had been moved to Blizna in Poland, and Bruno had been transferred to the Wasserfall Project. Now the V-2s were landing on London, over a thousand since September, and Bruno was glad not to be involved any longer.

He saw the flames flicker as the door behind him was opened. Albert ushered him in and then left, quietly closing the door behind him. Like himself, Vaas was not in uniform, and there was an awkward moment of silence before Bruno stepped forward, extending his hand. "Heinrich, how nice to see you again. Just like old times, apart from the absence of the ladies," he added, grinning.

Vaas studied the younger man carefully, curious to see what the years of war had done to him. He seemed cheerful enough, but he was thinner, lines had etched themselves into his face, and he looked tired. Possibly that was just the journey, but Vaas doubted it. He knew the strain, the pressure, to which the team at Peenemunde had been put. He knew it only too well; his own work on the nuclear program was constantly subjected to the same kind of pressure from Berlin.

"Come," Bruno said, "warm yourself by the fire—you look frozen." Vaas crossed the room and stood with his back to the blazing logs while Bruno ladled a drink from a wooden bowl. Albert had taken what little remained of the alcohol in the cellar and prepared a hot punch. It wasn't perfect, but it was warm, and Vaas accepted the small tankard gratefully. The hot drink steamed his glasses slightly, and he placed the tankard on the mantelshelf, meticulously wiping his tinted glasses clean with a spotless handkerchief.

Once again Bruno was fascinated by the disparate color of his eyes—one gray, one blue—though he tried hard not to let his interest show. He was well aware of how sensitive Vaas was about his eyes. It had been a source of embarrassment and humiliation for him, both at school and in the university. Some had merely stared and pointed; others, crueler, had been openly derisive. Later, when he had taken to wearing specially made tinted glasses, that too had become a source of amusement. "How's the world today, Heinrich? Does it look better through tinted glasses?"

Bruno sipped the drink and wondered why Vaas had arranged this meeting, but he was in no hurry. Vaas, as always, would broach the subject when he was ready, and not before.

The drink seemed to break the ice, and after the fire had warmed them and the punch had begun to disappear, so too did the reticence that had accompanied their first meeting in two years. Soon they were exchanging reminiscences about the university, the good times they had enjoyed in the hostelry. Albert provided them with the best meal he could lay before them under the circumstances: a huge bowl of succulent rabbit stew and vegetables. Meat was scarce in Germany, and the stew was delicious. The air raid came and went. They had become so inured to the accompanying din, the muffled explosions, that they scarcely noticed its passing. The mixture of alcohol and good food blunted the sensibilities and encouraged a sense of fatalism.

Albert came in discreetly and cleaned away the dishes, then reappeared carrying a small tray on which were three glasses.

Bruno looked up and smiled, "More surprises?"

The old man nodded gravely. "Gentlemen, I have saved this until last. It is something special for an occasion I thought I might never see again." He paused and coughed, clearing his throat. "Two of my students have come back and I would like to propose a toast."

Vaas and Bruno stood up respectfully. Albert handed each of them a glass. The golden liquid just covered the bottom. Bruno sniffed; it was brandy. He looked at the old man. "I should have come home earlier, Albert, much earlier."

Albert smiled proudly. "Thank you, sir. There is not a lot, but it is vintage." He raised his glass. "Thank you both for coming back, for sharing this moment here. A toast . . . to the university, to all of its students who used to come here wherever they may be." He paused, then added simply, "And to those that we may not see here again." The glasses touched, the brandy was swallowed.

Albert held out his tray. "Gentlemen, please, do not break the glasses this time—they may prove invaluable."

Bruno smiled and placed his glass on the tray. "Nevertheless, Albert, thank you for the meal, and especially the toast."

Albert's perennially grave expression softened a little. "Thank you, sir." He collected the other glass from Vaas and left the room quietly.

Bruno sat down and glanced at Vaas who was leaning on the mantelshelf gazing into the flames. "I think Albert is genuinely pleased to see us." It was a statement rather than a question, and Vaas did not reply at once. He continued to gaze into the fire; the flames, reflected in his opaque glasses, seemed to flicker within them.

"Your work at Peenemunde, it goes well, Bruno?" It was asked quietly, without emphasis, but Bruno was aware of a subtle change of mood.

"They are making good progress with the development of the A-10."

Vaas was curious. "The A-10?"

Bruno was in no mood to preserve departmental security. "It's a two-stage long-range rocket for targets in the United States."

"You say *they*, Bruno. Are you not engaged on this yourself?"

"I was but I have been transferred to a ground-to-air defensive missile called Wasserfall."

Vaas turned away from the fire and looked at Bruno. "You sound disappointed."

Bruno glanced up at him. "Is it that obvious?"

Vaas did not reply.

Bruno felt compelled to elaborate. "Of course I am disappointed. I have been working on the concept of a long-range rocket ever since I joined the team at Peenemunde."

"Indeed," Vaas interrupted, "I recall that your theories and research into the possibilities of space flight while at the university was what led to your recruitment for the Peenemunde team in the first place."

Bruno ladled himself more of the punch and offered some to Vaas, who declined. "I should have been on the A-10."

"Why aren't you?"

"I don't know." Bruno sipped the punch—it was cold. He poured it back into the bowl. "No, that's not true." He rubbed his eyes with the back of his hand; he felt tired. "Maybe they sensed that my heart was no longer in it." He looked directly at Vaas. "I'm not going back, Heinrich." He didn't know how he expected Vaas to react; he hadn't even contemplated telling him.

Curiously, Vaas almost seemed pleased. He sat down at the table opposite him. "Bruno, I did not just ask you to meet me here for old times' sake. You know that I have been working under Werner Heisenberg to try to perfect a German fission bomb from nuclear energy. We are very close now, and given time I know we can succeed." He stood up abruptly and resumed his position by the fire, his back to Bruno. "The Allies will be here soon, crossing the river." He turned and faced him. "There is no more time; we cannot split the atom and perfect a nuclear bomb before they are upon us."

Bruno shrugged his shoulders. "So, like us you need another year, perhaps more, but it just isn't available. Too much, too late. We have lost, Heinrich. It's over."

Vaas stared at him unblinkingly. The tinted glasses gave his eyes a slightly eerie, deadening effect, making it difficult to gauge what he was thinking.

He smiled suddenly. "You are wrong, Bruno, there is a way. When I left Hechingen I brought with me all the results of our work thus far. I intend to continue no matter what the Allies accomplish here in Europe."

Bruno may have been weary and slightly the worse for drink, but it was clear to him that Vaas was deadly serious. "How, *where*, will you get your resources? Build up a team that can deal with the problems you will face?"

Vaas sat down again facing him, staring at him intently. "I need you, Bruno. If I do perfect this bomb it has to be delivered, perhaps over a vast distance. If you had the resources and the space, could you build a rocket like the A-10?"

Bruno felt a mad desire to laugh. It was impossible, unbelievable, yet Vaas was sitting there just across the table, facing him. He could see himself reflected in the glasses. Bruno stood up and began to pace the room. He needed to clear his mind of the drink, try to get some straight answers. It seemed very far-fetched, and he knew Vaas in particular had other reasons for wanting to get out of Germany before he was captured. He had heard something of the medical experiments being carried out on people in the concentration camps. Passing huge levels of radiation through them in order to determine the possible results of an atomic bomb explosion. It didn't take much imagination to visualize the effects of such experiments.

Bruno decided to address himself to the problems, concentrating on the technicalities. "Who would provide the hardware? The capital to give the necessary backup? Where could you go where you would not be noticed, where you could disappear and carry out these experiments?"

Vaas deliberated for a moment, then, avoiding Bruno's gaze, he concentrated on what he was about to say. "Look, Bruno, I am not the sort of person who would decide to do something like this without a lot of planning and forethought." Bruno acknowledged that.

"Let me try and answer your questions. . . . I have, first of all, the background and the knowledge to complete the experiments; naturally I would prefer to complete them here, but it is not possible. The Allies will cross this river very soon now; we will all be captured and unable to help the Reich at all. Secondly, there are people who are willing to help, whose money is invested in a place where we could be assimilated, supported by people like ourselves. It is a place where *no one* would think of looking." He paused, and looked directly at Bruno for the first time. "Of course I cannot tell you where it is until I know you are with me. If you do not come, obviously you will be interrogated. Who knows what methods they may use? You may be forced to say where I am, then I could achieve nothing. Join me, Bruno . . . believe me, no one will ever find us."

Vaas stared up at him, waiting for an answer. Bruno turned away, disconcerted by the question, and the soulless glasses. Somehow he felt irritated with Vaas, angry at his intensity. He gazed sightlessly into the fire, trying to force the tiredness from his mind—analyze his reaction.

Why did it make him angry? For a moment he debated if this was the real reason for Vaas's running. It was attractive to believe that he was merely doing it to avoid retribution for his experiments, but he discarded that. It was Vaas's fanaticism, his Nazi ideology that motivated him totally. But Bruno had no desire to continue the fight for the Third Reich. He had seen too many things, and heard a great deal more about the solution to the Jewish problem presently under way in the concentration camps to think there was any point in prolonging the agony of this war. He wanted it over—he wanted just to go home. That was why he was here; he couldn't take it anymore. He turned and faced him. Vaas hadn't moved—he looked up at Bruno and knew he had lost. "I'm sorry, Vaas, I couldn't. I would be no use to you—not now. I need time to think things out—face up to whatever it is that will happen to me when the Allies get here. I can't bear the thought of hiding, being caught or betrayed. Maybe later things will change, perhaps I will want to work again . . . I don't know." He shrugged his shoulders and said simply, "I must stay, Vaas."

Curiously, Vaas didn't protest or bluster about duty or patriotism. They said their good-byes, then Vaas gripped Bruno's hand, squeezing it viselike until he felt the knuckles crack. It was agonizing, but Bruno did not cry out. Somehow he felt he was undergoing a test, not so much of manhood, as ideology. Vaas increased the pressure and Bruno felt the sweat trickling down his face, then suddenly the grip relaxed, and Vaas almost smiled.

"We shall see each other again, Bruno . . . I promise."

Then he turned and swiftly left the room.

Bruno stared at the door for a long time. He was shaken, disturbed—not so much by what had been said, but by its implications. He glanced around the room once, then picked up his hat and left. He thanked Albert, wished him a Merry Christmas, and promised to see him again soon. Then he picked up his bag and left the ancient hotel.

The sky was clear; the stars seemed bright and close, glittering in the cold night air. He wondered if Vaas would succeed in reaching his Shangri-la, if he himself would ever again get the opportunity of working on a rocket technology that would eventually enable men to reach the stars. Of that, at least, he was sure . . . one day, space flight would be a reality.

He carried his heavy suitcase over the bridge on the Rhine, the cobblestones slippery from the night frost, then trudged carefully up the steep hill opposite, to the house where his parents lived. He would say nothing to them of his meeting with Vaas. Something Vaas had said kept repeating itself in his tired mind: "No one will ever find us. . . ." Bruno wondered, was it possible?

4. Korea, Winter of 1950–51

It was bitterly cold and the long column of infantry shuffled slowly along the frozen, bumpy track behind the truck. A month earlier, when the Gloucestershire Regiment had first moved north of the 38th Parallel, the column had been longer. Now they carried their dead with them, piled high in the truck. This bare, rocky, hostile terrain was one corner of a foreign field that was never going to be England—the dead, at least, were going home.

Billy Redston was at the rear of the column; he stared contemptuously at the officer who was back marker. He was plainly scared shitless, glancing nervously from side to side, constantly adjusting the automatic rifle that he clutched in his mitten-covered hands. Even with the covering, his hands must be frozen by now on the cold metal. It was better to have the rifle slung over the shoulder and try to keep the hands warm, ready to use the goddamn thing. If the gooks jumped them now, he'd be useless.

The track started to wind upward between the high, rounded, bare hills. They were trying to reach the port of Hungnow before the American fleet of transports that had assembled there departed. Hungnow was their evacuation point. Their retreat to the south was cut off by the Chinese, and the fleet had been sent in to evacuate the thousands of American and British troops isolated north of the Parallel. Another Dunkirk, Redston thought bitterly . . . only this time it was the Yanks.

Christ! What a place. What the fucking hell was he doing here anyway? He'd tried to avoid being conscripted into the Army, anything but the Army. But his lack of education, due mostly to the destruction and dislocation resulting from the war, had prevented that. The RAF turned him down, and since the Navy seldom took National Servicemen, he'd finished up in this mob, hating every minute of it.

The track beneath his feet was hard, and he felt the tremor first, before he heard the explosion. He glanced up quickly. The truck at the head of the column was disintegrating under the impact of the mine, frozen, it seemed, in mid-air, bodies spilling from it as it erupted.

Instantly the rattle of machine gun fire swathed through the ranks of the men ahead before they could move. Redston leaped for the ditch, clawing himself into it as the track beside him was spattered with a concentrated hail of death.

The officer was beside him, unhurt but whimpering with fear. He grabbed his arm and hauled him down the ditch until they reached a small gulley bearing off from the track. Then, crouching, they ran across an open space for what seemed like an eternity until they reached a small clump of rocks on top of an incline, about a hundred yards from the track, that afforded some cover.

The yammering of the machine guns continued incessantly, but the short barking sound of the automatic rifles slowly died away until there was silence.

It lengthened. The pause became a minute, then two.

They waited, hardly daring to breathe. Then Redston heard the sound of gun metal scraping against a rock. He risked a quick glance and saw a drab flannel uniform disappear behind a boulder twenty yards away. At once a hail of rifle fire from all around them smashed into the rocks they were hiding behind, splintering and ricocheting like demented bees.

The officer was whimpering again, his face covered with blood, a red welt across his forehead, caused by a splinter or a bullet. Dazedly he wiped the back of his hand across his face, trying to stop the blood from running into his eyes. He stared at his bloodstained hand as though in a trance and began to cry. Sobs retched up from his stomach, wracking his body.

Redston looked at him in disgust, saying nothing, loathing this contemptible liability that left him without a chance. Was this how it was going to end? Eighteen years old, on a bare hill in Korea. He remembered another officer, in a wood, invading his private place. How he'd come to their house. His grandfather, lifting him clear of the porch, swearing at him, trying to prevent him from forcing them into the communal shelter. But his mother hadn't listened. Anything an officer said was bound to be right. Billy wished she could see this specimen now, but his mother would never know the truth about men like this—she never had.

He wondered if the gooks took prisoners. Suddenly the lead was spitting all around them again. As it died away, the officer finally snapped. He leaped to his feet, crying, screaming for mercy, spraying the rocks surrounding their cover haphazardly with his automatic rifle, his frozen hands unable to control the weapon. For some reason the gooks didn't kill him, and when his rifle was empty, hanging limply by his side, he just stood there crying, blood and tears running down his face.

Redston stood up behind him and said one word: "Sir?"

The officer half turned, looking toward the voice, seeing nothing through the blood. Redston shot him once through the chest. The officer was thrust backward by the impact of the bullet. He fell like a rag doll outside the rim of rocks that had been their shelter.

Redston threw his rifle to the ground, and slowly raised his arms.

The cell was small, barely big enough for him to stretch out, and it was impossible for him to stand upright. He was lying on a low cot next to the wall; there was one blanket, and a bucket in the corner. The cell was windowless, the only light, a single bare electric bulb that burned continuously, and he had lost all track of day or night. Perhaps his interrogator before the long forced march northward had not believed him—more likely they were making sure that he would be fully cooperative when the moment came.

He had no way of knowing how long he had been in this low, narrow cubicle, and his mind was beginning to play tricks on him. Sometimes it seemed he was in darkness, dust choking his mouth, filling his eyes. He could hear the faint sounds of men moving far above him, searching, calling his name. Then he'd see his grandfather's face peering at him, crying. Cursing the soldiers, blaming them, his voice was thin, distant, coming closer. "You forced us from the house—you killed his mother— you killed his mother—you killed his mother."

Billy sat bolt upright, sweating, staring at the light— thank God for the light; they'd found him, soon he'd be able to move again. His eyes slowly focused on the cell he was in—the bucket in the corner—the smell. He fell back on the low cot, covering his eyes, realizing where he was. "Oh God, please let someone come soon." In his despair he repeated it endlessly, then he stopped, listening. He heard something, footsteps, getting closer, coming toward him.

They halted outside the cell door behind him, and he heard keys on a chain, then the bolts being drawn back. He sat up and faced the door. A Chinese soldier stood in the doorway, pointing a rifle. He jerked it toward him, indicating that he should leave the cell. Billy scrambled to his feet, stooping to avoid the ceiling. He ducked under the mantel of the door and found himself in a narrow stone passage. He could stand upright now and the sheer physical relief was enormous. The soldier pushed him forward and he began to walk slowly, unsteadily toward the end of the passage. There were some circular stone steps to climb, and twice he had to pause before reaching the top. Each time he was prodded painfully in the ribs with the rifle.

He found himself standing in the middle of a high-ceilinged huge room, almost the size of a barn. There were no windows at ground level; the light filtered in through long narrow glass panels set horizontally into the walls near the ceiling. The walls were of bare stone and it seemed almost like a church, a monastery perhaps? It might explain the lack of furnishings. Just the two chairs standing in front of a huge log fire. Then he saw the hand resting on one of the arms, holding a glass, and he realized someone was sitting there.

The guard stood impassively behind him. Billy didn't move. "Come in, Redston." The voice boomed and echoed around the room. It was the first time he had heard English spoken since his interrogation immediately after he was captured. He moved tentatively forward a couple of paces—half expecting the guard to stop him. The voice boomed out again. "It's all right, Redston, no need to be afraid."

He walked toward the fire, then realized how the occupant of the chair knew what he was doing. On the high mantelpiece there was a round silver tray inlaid with glass, which reflected rather like a mirror.

He heard the man laugh, then he stood up as Redston approached and he held out his hand. He was enormous—tall for a Chinese, thickset, and running to fat. He was wearing the normal high-collared tunic of the military, but it was undone and he was in stockinged feet. His boots were slung beside the fire where he had been warming his feet. He crunched Redston's hand in his and told him to sit down. Redston did so gratefully, basking in the glow from the fire. The massive Chinese poured another drink from a bottle standing on the mantel and offered it to him. "Wine?" he said. "It's not French, but it's not bad." Redston took it and swirled it around in the glass, then took a swallow. The pungent smell of the warmed wine assailed his nostrils and almost made him feel sick. He'd forgotten how hungry he was. He put the glass down.

"Can I have some food? I can't drink this on an empty stomach."

The Chinese looked concerned. "Of course, how stupid of me." He said something to the guard, still standing immobile by the circular staircase. The guard turned and left the room, the high double doors banging noisily shut behind him.

The Chinese sat down in the other armchair with some difficulty, dwarfing it with his size. He stretched out his legs, placing his feet on the metal curve around the fire, warming his feet luxuriously. He glanced at Redston and beamed. "I hear you don't like the British Army."

Redston turned from the fire, his face slightly flushed

by the heat. "I hate it," he said tonelessly. His voice seemed to echo back from the empty room behind him. The light from outside was fading and the flames from the fire cast strange shadows on the wall behind him. One of the logs spat sharply, and a spark fell on the stone floor by his feet. He stared at it fixedly. He heard his grandfather's voice again. He was sheltering beneath the van. . . .

Where's your mother, Billy, is she all right?

The Chinese sat and watched him silently. Only the fire made a sound.

5. Barossa Valley, 1970

The red car breasted the top of the incline and coasted down the curving road toward Gawler. She was now leaving the region of Barossa Valley, and once through the main street of the small town, the road widened into a two-lane highway, stretching away in front of her as far as she could see. She never ceased to be surprised at the complete change in the character of the country once the valley was left behind. Here the plain spread out flatly on either side of the road, which seldom deviated from a straight line, unlike the narrow twisting roads of Barossa, bordered by woods and vineyards.

It was very much a physical as well as environmental change, a complete change in perspective, almost a different country. The sky, a blue empty bowl, the road ahead quivering slightly in the heat haze, typical of this part of southern Australia, but very different from Barossa.

Sharon Langbein glanced around at the back seat where her daughter was fast asleep. Trudie was only four, but already a very determined and self-sufficient little girl who could be quite a handful. Sharon was glad she was asleep. Adelaide wasn't far from Barossa Valley by

Australian standards, about 35 miles. But if her daughter had been awake Sharon knew there would have been an incessant barrage of questions all the way. She was glad of the respite, and looking forward to the beach, the sun and space. She recognized that she was glad to escape occasionally from the somewhat claustrophobic atmosphere of the tightly knit community, much as she loved the beauty of the valley.

There were other reasons, too, why she was glad to escape. It hadn't been easy for her to bring up Trudie without a husband. The Lutheran tradition was very strong in the valley. Indeed up until the early sixties, girls who had been unlucky enough to get themselves pregnant outside marriage were still expected to stand in front of the congregation on a Sunday and, together with the prospective husband who was responsible for her condition, publicly admit their sin.

However, the strict religious morality had eased over the last few years, but there had still been a lot of hostility toward her and her daughter, although she had not run, and had no intention of doing so. She liked her small antique shop in Tanunda. She had worked hard to make it prosper, and now that it was beginning to do so, she did not intend to be driven out—not by anyone. Even her father had at last accepted Trudie. Eventually, she was sure, he would once again accept her.

She drove down through Elizabeth, turning westward after Geeps Cross away from the city center, along Grand Junction Road toward the coast. She crossed the bridge that spanned the Port River and railway in Port Adelaide, then turned left down Military Road, running almost parallel to the beach. She glanced at her watch; it was still fairly early, just after ten. She knew a stretch of beach that was not over-looked, and at this time on a weekday would be practically deserted.

Off to her left were marshlands where the river petered out, and on her right the housing gave way to high sand dunes that stretched down to the Gulf of St. Vincent beyond. She glanced in her rearview mirror—there was very little traffic about—then slowed down, turning right off the road onto a sandy track that slowly disappeared into a small hollow between the dunes. She parked the car and started to collect all her bits and pieces and put them into a capacious string bag. Trudie began to stir, woken by the lack of motion and silence from the engine. Sharon put a floppy yellow hat on her to protect her head; the sun was fierce on the beach even for those who were used to it. Then making sure she had collected everything, she led Trudie down through the sand dunes to the wide white beach, empty and silent except for the squeaking of the gulls, the sound of the waves, the excited squeals of delight from her daughter.

Erich Spengler swallowed the last of the beer from the can and threw it away, rolling over onto his stomach and slowly adjusting the binoculars until the woman and the child were clearly defined. He wiped the sweat from his eyes, rubbing the lens on the lapel of his jacket. He then had another look. The child was a girl, about four or five years old. He had asked for a girl this time. Spengler had another look as they settled down on the beach. The woman clearly intended to sunbathe, while the child had already begun to build a sandcastle. The child would do.

6. Norwood, Adelaide, 1970

He blinked. The din was reverberating inside his skull like the bells of Notre Dame. He had a choice; either he could wake up and stop it, or he could suffer permanent brain damage—not much of a choice at that. Slowly he stretched out an arm and felt around until he found the clock. It seemed to take an eternity, but finally his finger found the button and pressed it. The din stopped but continued to reverberate inside his head for a few seconds. He ran his tongue around his teeth. They were furred and tasted like sour cream. Jesus, he felt awful, but somehow he had to get himself to the production meeting that began in an hour.

Take it easy, he thought, one thing at a time. First, the legs. He tried to move the right one. It wouldn't budge. Goddammit, something was holding it down. He thrust an arm under the sheet and felt around. It was a leg, another leg? He felt again. There was another leg, thrust across his own, pinning it down. He moved his hand slowly up the thigh until it reached the top. It was a woman—thank God. . . .

He lay there for a second, trying to remember. Nothing,

blank! He turned his head slowly and opened one eye. Her hair was spread out over his pillow, obscuring her face. Gently he removed a few strands until he could see it. Still blank! He didn't remember a thing. Leon's Bar was the last thing he remembered. And the stuff they served there must be dynamite. Either that or he was getting old. Still, there was the leg, in fact a pair.

He raised his knee, and the strange woman groaned and turned over but didn't wake up. Good, he thought. Maybe he could slip away before she did. She could find her own way home.

He crawled gingerly out of the bed, pulled on his shorts, and made his way groggily to the bathroom. He could hardly move the leg that the woman had been lying on; it was numb.

There was another strange person in the bathroom, a man staring at him from the mirror with red-rimmed eyes and a black growth of beard. He shut the bathroom door, wrapped a sock around the electric shaver to deaden the noise, and began to effect some repairs on the old man's face that gazed at him reproachfully from the mirror. Would he ever look thirty-eight again?

His eyes were normally blue—though this was difficult to perceive in the bleary orbs staring at him right now. He pushed the thick black curly hair away from his forehead —the gray hairs were spreading like wildfire, he was getting old. He sighed and refused to look any more, pushing his head beneath the cold tap and willing himself to turn it on.

After shaving, washing, cleaning his teeth, and gargling he began to feel averagely awful and steered himself back toward the bedroom. The woman hadn't stirred. He got dressed, wrote a note explaining that he had gone to work —that the whole thing had been wonderful, and would she mind making sure that the door was locked when she left. He pinned that to her panties, then slipped quietly outside the single-story bluestone cottage.

Jesus, why did the sun always shine so brightly in Adelaide? He groped his way to the car and fumbled inside the glove compartment until he found his shades—at least now he could see. He drove carefully down Edward Street, turned left into the main road, and tooled his ancient Holden toward Collinswood and the Australian Broadcasting Commission Studios.

Christ, he hated Australia. This morning he really hated it. He hated the wide, open roads, the low buildings, most of them single-storied until you reached the city center, where a few tall office buildings were beginning to raise themselves, huddled together as though for protection. It reminded him constantly that he was not at the center of things anymore—not where he wanted to be.

Brockway missed New York, he even missed the traffic jams. The hustle and the bustle. He had to get back, he knew that . . . he'd always known it. All he needed was the right story, then the offers would come and he could quit this place. Harry Brockway had arrived in Adelaide five years before. He had spent most of his working life in the media, first in radio, then television, but by the time he was thirty-three he realized he wasn't going to get the breaks he was looking for in New York, or he just wasn't goddamn good enough.

He wasn't prepared to accept that the latter was true, so he cut the connections and upped stakes, arriving in Australia with a bunch of tapes and what little remained of his capital. ABC had listened and looked, done some checking in New York and had given him a reporter's job on a nightly TV slot out of Adelaide. He was hard-nosed and ambitious, prepared to sell anything, do anything, to get the story across. He had upset a lot of people at ABC but the public seemed to like his brash, unequivocal approach, and he was beginning to make a reputation for himself where it mattered.

Brockway knew exactly what he was doing, but it still pained him that he had been forced to quit the States.

There was an old yellow sandstone house in front of the studio complex at Collinswood, called Tregenna House. It had an iron roof with a painted spire and had once been the home of a family who ran a chain of drugstores in Adelaide. More recently it had been used by ABC as a newsroom, but now it was being torn apart by a demolition firm, to be replaced by a huge building for production offices. It wasn't until after Harry parked his car that the clamor and din of the operation hit him. He winced and made his way quickly to the sanctuary of the production office where it was still audible, but bearable. After three cups of black coffee and something to settle his stomach, he began to feel better. The morning conference got under way on time. There were three other reporters apart from himself—none of whom had much time for Harry. But his producer knew that he got results. He was a good deal older than the reporter, and Harry had the uncomfortable feeling that George Greenfield understood the motives that lay behind his methods a good deal more than Brockway himself. The meeting followed the usual pattern. They knocked around a few ideas for that evening's show, had a look at the news, but because of the time difference nothing had happened in Europe yet. They discussed some current events and had a look at what celebrities were available—which wasn't a lot. Adelaide was not exactly the center of the entertainment business, though they did have an excellent Arts Festival once every two years.

A few suggestions were made about what story should dominate the program that evening. Brockway said nothing—he still felt wooly and incapable of saying anything constructive.

The report was telephoned into the program at ten past eleven. George picked up the receiver. The group around the table slowly quieted down as it became clear from the producer's reaction that something significant was coming through. His questions were precise, cogent, and he made a few notes on a pad. He put the phone down and looked up at Brockway. "Another child is missing. She vanished from Tennyson Beach, north of Grange, about forty-five minutes ago."

Brockway was already out of his chair and heading for the door. He had covered the last two disappearances; no trace of the children had ever been found. This one made five altogether. He was almost out of the room before the producer could call him back.

"Brockway," he yelled.

The reporter poked his head back around the door. George held up the piece of notepaper. "You'll need this." The other reporters around the table eyed him mockingly, clearly amused. Brockway walked slowly over to his producer and took the notes. George looked up at him resignedly. "Listen, Brockway, I know this is your story, and I know how you work. Get what we want, but this time don't press the mother too hard, understood?" Brockway nodded his assent, got back to the door, then glanced back at the reporters who still sat around the table. "Guess whose story's gonna top the program tonight?" Then he grinned and left the room.

7. The Beach, South of Semaphore, Adelaide

It was hot, the wide white sandy beach deserted, unblemished, except for the two sets of footprints leading down to the shoreline. Trudie was quiet now, intent on her digging, filling her plastic bucket, pounding it down and turning out the rounded shapes that would form the turrets and towers of her sandcastle.

Sharon spread the blue blanket that she had taken from the car over the hot sand, then sat cross-legged on it, pulling a bottle of oil from the string bag. She began smoothing it into her skin, brushing it lightly onto her legs, then pouring a little oil onto her stomach, spreading it across her body and around her breasts, covered by the top of her two-piece swimsuit.

She glanced up and down the beach; it was still empty, a heat-haze shimmering near the horizon where the cloudless blue sky and shore merged. She would have liked to remove the top, but something held her back. However much she tried to ignore the Lutheran restraints of Barossa, they still ran deep.

She lowered herself backward, stretching luxuriously on the blanket, then took off her sunglasses, shaking loose her long brown hair, before lying on her back. A cooling breeze blew in off the sea. She closed her eyes. The sound of the waves lapping the shore, easing themselves up the beach smoothly, lazily, then rolling back again was rhythmic, soft. . . . She began to drowse. . . .

Spengler could see the oil gleaming on her skin, her breasts rising and falling regularly as the woman was lulled to sleep. He quartered the beach with his binoculars, meticulously checking that the area was empty, that no early-morning sunbathers had escaped his attention. The woman hadn't stirred for nearly ten minutes. He felt he had waited long enough. From his pocket he took a small handmirror and focused it on the child, who was still building the sandcastle. He manipulated it until the reflection of the sun caught the child's face. Trudie shaded her eyes, looking toward the light glinting among the sand dunes off to her right. She glanced at her mother; her eyes were closed and she appeared to be sleeping. Still the light shone and flickered like a star on a cold night. The child was curious. She dropped the plastic bucket, but still carrying the spade, she began to walk toward the light, her feet sinking into the soft sand as she neared the dunes. Once the child was cut off from view of her mother by the small hillocks and clumps of saltbush, Spengler made his way swiftly around behind the girl.

Trudie had stopped. She couldn't see the light twinkling any more and she gazed around her uncertainly, wondering where it had gone. She heard something behind her and began to turn. An arm swept down and around her chest, gripping her tightly, lifting her off the ground. She opened her mouth to scream but something soft and clinging came down onto her face, blotting out the light from the sun, covering her face and mouth. A funny antiseptic smell, like a doctor's office, assailed her senses as she tried to breathe.

The child went limp in his arms, and Spengler removed the chloroform pad from her face, thrusting it back into his pocket. Quickly he carried the child through the sand dunes until he came to the place where he had left his car. He wrapped the girl in a blanket and laid her onto the back seat with a pillow under her head. Then he closed the door, got into the driver's seat, which was hot to the touch from the sun, and drove as quietly as he could toward Military Road.

The sound of the car's engine woke Sharon. She felt around for her sunglasses, then sat up, glancing instinctively toward the half-completed sandcastle. She stood up, shading her eyes, looking up and down the beach. There was no sign of Trudie; it was deserted. Panic swept through her, engulfing her in a cold sweat of fear. Her throat and chest constricted, making it difficult for her to breathe. She looked out toward the calm sea—empty. She ran toward the water's edge calling her name, her voice shrilly close to hysteria. "Trudie, Trudie, where are you?" There was no reply—just the sound of the waves slapping onto the shore. . . .

8. Semaphore, Adelaide

The Toyota Land Cruiser skidded around the corner of Semaphore Road into the Esplanade, then cut across the oncoming traffic, coming to a halt outside the single-story brick police station. His camera operator and sound engineer were already assembling their equipment as Brockway jumped down from the cab and made his way inside through the glass-fronted double doors.

There was a police sergeant behind the desk, but Brockway spotted a plainclothes detective yelling into a wall telephone. He'd worked on one of the earlier cases that Brockway had covered. He waited until he replaced the receiver, then tapped him on the shoulder. Detective Sergeant Phil Clayton turned, recognizing him.

"Is it the same?" Brockway asked.

The detective nodded. "Yeah, least we think so, little girl this time, four years old—they were down on the beach. The mother fell asleep, when she woke up the kid had gone—course she could have walked into the sea, but we don't think so. We found the kid's shovel among the sand dunes, and there were fresh tire tracks nearby."

Brockway put an arm around his shoulder, turning him away from the sergeant behind the desk. "Listen, Clayton, I've been reporting and following up these cases for over a year now—I've gotten nowhere." He paused. "I have to interview the mother this time."

The detective stopped him, holding up a hand warningly. "Forget it, Brockway, what are you trying to do? You know what the situation is in a case like this. She's taking it pretty well right now, but an interview might tip her right over the edge."

Brockway decided to change his approach. "So far five children have disappeared, right? *None* of them have been found—not even bodies. Now I know the police are under a lot of pressure and I don't want to make it worse." He paused for a moment to let that sink in then added, "But if I can get this woman on camera *now*, then maybe we can heighten public awareness, give ourselves a chance." He could see the detective weakening. "I promise I'll take it easy—no rough stuff. I'll also make sure that the public knows the police are covering every angle."

The detective studied him carefully for a moment, then made up his mind. "Right, it's a deal. But no histrionics, understand." He turned and made his way to a back room, calling out over his shoulder, "You wait here."

Brockway let out a long sigh of relief as the detective went to fetch the mother. The effects of his hangover had disappeared. The adrenaline sharpened his thinking and he was systematically evaluating all the possibilities. Instinctively he sensed that this story was a "big one." Maybe if he handled it right he could get what he wanted most. His own documentary slot—with him up front.

The door to the back room opened, and Clayton came out leading a young woman by the arm. She shook loose from him and said, "It's all right, I can manage."

The detective smiled, slightly embarrassed, and introduced the reporter. "This is Harry Brockway from ABC Television. Harry, this is Mrs. Langbein."

The woman pushed back some hair that was sticking to the suntan oil on her face. "*Miss* Langbein," she emphasized. She held out her hand. "How do you do, Mr. Brockway. Can you help me?" Brockway felt her hand tremble slightly as she asked the question, but he was surprised at her coolness—he might have to do something about that.

She was about twenty-five or twenty-six with hazel eyes and fair hair, bleached almost white by the sun. Her chin was firm, the mouth wide and generous, but it was her composure that he found remarkable. That worried him; it was not what he wanted for this interview. He donned his professional approach, calm, confident, and sympathetic. "Yes, I think we can," he said reassuringly. "I would like very much to get the situation across to the public as soon as possible. I realize, of course, the stress that you are under, how difficult it must be to even think about an interview at this moment, but believe me"—he lowered his voice to emphasize his concern—"if we can get this on television now, I think the public will respond, and it may help the police to get your daughter back."

"Yes, yes, of course. What do you want me to do?"

Was that her voice? It sounded so calm—so controlled; inside was screaming hysteria, panic. She knew that if she allowed anyone to show too much concern she would snap and probably need sedation. She *had* to stay calm, keep her mind clear, remember everything that might be of some help to the police—to this reporter. She didn't hesitate for a moment. If going on television helped her to get Trudie back she would do it—she'd do anything. "Where shall we go?" Once again that strange, unnaturally controlled voice was coming from her mouth.

Brockway looked at the detective. "Is there a room somewhere we can use?"

"Sure," Clayton said, "I'll take the lady, you go and get your crew." He led the woman back to the room they had come from. Brockway didn't like being separated from her, but Clayton had been too quick for him. He glanced back toward the entrance of the station. Outside on the pavement Mike Hardy, his camera operator, and the sound engineer, Roy Francis, were assembling their equipment, which was simple and effective. A 16mm film camera, a box containing film stock, a boom sound microphone, and tape recorder. Australian crews traveled light, and this one had been with Brockway on nearly all of his assignments; they knew what he wanted and were aware of Brockway's potential.

The detective sat on the edge of the desk trying to evaluate just how calm this woman really was. He offered her a cigarette which she declined. "Look, er, Miss. . . ." He hesitated for a second, not sure if that was the correct way to address her. "Look, I want you to know that you do not *have* to do this interview for Brockway—it's not going to be easy for you and if you had rather not, well, I can just tell him to forget it." He waited. Sharon looked up at him directly from her chair where she was sitting, emphasizing her determination.

"I want to do it. It doesn't matter about me, all that matters is that I find my daughter. . . ." Her voice trembled slightly, but she controlled it swiftly. "I want you to know that I will do anything—*anything*—that will help you find her."

The detective nodded. He was impressed. He had seen other parents in this situation, but none had reacted as positively as this one. "Would you like some tea?"

There was a knock on the door and Brockway's head appeared around it. "Can we come in now?" The detective waved them in, and they trooped through the door with their equipment. He repeated the question, clearly resenting it. "I suppose you would like tea as well?"

"Coffee for me," Brockway said, then grinned as the detective rolled his eyes upward in supplication. "Black," he added as Clayton was about to leave the room. The detective stopped momentarily, then shut the door fast before anything more was added to the list. The crew quickly began to set up and Brockway squatted down in front of Sharon.

"Miss Langbein." He paused. "I'm sorry, I don't know your full name."

She told him.

"Sharon," he said. "Do you mind if I call you that?"

She shook her head. "No, I don't mind," she said disinterestedly. Brockway could see she was only half listening to him, her mind elsewhere, thinking about her daughter. He decided that he wouldn't probe at this stage —he wanted that on camera. He engaged her in mundane conversation, skirting carefully around anything that might touch on the child's disappearance.

The detective reappeared with the tea and some weak black liquid that tasted of nothing in particular, least of all coffee. Mike was checking the shot through the view-finder of his camera, which he had set up in front of Sharon, and he gave Brockway an almost imperceptible nod to indicate he was ready to roll. Brockway glanced at his sound man. Roy was set. He picked up his cup and handed it back to the detective. "Thanks, Clayton, the coffee was great—I think we can manage now."

The detective got the hint and carried the cup to the door, then glanced back toward Sharon. "I'll just be outside if you need me."

She looked at him and smiled. "Thank you, I'll be alright."

As the door shut behind him Brockway gave his crew a signal. "Okay," he said matter-of-factly, then sat on the edge of the desk out of frame. He heard the camera begin to whir. Mike said quietly, "Turn over." Brockway glanced at Roy who had started to record and was holding the boom down between him and Sharon. "Running," he said. It had all been done so unobtrusively that Sharon only gradually realized that the interview was under way.

"Where do you live, Sharon?" Brockway asked.

"In Barossa Valley."

"And why were you in Adelaide today?"

"I came down for the day. I've been very busy lately and I wanted to give Trudie a bit of a break. I had promised her a day on the beach some time ago."

Brockway could see the distress in her eyes, but her voice did not falter. "So you drove down from Barossa this morning?"

"Yes."

"Where did you go to?"

"There's a place on the beach that we have been to before, north of Grange, that is not over-looked. There are no houses there." The voice was tight but still under control.

"What happened after you left the car?"

She paused for a moment, trying to remember the details. "I'm sorry," she apologized. "I was thinking."

"That's all right. Take your time."

"First I started to get our things together to take down onto the beach, then I locked the car."

"Where was that?"

She frowned. "There is a track off the main road that ends in a sort of sandy hollow between the dunes."

"Go on."

"Well, I took Trudie down onto the beach, found a place—"

He interrupted her. "There was no one around?"

"No, it was empty." Her voice quivered slightly for the first time.

"What did you do then?" he asked gently.

"I—we, we took off our outer clothes—we were both wearing bathing suits underneath. . . ." She stopped, then continued firmly, "And Trudie began to play."

"Did she go far away?" Brockway asked quietly.

"No," she replied sharply, "she started to build a sandcastle no more than four or five feet away from me."

"What happened then?"

She averted her gaze from Brockway. "I think I must have dozed off," she said almost under her breath.

Brockway repeated it with just the right amount of incredulity. "You dozed off?"

"Yes," she said, still gazing at the floor.

Brockway pounced. "You took your daughter onto a deserted beach, then fell asleep?"

"Yes, but I was tired," she said defensively. "We had both had a bad night. Trudie was very excited about the trip—she couldn't sleep and kept me awake practically all the night."

"What about your husband?" Brockway said innocently. "Couldn't he have looked after her for a while?"

She looked up at him, "I'm not married," she said tonelessly.

"Divorced?" he asked, smiling.

"No." Her voice was still dead, empty. "We did not marry."

Brockway shifted his ground. "So you brought your daughter down to an empty beach and you were tired?"

"Yes," she said sharply, trying to fight back. "Nothing wrong in that, is there?"

"But didn't you think that was risky?" Brockway knew he had her now.

"No," she said uncomprehendingly. "We had been there before many times."

"But what about the other children that had disappeared?"

Her mouth dropped, she stared at him horrified. "Other children?"

"Yes," Brockway said quietly, driving in the last one up to the hilt. "Four other children are missing as well, Miss Langbein."

She felt sick, anguish beginning to well up inside her as she realized the full implications. "Oh God," she said, her eyes clenched shut, trying not to cry. It was impossible; she felt the wet tears running down her face. She looked up at him desperately. "What shall I do?" she said, choking up. "What shall I do?"

Brockway kept the camera on her as she began to sob uncontrollably, then moved in himself, putting his arm around her shoulders, solicitous, eager to let the viewers see that he was concerned by her distress. "Don't worry, it will be all right. The police will find her, I'm sure." A moment or two later he passed his hand across his throat, indicating a cut to his crew. Sharon heard the camera stop, his voice droning on. "Try not to upset yourself, we're all on your side, looking for her. The police have some clues and the interview might help."

Through her distress, her grief, she was beginning to feel something else. A loathing contempt for this man. She knew now that she had been set up—lulled into believing he was on her side. She reached for her handbag and took out a handkerchief, wiping her eyes. "Take your hands off me." Her voice was icy, calm.

Brockway was surprised by the tone. He slowly raised himself to his feet.

She stood up, facing him. "Why did you ask me about my husband? You knew I wasn't married."

Brockway smiled and shrugged his shoulders. "I'm sorry about that, but I think it's important for the public to have all the facts. It can only help Trudie, because I'm sure that when people see this they'll be sympathetic." Sharon shook her head in disbelief.

"Oh, you're good, Mr. Brockway, you really are very convincing. I could almost believe that if I didn't know what a shit you really are." The expletive seemed shocking coming from her. "You used me. I was just fodder for that machine there." She glanced at the camera, then at Mike and Roy. "And you two aren't much better. I hope your paychecks are big enough to make it seem worthwhile." She turned and faced Brockway again. "But that's not what you want, is it? It's not just salary that turns you on." She looked at him contemptuously. "What is it? Suffering? Grief? Or do you just want to be famous?" For the first time Brockway was shaken by her outburst. His composure cracked for an instant, and she saw it in his eyes. She nodded to herself. "Yes, that's it, isn't it? That's what you are after, you want to become the 'big newsman' riding in on the backs of little Hausfraus." She smiled bitterly. It was quiet in the room—nobody spoke. Sharon walked slowly across to the door, then faced him. "I don't care what you do about me, Mr. Brockway, but you are *never* going to use the fate of my daughter to boost your contemptible ambitions—that I promise." She stared at them all for a moment, then quietly left the room.

The silence lengthened. Mike and Roy exchanged glances, then slowly began to pack their equipment away. Brockway felt ill. There was bile in his mouth from the night before, but there was something else, too. He knew she was right and he'd had to swallow it. It hung heavy and hard in his stomach, an indigestible lump of truth. He had led her on, manipulated her into reacting on camera exactly as he wanted. Done it deliberately and now she was aware of it, had seen him for what he was. Given him a cold, hard look at himself. Brockway knew he was no angel, but he hadn't liked what he had seen through her eyes.

He picked up the telephone and he rang the film process labs. He heard it ringing for a few seconds before it was picked up; he recognized the voice. "Hello, Arthur— it's Brockway—I need a favor. I've got some stock here that we have just shot. If I bring it straight around, can you process right away?" There was a pause while Arthur considered this and checked out his options. Mike and Roy were looking at Brockway inquiringly, waiting for the verdict.

Arthur came back on the line. "If you get it here in the next fifteen minutes, you're on."

Brockway gave a thumbs-up to his crew, thanked Arthur, and slammed the phone back down on the cradle. He looked at Mike. "We've got fifteen minutes to get it to the lab."

Brockway got back to the police station at Semaphore around 6:30 that evening. Nothing had changed. The sergeant was still behind the desk and Clayton was on the phone. He gave the sergeant a friendly nod and slipped into the back room before Clayton spotted him. He guessed right; she was still there, still waiting. She was sitting in the chair by the desk, her head resting on one hand cupped under her chin. Her eyes were closed, and he could see the strain on her face. He closed the door gently behind him, and she opened her eyes.

Her face hardened as she saw him. "I'm surprised you have got the nerve to set foot in here."

He looked at her intently for a moment, then nodded his assent. "So am I."

She turned her head away, not saying anything, and started to fiddle with the cold cup of tea on the desk. He stood by the door wondering how the hell he was going to broach the subject. He cleared his throat. "Look, er, about this morning. You were quite right." She didn't turn around. "You were right to say what you did. I deserved your contempt."

This time she did look at him, appraising him—trying to judge his sincerity. Not that she gave a damn. "I just hope you think it was worth it for your program," she said bitterly.

"It's about that that I have come to see you."

She started to twist her handkerchief around in her lap. Her eyes were swollen from crying. "I don't care about your program," she said tiredly. "Just leave me alone, will you?" The tears began to trickle down her face and she turned away in the chair so that he could not see her obvious distress.

He walked across the room and knelt down in front of her. "Listen to me. I know there is no reason why you should believe what I am saying, but I swear it is the truth. I have done something for the program which is already taped; it will be going out soon. Now I want you to see it, Miss Langbein—not because of what happened this morning, but because it might do some good for your daughter."

She looked down at him kneeling in front of her, wondering if there was any truth in what he was saying. "Why should I believe you?"

"No reason, except that I have come back, and I want you to look at it." He could see the uncertainty on her face. "It doesn't matter what you think of me, that isn't the point—but I think for your daughter's sake you ought to know what is being said, what is being done."

Sharon realized there was some sense in that. She felt

her spirits rising; maybe it would help—at least she could find out. "Where can we watch it?"

He stood up, relieved. "I've arranged for a TV set in a hotel around the corner."

She gave him a hard look. He held out his hands placatingly. "Just in case," he said defensively—then grinned.

She got up out of the chair, unsmiling. "Where is this place? I am not going to be sitting in some hotel lounge, am I?"

"No," he said quickly. "I have got a room for you—it's private." As they left the room the detective spotted them and grabbed Brockway's arm. "What the hell are you doing here?" He pulled him around, facing him. "I warned you, Brockway."

Sharon interrupted. "It's all right, Mister Clayton. I am just going to get a breath of fresh air—I don't mind him."

Clayton did not let go of his arm. "Okay, if you say so," he said reluctantly. Then to Brockway, "You step out of line this time, and I'll come looking—I promise."

Brockway acknowledged the warning and slipped from his grasp. "Okay, I promise." He held up a hand as though he were being sworn in, and steered Sharon toward the door.

He switched the set off. She seemed a little dazed, so he poured out a cup of fresh coffee and handed it to her. "Thanks," she said, looking up at him, "I don't understand."

"What?"

"The interview, it wasn't a bit like it seemed at the time."

"I edited it, shuffled it around, and made some cuts. It's just technique—I think it was better for it."

"Oh, yes," she said hastily. "It was better, and the way

you began and ended it, I think"—she fumbled around for the right words—"I think it might help us find Trudie."

"Don't worry," Brockway said confidently. "We'll find her."

She regarded him seriously for a moment. "Do you really think so? What makes Trudie any different from those other children that disappeared and haven't been found?"

"Because every time this happens it's a new risk for the sick bastard that's doing this. Another chance for the police to pick up a few clues." He went on, "They found car tracks in the sand near the place where Trudie's shovel was found—and this time," he added firmly, "I'm gonna be with it every step of the way." He gazed at her steadily, looking directly into her eyes. For the first time Sharon believed him.

9. Africa, 1970

The helicopter swooped low over the African plain. A herd of wildebeest, startled by the sound of the chopper's blades, began to flee westward in front of the machine.

Soon they were left behind, and Redston could concentrate his attentions on the terrain. This part of Shana Province was several thousand feet above sea level and from the reports that he had already received Redston knew that SSS expected to find mineral resources in the area. They controlled an area almost half the size of West Germany and under the agreement they had signed with the president of the African state, not only was SSS completely autonomous from it, but they had their own communications network, ran their own airline, and also policed the forty thousand square miles under their control.

Redston had kept careful scrutiny on the company's activities ever since he had been informed of the possibility of such an operation several years before. Contact had been made at their headquarters in Stuttgart, and they were informed of his interest. Now the whole purpose of this gigantic operation was about to be tested for the first time, and Redston intended to be there—to see if it would work. If it did, then the possibilities were limitless.

The German pilot had relapsed into silence after trying to engage him in conversation several times. Redston preferred to remain uncommunicative. They knew he was coming and had no doubt briefed the pilot to extract as much information from him as he could, but Redston had been laconic; niceties didn't interest him.

They would learn nothing from him until he was satisfied as to their true potential. He knew the operation had evolved from the highest levels of power and influence, and had been conceived with the tacit approval and help of the West German government in Bonn, though the company itself was a private enterprise venture, and owed its existence almost entirely to the work of one man.

The tax concession laws, always generous, had in this case been stretched abundantly, allowing anyone who cared to invest in SSS a 260 percent tax loss against investment. Thus for every one thousand dollars invested, two thousand six hundred could be written off against tax. The sixty million dollars needed for the operation had been raised secretly and with stupendous ease; private investors had lined up to place their capital. Yet it was all completely legal, with a copy of the contract between the company and the African state on file in Bonn.

The terrain began to alter. The ground started to rise gradually, outcroppings of red sandstone breaking up the surface of the plain. The helicopter gained altitude, and as the range of his vision increased Redston caught his first glimpse of the high rocky escarpment. The base of the escarpment shimmered in the heat haze, and for a moment Redston thought the massive plateau must be a mirage. But the top was etched clearly against the blue sky, and as they drew closer he could see the high metal tower of the launch platform dwarfed by the massive natural fortress on which it stood.

This was the base from which SSS would get lift-off for the first all-German rocket since the V-2. It was the center of a command structure for the largest rocket range in the Western World, owned and controlled by a private German company. Around the landing site Redston could see concrete bunkers for protection against the blast. The top of the plateau was about two miles long and almost as wide. Stripped of nearly all of its natural vegetation, it was now a complex maze of communications structures, laboratories, and quarters for the German personnel who ran this massive private enterprise, inaccessible except by air with a runway crossing from north to south on top of the plateau. Redston could see several transports as well as private aircraft parked at the terminal near the center of the runway.

The pilot brought the helicopter to a rest beside the terminal building, and Redston saw a group of three men emerge, waiting to receive him.

Redston scrutinized them carefully while he waited for the blades to stop turning. He recognized all of them from their dossiers. Kurt Weiss was the chairman of Satellite Surveillance Systems. Youthful for the position he held, in his late thirties, he had been the middleman, the organizer at the German end, whose contacts in high places had made the financing possible.

Nothing, however, could have been organized without Christian Streicher. Redston had heard about Streicher before this operation. He was an agent, a self-styled international financial consultant. He had been brought in because it was known he had considerable influence with the head of the African state; indeed he had already managed several slick business deals with African leaders, and was able to use his influence to bring both sides of the operation together.

But it was the third member of the group who interested him most: Bruno Heissler, 50 years of age, formerly a director at the Kennedy Space Center. He was the real motivator for this incredible venture. A brilliant rocket scientist, his glittering success for the Nazis at their Peenemunde Rocket Establishment had led him naturally into the American program under Werner Von Braun.

The blades had almost stopped, and Redston waited no longer, leaping down onto the tarmac before the short ladder could be wheeled in. He walked swiftly toward the small group, and Heissler stepped forward, extending his hand. The handshake was warm and friendly; he introduced Kurt Weiss, then Christian Streicher. Redston gave Streicher a cursory glance. He was wearing a wide-brimmed hat and a khaki bush jacket that seemed somewhat flashy and out of place in a modern operations center like this, in spite of the African setting.

After the introductions, Heissler led him toward the main building. "I expect you'd like something to drink after your journey—I get very thirsty, even at this height and distance from the plain."

"How high is the plateau?"

"Nearly four thousand feet. It's high, but it does improve the climate."

Redston took the opportunity to study Heissler. He looked far younger than his years. His face tanned by the sun, his fair hair bleached almost white. He seemed in excellent spirits, but Redston detected a slight air of tension, due no doubt to the imminence of the launch.

The building was pleasantly cool inside due to the air conditioning, and a well-appointed room had been set aside for their meeting. Plainly no expense had been spared on the base camp. A table was laden with cold meats and salad, and there was a fine selection of German wines, including an excellent hock. They sat around the table and Streicher immediately began helping himself. The pleasantries might have continued, but Redston wanted to know more about Heissler—he decided to go fishing.

"The concept of a low-cost rocket seems extraordinary under the circumstances."

Heissler raised his eyebrows curiously. Redston explained, "Well, until recently you had been working with billion-dollar budgets for the U.S. space program—why the sudden switch?"

Heissler smiled. "Not that extraordinary, surely, though I suppose it might seem that way to someone in your position." He paused for a moment, reflecting. "Of course my ultimate aim has always been the fulfillment of space flight, but once we had landed Armstrong and Aldrin on the moon last year, I knew the U.S. program would begin to wind down. There is neither the public interest nor the government will to take it any further at this moment; I certainly didn't want to be around just picking up the pieces. For a long time I'd thought about the Third World countries, and the need they have in a volatile situation for satellite surveillance capability, especially countries with unstable borders. Russia and America refused to provide it for security reasons, but I don't believe it would trouble them so much that they would interfere. A surveillance satellite is no danger to the rest of the world, so, a low-cost rocket seemed to be the answer; it provided me with a challenge and soon we shall know the answer."

Redston knew this was only half the truth and he felt it was time to get past the PR level and shake them up a bit. "But this isn't just a private venture, is it, Heissler? Isn't it true that SSS received a research grant from Bonn—the

Social Democratic Ministry of Research and Development to be precise—backing you to the tune of two and a half million pounds." The others were sitting up and listening now, and Streicher put the forkful of meat he had been about to eat back on his plate. This needed straightening out.

"I won't deny that, but the president of this country has an excellent relationship with our Defense Minister in Bonn who takes the view that this is a private investment by a German company in Africa and a major bulwark against the spread of Communism here."

Redston remained impassive. "Is that why SSS was given the free use of the Government Rocket Test Center near Stuttgart?"

Streicher looked to Kurt Weiss for comment, but he sat back in his chair, shook his head slightly, and said nothing. Heissler reached for the bottle of hock and proffered it to Redston who declined. He poured some in his own glass. "Clearly you have done your research well, Mr. Redston, but you need have no fears about the Bonn connection. They were helpful in the early days, it's true, but they have already gone cold on us. The Russians do not take kindly to our presence here, and they have been applying pressure on the chancellor. Bonn would like nothing better now than for us to fail and come home." Redston did not reply. It was obvious to Heissler that Redston did not want his interest or those of his clients revealed to any German government connections—he would have to know more. "Besides, this venture goes back a lot further than their initial interest." Redston waited while Heissler took another sip of the hock. "I told you that my overriding interest has always been space flight—that's why I was at Peenemunde during the war, though I don't expect you to believe it. However, it is true."

Redston nodded his head. "I don't doubt it."

"Thank you." Heissler smiled wryly. "Well, the V-2 was the closest we came to that and it has been the basis of everything that has followed. Curiously, Hitler regarded it as a failure and wanted it abandoned. Werner Von Braun and myself had to fight hard to keep it alive—we were even working on plans for a two-stage rocket, the A-10, that could have reached out into space." Heissler omitted to mention that its target had actually been the U.S. "Toward the end, money, supplies, parts—everything —was almost impossible to obtain, so a cheap method of propulsion was vital. That's when the idea was born. The Wasserfall Project, a ground-to-air missile, used compressed air for forcing the liquid fuels in the rocket instead of costly pumps. It's something I have been researching, on and off, ever since." He paused, and gazed hard at Redston. "This company is mine, Mr. Redston—nobody else's, and if we launch successfully later today, it will be the first all-German rocket since the V-2." He raised his glass, his eyes never leaving Redston's face. "Let's drink to that, shall we?" Redston studied him for a moment, then smiled. He'd gotten what he'd wanted. He raised his glass and drank.

Later that day he stood in the concrete bunker and listened to the countdown in German. It was eerie, strange. He'd watched the Germans launch their V-2's on newsreels many times, and it had always affected him deeply. Now the Teutonic cadences reminded him of another concrete structure, one that he couldn't forget—the pattern was recurring.

As the blast-off drew close, he began to sweat. The bunker was small, claustrophobic, and an unreasoning sense of panic began to creep insidiously through him; his nightmare wouldn't go away.

He knew it was stupid, without reason, and he fought

desperately to control the urge to run. The countdown was nearing completion, and he could hear it echoing around the site *zehn, neun, acht, sieben, sechs, fünf, vier, drei, zwei, eins.* There was a moment of silence, then a deafening roar as the rocket ignited. Redston ducked instinctively, covering his ears. Sheets of flame poured from the side outlets, and he waited for the concrete roof to bulge in toward him as though it were made of jelly, just as it had, those many years before, smothering him. Trapped between the narrow alcove of concrete blocks that had crushed the life from his mother, but had spared him. A dark, cold tomb, where he had seen no light, felt no pain, and hardly dared to move until his rescuers had finally found him.

But it didn't happen—not this time. The pencil-slim rocket slowly, effortlessly, lifted itself clear of the platform and soared into the African sky on a tail of blue flame. It had worked perfectly—the first piece of Redston's jigsaw fell neatly into place.

10. South Australia

The headlights shimmered on the dark wet surface of the road, and the side wind continued to slant the rain viciously into the car, making driving difficult. Sharon glanced at Brockway from the corner of her eye. He seemed relaxed behind the wheel in spite of the dreadful conditions. His eyes creased at the side as he peered into the darkness.

Again she wondered exactly why he had insisted on driving her back to Barossa Valley after it became clear there was no point in her staying at the police station any longer. Was it purely because, as he said, he felt responsible for her in some way, or was there another motive? She was beginning to trust him after the trauma of the interview, but there was a side of Brockway she would never be sure of. A slight ambivalence that disturbed, but also intrigued her.

She became aware that, for minutes at least, Trudie had not crossed her mind. At first she was shocked and felt guilty, but then the more practical side of her character reassured her that this was natural, perhaps healthy, for

Trudie had not been out of her thoughts for more than twenty-four hours.

Brockway turned right off the main road in Gawler and pushed the gear into third as the car started to climb the long shallow hill toward the valley. The road began to narrow as it curved around the slight bend at the top, and trees closed in on either side as it began to wend its way between the vineyards of the valley.

On his left he caught a glimpse of a sign high up on a tree. It was shaped like a shield and glinted wetly in his headlights. In heavy black German lettering it said "Barossa Valley." He glanced around at Sharon. "It can't be far now."

"No," she replied, "just about twelve miles."

He looked at her curiously for a moment. "It's funny, but I've never thought to ask what you do."

She smiled. "What makes you think I do anything?"

"I don't know, it's just that I can't imagine a woman like you doing nothing."

"Is that supposed to be a compliment?" she replied.

"Well, yes, I think so." The voice was serious but his eyes were twinkling.

She let him off the hook. At least he had made her smile.

"Yes, I am a working girl. I run a small antique shop in Tanunda. It's beginning to do quite well," she added.

He weighed his next question carefully. "Is it difficult?"

She stared straight out through the windshield at the rain slanting through the headlights. "Yes," she said quietly. "It *was* difficult." The silence lengthened, just the sound of the wipers slapping back and forth, fighting a losing battle with the rain. He thought that was it, she had clammed up on him, but then surprisingly she continued. "I started the shop with Nic about four years ago. We had met at university in Adelaide. It was his idea, not mine—he felt that tourism was bound to develop in the valley and there must be a place for a business like that." She fell silent, thoughtful.

He tried once more. "What happened to Nic?"

She looked at him sharply, surprised by the question, but he continued to gaze steadily ahead.

"He quit, after Trudie was born. Decided he didn't like the valley or the people. That it was too close-knit—intolerant, he called it. Well, probably he was right, it's just that I am used to it, and to be fair he did say he'd wait for me if I cared to go with him. That he would look after me and the baby." She paused for a moment then said, half to herself, "Why am I telling you all this?"

He glanced at her. "No reason, maybe it helps to talk to a stranger." Then he added, "You didn't go, though?"

"Go?"

"Leave the valley?"

She shook her head. "No, I couldn't. I was confused about him. He didn't seem to be the same person I'd known at university. Besides, my parents were not talking to me—they were shocked, embarrassed. More than anyone else. We have some pretty strong traditions up here, and a woman and a baby without a husband is not one of them." Then, quietly, "I knew that if I left the valley with Trudie there would certainly be no chance of a reconciliation with my parents."

"As bad as that?" he said.

"Yes," she said simply. "That's the way we are up here. It's pretty isolated, but things are slowly changing now—not least because of you lot."

"You mean television?" he said.

"That's right. Who knows," she said bitterly, "dad may even talk to me now."

Brockway turned to look at her curiously. In that instant the road veered sharply left, then right, prior to crossing the railway line, and he heard her scream a warning. His eyes flicked back to the road. He saw the ditch and tried to keep the car on the road without touching the brakes. They would have made it, too, but the road was wet, his speed too high, and the back of the car began to slide away from him. It moved inexorably sideways into the ditch; the front buried itself in the bank and it came to an abrupt halt. Brockway's head snapped forward and crashed into the corner of the windshield and the door.

He could hear someone slapping him, though curiously he couldn't feel it. It was disorienting, like a bad dream. Then the pain hit him, thudding in his head like a sledge-hammer. He groaned and opened his eyes. Sharon was driving the car, casting quick, anxious looks at him. She was saying something, but it was difficult to understand through the throbbing in his head and the sound of his face being slapped. Then he identified the sound; it was the wipers still coping inadequately with the rain pouring across the windshield. At least that hadn't broken. Then it all came back with a rush, and he tried to sit up, gingerly feeling the painful corner of his forehead. Sharon had tied his handkerchief around it. She repeated the question anxiously. "How do you feel?" He glanced at himself in the rearview mirror; the handkerchief was stained with blood and he felt it tenderly.

"A bit like a wounded soldier," he said, and tried to smile reassuringly, but changed his mind and winced at the pain caused by the effort. "Not so good," he allowed. "Almost as bad as a hangover," he cracked, unable to resist the humor. Then he remembered. "The car, how did you get it out of the ditch?"

"Never mind about that. You sit still until I get you to the doctor." Then, answering his question, "It wasn't too difficult. We were lucky—the ground was soft and the offside wheels were still on the road." Brockway relaxed slightly, moving his limbs to see if he hurt anywhere else, but it seemed to be just his head. "Are you okay?"

"Sure, not a scratch. Now be quiet—you've got a nasty bang on the head."

"Jesus, I'm sorry. I could have gotten us both killed."

"You would be well advised," she said severely, "not to use that kind of language up here. Now will you please shut up, for God's sake?" and grinned at her deliberate "blasphemy."

Brockway relapsed into silence, nursing the pain in his head, enjoying the intimacy of her concern. It was impossible to see beyond the two pools of light dancing along the narrow road in front of the car, just a vague impression of an occasional clump of trees, and the constant drilling of the rain onto the roof of the car. Sharon eased her foot down on the brake and put the car into third gear as they swung around another S-bend first to the left then to the right, and began to climb the shallow hill into Tanunda.

"Almost there," she said, breaking the silence. She glanced at him. His face was pale and bloodstained beneath the bandage, and he would probably need stitches, she thought. They passed beneath the wooden arch slung high across the road advertising a local winery, then they were in the main road of Tanunda, which was deserted at this time of night.

She turned right by the small two-story museum on the corner, past the white building that served as a bandroom for the local brass ensemble, and pulled into the driveway of the hospital on the right.

It was a high, modern brick building, constructed in the early postwar period, that dealt almost exclusively with private patients, its clientele stemming mostly from the upper echelons of the community.

Sharon knew one or two of the staff through her father, who was a company manager for one of the wineries further up the valley. She helped Brockway out of the car, and supported him into the reception area. Brockway felt ridiculous as he stumbled once or twice, but his head was swimming now that he was upright, and it was difficult to focus. He saw the male orderly coming toward them and he said to Sharon, "Okay, I'll be fine." Then he passed out.

Three hours later he woke up for the second time. He was in a small white-walled room with just a wicker chair and a religious picture on the wall for furnishings. The pain in his head had lessened, and he was wearing nothing except a long white nightshirt and a bandage around his head. He tried to call out. "Nurse," he croaked, his throat dry, the voice almost inaudible. He cleared it and tried again. "Nurse!" It sounded better, echoing around the small room, but it brought no response. He glanced around the room to see if there was a buzzer—some way to attract attention, but there was nothing. *Shit*, he thought, *there must be someone around.* He eased his feet out of the covers and placed them on the floor. The linoleum was cold. He stood up slowly. His head felt muzzy, but the pain stayed in one place. He looked around for something to put on his feet; the room was empty. Slowly he made his way to the door. It opened silently, and he glanced up and down the passageway outside—still no one. He turned right and started to walk groggily along the passage. Suddenly he began to feel nauseous; the strength drained from his legs and he felt his face go cold and his lips bloodless. The passageway began to sink beneath his feet, and he grabbed at the metal rail beside him. He tried to keep moving, but he seemed to pass out for a moment and when he opened his eyes he saw the elevator. It was at the end of the passageway, a metal door, quite narrow, with a single button in the wall beside it. He groped his way toward it and pressed the button. The metal door slid open noiselessly. He stepped inside, supporting himself in one of the corners. He saw the panel in front of him and pressed a button marked "G." Nothing happened. He could feel the cold sweat breaking out on him again, and frantically he pressed it three or four times. This time the door closed and he felt the elevator begin to descend. It seemed to continue downward for an eternity. *Christ, this must be a tall building*, he thought, then it jerked to a halt, almost flinging him to the floor in his weakened state. The metal door did not open, so he pressed the button again. The door slid back. He seemed to be in a huge white room that spread out in front of him, indefinable and empty. Again he felt disoriented, then he heard a door thud shut and saw a man emerge, it seemed, from one of the walls. He staggered toward him trying to speak—to ask where the hell he was. The man caught him before he fell, and Brockway had a vague impression of the man's feet encased in huge yellow shoes. He felt indescribable relief at having found someone, then relapsed into unconsciousness.

11. The Birdsville Track

Jiggs prodded Molly with his stick, urging her none too gently to increase her pace. The camel grunted indignantly but moved imperceptibly faster, dragging the reluctant Bess along behind her. They had just crossed the Birdsville Track and were heading westward toward the dry salt beds of Lake Eyre.

Jiggs wanted to be well clear of any possible users of the track before he lit his campfire that night. The sun was well past its zenith, but still blazingly hot, bouncing off the hard sandy surface as it sank in a giant orange ball toward the horizon in front of him.

Jiggs didn't have to consult his watch to know what time it was, but it was a familiar ritual that he enjoyed following, one of the few links that he cared to retain with the society that he had fled from thirty-odd years before. It was an old-fashioned fob watch, made of solid gold. First he took a leather pouch from a pocket in his tattered bush jacket. He removed the watch carefully, and it shone brightly, reflecting the fierce light of the sun. The pouch protected it perfectly from the sand and the heat of the desert—and it remained faultless and accurate in spite of the conditions. He snapped open the gold face cover and looked at the familiar inscription his wife had placed inside it on their wedding day thirty-nine years before. He always read it, then held it to his ear, balancing himself astride the camel instinctively. The watch continued to tick comfortingly; he checked the time, nearly five o'clock. He wound it slowly and put it back into the pouch, and thence into the pocket reserved for it in his threadbare jacket.

Having checked the time, he carefully eased from its goatskin satchel a battered but still serviceable radio. Jiggs didn't tune it, he didn't have to. It remained constantly set on only one station: 5LC, broadcasting on the National ABC Network. There were others he could get if the conditions were right, but there was no interference on ABC. Besides, he didn't like the commercials.

He switched on and heard the familiar voice of the announcer beginning to read the news. It dealt mainly with the forthcoming visit of the Queen to celebrate Australia's bicentennial. Jiggs passed it on to Molly and Bess for what it was worth. "Can't think why they don't leave the poor woman alone, dashin' her 'round all over the place, and what does she see when she gets there," he said rhetorically. Molly grunted. "That's it—nothing. Just a load of old mayors and councilors. Red carpet over everything. How's she ever gonna know what Australia really looks like?" He smiled grimly to himself. "Bet they even kill off all the goddamn bloody flies before she sets foot in the place."

Molly didn't comment, just raised her head imperiously and curled her lip with contempt.

Jiggs laughed at the display of temperament, then listened intently as Bill Cameron's program came on. It was a mixture of old songs and news items from the 30s and 40s called "Memories." Jiggs liked it. The first record was an old favorite. A monologue by Stanley Holloway that he knew by heart. He joined Holloway in the recitation so that his camels could have the full benefit of its quality. "Sam, Sam, pick up thy musket. . . ." His recitations were a great feature of the day, and both Molly and Bess cocked an appreciative ear. Halfway through, Jiggs stopped abruptly, and Molly grunted her displeasure. He switched the radio off and halted the two camels, returning the radio to its satchel. He shielded his eyes from the setting sun and scrutinized the long dust cloud carefully.

The vehicles causing it must have been a good five miles ahead of him, moving northward from left to right across his path toward the Simpson Desert. Even at this distance it was clearly more than just a single vehicle; he estimated at least ten. Jiggs didn't like it—he felt an almost proprietary interest in this stretch of subdesert between the Flinders and Coober Pedy, and while the odd four-wheel-drive sometimes ventured off the trail, he had never seen anything like this before. He prodded Molly into motion—he wanted a look at those tracks before nightfall.

The shadows of the two camels were lengthening, and it was noticeably cooler by the time he reached the tracks of the convoy. He reigned Molly to a halt, forcing her to her knees, and then dismounted and began to examine the tracks meticulously. His estimation didn't alter: about ten, possibly twelve vehicles in all, some of them heavily loaded. The wheels had sunk deeply into the hard dry surface.

Jiggs stood gazing in the direction that the convoy had taken, trying to evaluate the reason for their presence. He rubbed his gnarled hand over the gray stubble on his chin thoughtfully. There were no minerals in the Simpson, nothing he could think of to draw them in that direction.

He glanced at Bess who was chewing on some saltbush. "Wonder what they want?" he said aloud. "Could be with some oil company, I suppose, unless it's another one of those speed merchants," he said, remembering Sir Donald Campbell's attempt on Lake Eyre to get the land speed record in '64. "The bloody lake filled up with water that time," he laughed. "Never happened before." Then, more seriously, "Just as well, though, Bess—that put everyone off."

He clambered onto Molly's back, prodding her with the stick. He intended to stay on the trail of the convoy until it was dark; he had to know their destination.

Although Jiggs had virtually been a recluse for the last thirty years, he was still an insatiably curious man.

There was another reason, too. Jiggs regarded this area as his patch, and anything untoward that happened within it, or ventured upon it, might be a threat to his remote valley in the Flinders, so he stayed as close as he could. The convoy continued to move northward, skirting the easterly side of the dry salt Lake Eyre. Gradually they drew away from him, the dust cloud no longer visible, and their tracks became impossible to see as the sun dipped below the horizon.

Darkness came quickly and Jiggs made camp, hobbling his camels so that they couldn't wander. It was vital with camels. Bess had once slipped her leather hobble when the buckle had broken, and strayed nearly twenty-five miles that night. He'd spent nearly a whole day searching for her.

With darkness the temperature dropped swiftly and the bush flies disappeared. Jiggs lit a fire, warmed some beans, and boiled his billy to make tea. That and some dried roo meat was his meal for the day. The camels survived on saltbush and spinefex. He would have to use his supplies sparingly; he had not anticipated this diversion.

Usually the two-hundred-and-fifty-odd-mile journey from his valley in the Flinders to Coober Pedy took five days, but now that could be more than doubled. He had to be careful. The delivery of his opals could wait. His visits were regular but haphazard, and his agent was not expecting him, although this time Jiggs felt sure he would be pleasantly surprised. He'd been gouging a dig in some sandstone beds at Tibooburra, one hundred and twenty miles northwest of White Cliffs. The sandstone had come out in flat pieces that fitted together like a jigsaw puzzle. Beautifully veined with opal, it was uncrazed or blemished, and easily cleaned. Though money was of little concern to him, Jiggs knew it would fetch a good price.

He bedded down for the night, his saddle for a pillow, and a tarpaulin and a blue blanket his bed. He would start early, at first light. He intended to track this mysterious convoy to its destination. . . .

By noon next day he was already working his way up between the high, ochre-colored sand dunes of the Simpson Desert. Awe-inspiring to those who had never seen them before, the ridges of sand, sometimes up to two hundred feet in height, stretched in long symmetrical lines from north to south.

Formed some ten thousand years before in the Pleistocene Era by high longitudinal winds, they ran for hundreds of miles across the Simpson, making it virtually impossible for vehicles to travel across them from east to west. The gentler westerly winds that now blew across this desert had banked each ridge on its westerly flank so that the incline was much shallower than on the east, where it dropped away steeply enough to make even a four-wheel-drive vehicle bottom out. However, provided they stayed in the corridors between the ridges, slow northerly progress could be made.

Once into this terrain Jiggs knew he was maintaining his position, and possibly gaining on the convoy. Several times he had seen the dust cloud churned up ahead of him, and from the amount of rubbish left at their campsites, he estimated that their numbers must be between forty and fifty men.

Late on the evening of the fourth day he was close enough to see the smoke from their campfires. If he hurried there might just be enough light left to get his first look at them before nightfall.

Jiggs was puzzled. He couldn't fathom why they were here in the heart of this barren desert. There were no minerals, certainly not oil. A French oil company had built a track across the sand ridges in 1963, some fifty miles further north, but they had abandoned it and any further exploration two years later. He hobbled Molly and Bess and pulled out an ancient brass telescope from Molly's pack, then he set off on foot.

He climbed the shallow incline of the ridge to the east until he reached the top, emerging into the sunlight that was still catching the crest. He looked eastward; it was an incredible sight. The sun was now casting shadows right across the corridors between the ridges, each red crest caught by the sun emerging in succession from the dark shadows in between. The ridge tops were like ochre stepping-stones across a vast black sea.

He began to walk northward along the top until he saw the lights from their campfires ahead. He lay on his stomach and pulled out the telescope, focusing it until he had the shadowy outline of the vehicles in his sights.

There were twelve of them, drawn up in a semicircle; already a considerable amount of unloading had been done, and suddenly he realized that this was their destination. The light was fading fast, but Jiggs was able to discern what looked like the sides of some prefabricated buildings lying flat upon the floor of the corridor, prior to construction.

Jiggs did not light a fire that night; he could not risk being seen. Next morning at first light he rode his two camels over the ridge into the next corridor in case anyone from the convoy decided to retrace his steps. It was unlikely anyone would cross over the ridge on foot, and the camels would be safe from detection here. Once again he hobbled them, giving them enough freedom to move around and graze on the occasional clump of saltbush and porcupine grass. Then he walked northward along the corridor until he estimated he was opposite the base site. Slowly he climbed the steep easterly side of the ridge, his feet sinking into the soft sand, sometimes up to his knees. As he neared the top he began to hear the activity from the site beyond. He reached the crest and raised himself slowly on his elbows. Already two of the prefabricated buildings had been erected, and equipment was being installed. Most of it was electronic and it was clear to Jiggs that this was not a potential mining site. One of the six-wheeled drive trucks was carrying a generator, and cables were being laid to the main structures. He hollowed out a shallow depression in the crest that gave him some cover yet enabled him to lie across the top of the ridge. All day he watched them, occasionally taking a sip of water from his flask. The heat was intense but it had little effect on him. Years of conditioning had given Jiggs the resistance to cope with his environment. The site grew visibly before him, but he surmised that it must be temporary, since the sheer logistics of serving a base of this nature for any length of time would be almost impossible.

Whatever its purpose, Jiggs resented the intrusion, but he could not afford to hang around any longer if he was going to get to Coober Pedy before his supplies ran out. Nor was there much to be gained by staying here. He would come back after he had seen his agent and made his opal deposits—perhaps someone in the mining town would know something about this. News had a funny way of traveling fast out here in spite of the distances. Before the shadows began to lengthen again, Jiggs half slid, half jumped his way back down to the floor of the corridor, then walked back to where he had left his camels. He climbed on to Molly's back and set off southward, eager to get far enough away so that he could light a fire when it was dark, and cook some food.

He expounded at great length to Molly and Bess about the day's events, at one with his animals and the harsh environment, yet uneasy about the unexplained presence of a complex modern unit in the heart of this vast and barren desert.

12. Tanunda, Barossa Valley

Doctor Kauffmann accompanied him down in the elevator to the ground floor. There was no sign of the room he had stumbled into, just the normal hospital reception area, and Brockway concluded that he must have been suffering from the aftereffects of concussion and an overdeveloped imagination. The tall, elderly doctor warned him to take things easy for a while. Brockway fingered the piece of tape on his forehead that covered the three stitches they had inserted in the wound, and thanked him.

"Sure, Doc, don't worry, I don't want to have to go through that again." He acknowledged the receptionist's cheerful "Good-bye, sir" and stepped out into the bright sunshine, putting on his shades.

Sharon was waiting in the familiar, slightly battered red car that they had driven up in from Adelaide. He was surprised; she was the last person he had expected to see. He wondered if anything had happened. He walked slowly down the steps, and leaned down beside the open window. Her face was drawn and pale despite the make-up, but she was making a brave effort to appear cheerful.

"Hello," she said, "I thought you might be able to use a

lift." She smiled half-heartedly, the strain never leaving her eyes.

"Thanks," he said, "that's kind of you."

She patted the seat beside her. "Come on, hop in."

He walked around the car and slipped into the seat. "How did you know when I was coming out?"

"I rang Doctor Kauffmann, he told me." She fiddled with her handbag. "I hope you don't mind." She glanced at him briefly. "I couldn't stand being alone in the house anymore, waiting for the phone to ring."

"No," he said quietly, "of course not." He paused momentarily. "They know where you are?"

"Yes." Then with forced gaiety she added, "I told them I was going to a restaurant . . . would you like to come?"

She was desperately trying to hold onto some sort of normality. "Sounds great—what are we waiting for?"

She turned and looked at him. She was grateful, but said nothing. The car started at once; she drove down to the main street, turned right, and parked outside of a restaurant on the left called Die Galerie. It looked like a shop from the outside, but inside it was cool and spacious. On the left was a bar where Sharon ordered some wine. Brockway was content to let her handle it; he was feeling a little woozy and was glad to be inside out of the heat. After dealing with the wine order the man behind the bar led them down a couple of steps to the restaurant, a long low, wood-beamed room, with heavy wooden tables and canvas-backed seats that vaguely reminded Brockway of the chairs he had seen on some movie sets.

This room was very real, however, with oil lamps set in brackets high on the walls and old black and white photographs hanging on them of what looked like some of the original settlers in the valley. They gazed seriously from their fixed poses at the diners, sturdy and implacable.

Brockway had the impression that they would have approved of the slightly uncomfortable chairs and the flagstones on the floor. The man placed the bottle of wine on the table between them and asked if he should pour. Brockway looked at her inquiringly, and she nodded her agreement. The hock was superb, and Brockway quickly refilled their glasses.

"You like it?" she asked.

"Yes, I do—it's terrific, a good choice."

"If there's one thing they can do well round here—it's this." She took another sip from her glass.

Brockway felt better already and realized he was starving. "Do we get a menu?" he asked.

"I think he's bringing it," she said.

He arrived and placed a blackboard down beside them, smiled and left. On it the menu was written in chalk:

Kaminchen mit Schwarz Olive,
Wiener Schnitzel,
Sauerbraten,
Apfelstrudel
and
Black Forest Tart.

He glanced up at Sharon and grinned. "If I didn't know better I'd say that we were in Munich."

"Don't mock, the Sauerbraten is good."

"What is it?"

"Marinated beef—it's traditional," she added.

"Is it all like this?"

"What?"

"The valley, the German influence."

She sipped her wine and looked at him over the rim of the glass. "Yes, I suppose so. I haven't really thought

about it for a long time." She gestured with her hand.
"You get used to this, although I suppose it must seem a
bit odd to strangers."

Brockway nodded in agreement. "Yes it is, but interesting, though. A pocket Rhineland in the middle of Australia." A new thought struck him. "Might make a good
documentary. Maybe I ought to mention it when I get
back."

Sharon picked up on this, thankful to have something
else to think about. "Yes, it might. It's interesting, actually, although Barossa is not a German name; it comes
from the Spanish town of Barossa—they make a lot of
sherry there—I suppose that's the connection."

"But how did it begin? It's all around us. The churches,
the architecture. It's not like anywhere else I've seen in
Australia."

"The churches are mostly Lutheran—that's how it
started, basically. The Lutheran community began settling here in the eighteen-fifties because of persecution in
Prussia. The German influence has always been very
strong."

Brockway was getting interested; there *was* a program
here. "Yeah, but what happened during the war? In fact
both wars. You mentioned persecution in the nineteenth
century, but did anything like that happen here?"

Sharon thought about it for a moment, wondering how
much she should tell Brockway. She knew how ambitious
he was, but even if it did result in a TV documentary, it
could only be good. "Yes, yes, there was persecution,
xenophobia during both wars. My father remembers the
schools being closed during the first war—he was just a
boy then. There were no church services, and many of the
German place names were changed. There was a lot of
bitterness. I remember him saying that some families

were almost starved out." She picked up her glass, smiled nervously, and sipped.

Brockway sensed that she was holding back. Maybe her father had gotten involved somehow? "This bitterness that you mentioned from the First World War. How did the German community here in the valley respond to Hitler?" He gestured with his hands. "I don't mean when the Second World War was taking place, but before—in the thirties?"

Sharon nodded her head. "Yes, I believe a lot of his propaganda was accepted uncritically. The autobahns in Germany, getting rid of inflation, people working again—that sort of thing." She remembered something else. "They appointed a consul general down in Adelaide. My father told me he met him once; apparently it was very grand."

Brockway decided to check that one out later. He broke a piece of the bread and started to butter it. "How are your parents? Did you see them?"

"Yes." She looked through the window into the garden. "They were shocked and very upset, of course, though my father tried hard not to show it, but I could tell." She smiled, that tight little smile again.

"How was he?"

"You mean did he speak to me? Yes, he did. So I suppose that's something to be grateful for." Her eyes were lowered; she was fiddling with the red napkin. "He was sweet, actually, though he's not an emotional man." She glanced up. "Very traditional."

As though on cue a brass band struck up from the garden outside. Brockway laughed, breaking the mood, then leaned over to make himself heard.

"Is that traditional, too?"

"Yes," she said, "when it's sunny."

A pert young waitress arrived and began to recite the menu, pronouncing the German words perfectly with a strong Australian accent, which Brockway found amusing. He ordered the Sauerbraten and drank some more of the hock. He knew that no trace of Trudie had been found and he was quite deliberately trying to keep the conversation light and away from the subject. He suspected that she was doing the same, and the more he got to know about this woman the more he respected her, but it went deeper; her physical attraction had always been apparent, but it was her fiercely independent spirit that drew him closer, and although he was not fully aware of it, he was beginning to feel a strong sense of responsibility for her.

They were both looking into the garden enjoying the music and were unaware of the man's presence.

"You are Sharon Langbein?" he asked. He was about twenty years old, unimpressive, standing awkwardly beside their table.

"Yes," she said, surprised by the question, suddenly apprehensive.

"I am sorry to interrupt your meal"—he smiled nervously at Brockway—"but it's about your daughter— Trudie, I believe?"

Now she was really frightened; Brockway could see it in her eyes. "What about Trudie?" she said sharply. "Has something happened?"

Again he seemed embarrassed. "Well, no, not exactly. You see, I am with the local newspaper and I am covering the story . . ."

Brockway stood up. "Wait a minute." He leaned down and said quietly to Sharon, "It's all right, I'll deal with this. I'll be right back. Okay?" Her eyes were still frightened, shocked. "Okay?" he repeated firmly.

She nodded her agreement.

He turned, gripped the young man's arm and began to

propel him quickly out of the restaurant. He protested feebly, but didn't resist. When they were outside Brockway faced him. "What do you think you're doing—is that how they teach you to approach a bereaved victim in journalism school?"

"Well, no," he stammered. "I've never covered a story like this before."

"Right. Now listen to me, and write it down." The young reporter fumbled in his pocket and produced a pad and pencil. "Ready?" The young reporter nodded. "Sharon Langbein's daughter Trudie was kidnapped by someone from Tennyson Beach in Adelaide, while the child was playing. This is the fifth child to disappear in this way during the last three years, and the first girl." He paused. "Got it?"

"Yes, yes I think so."

"Good. Now listen, and you can also write this down if you want to. She lives here in Tanunda, and if I ever hear you so much as pass the time of day with her in the future I'll kick your ass so hard, you won't be able to sit on it for a week—do I make myself clear?"

The young man nodded nervously. "Yes, yes, of course —I didn't mean to upset her—"

Brockway interrupted him, "Then learn how to do your job properly. Now go!" He almost shouted the last two words, and the reporter moved off sharply down the street.

Brockway straightened his tie and glanced nervously around, grateful that his crew had not witnessed the incident. They would never have believed it. He found it hard to believe himself.

They didn't stay in the restaurant. Sharon was shaken by the incident and Brockway drove her back to her house on Elizabeth Street. It was a pretty sandstone single-story place, backed off from the road opposite a park.

There was a verandah at the front, and Brockway parked the car between two trees that verged onto the road.

He sensed that this was not the right moment to make any cracks about getting her safely home, and there was a moment or two of silence between them. Sharon spoke first. "I'm sorry you didn't get your lunch."

"Forget it—I wasn't too sure about that Sauerbraten anyway."

She glanced at him from the corner of her eye. "I could fix you something—I've got some steak."

"Steak," he said, thinking about it—he was hungry.

"Grilled or fried?"

"Whatever." He glanced at her; the tension had gone. "It's a deal."

"Come on," she said matter-of-factly. "Let's eat."

After the meal he helped her wash the dishes and tidy a few things away, then they sat down together and had some coffee. "Sugar?" she asked.

"No, thanks, I like it the way it is."

She put a spoonful in hers and stirred it slowly. "Thanks for taking care of that reporter"—she glanced at him sipping his coffee—"though I was a little surprised at your reaction."

He shook his head. "Yes, well, I was a little surprised myself, since *I* didn't do too well the first time."

She looked at him steadily. "Nevertheless, I am grateful."

He found her look disquieting and put his cup and saucer down on the coffee table. "Look, er, do you mind if I use your phone? I need to find some transportation to get back—I guess they're wondering where I am." He stood up, moving toward the phone.

"Harry—" He stopped. There was something about her

tone, an urgency, intense. "Harry," she repeated, "please don't go, not now—stay with me for a while—please."

Brockway knew it was a mistake—if he didn't leave now, in a way he never would, but she was looking at him, her eyes full, a desperation behind them that she was trying hard to control. Brockway never really had a choice, but he never regretted it.

She made love to him with a passion, a need that he responded to tenderly, sensing her vulnerability. Sometimes she cried with the pain of her loss, the love for her child. Her need for this man whose loving was sensitive, responding to her changing mood, stimulating her with his touch. His hand stroked her breasts gently, his finger tracing a circle around her nipple. Then it slid down over her stomach between her legs as his lips closed over her nipple, his tongue caressing and stroking each breast. . . .

He could feel the wetness between her legs and slowly he slid himself into her. She grasped his hard, muscular buttocks, pulling him into her as far as he would go, trying to blot out the pain, the loss. Feeling him inside her, each thrust seemingly deeper, stronger, she responded instinctively, gasping with relief at the pure, physical release of this moment. He lay heavy on top of her, kissing her damp hair spread across the pillow. Then he rolled off and held her head gently in the crook of his arm. She felt a great wave of tiredness engulf her. She relaxed at last, and slept peacefully, quietly, for the first time since Trudie had disappeared.

13. Pine Gap

The Pine Gap project had become fully operational by the early part of 1969. Described at the time by the Minister for Defense, Mr. Fairhall, as a base for investigating "upper atmosphere and space phenomena, some of which may conceivably have a defense significance." This description was at best misleading, and at worst nonsense.

Situated twelve miles southwest of Alice Springs, it had been built by the Americans' Advanced Research Projects Agency (ARPA) which was responsible not only for research and development of missile systems but also for their operation.

Clearly it was a part of the "spy in the sky" concept, in effect a research and control center for spy satellites, which would now permit satellites to take orbital paths over areas of China and the Soviet Union, as it was difficult to monitor them from a North American site. It was also believed that the project in Pine Gap would assist the Americans to find a counter to the anticipated development by the Soviets of the Functional Orbit Bombardment System (FOBS). Thus a part of Australia had, for the first time, become a prime nuclear target, and this struck a very raw nerve among most Australians who had comforted themselves for years with the thought that in the event of World War III, they at least might be spared. A naïve theory, but it had gained credibility through repetition in the Australian press.

It was dark when the phone rang in Sharon Langbein's house on Elizabeth Street. Brockway was half asleep and tried to reach it before it woke Sharon, but she was still lying on his arm and it was numb. His movement, and the phone, woke her, and she called out sharply "Wait!" before he could reach the receiver.

"I'll get it," she said, brushing the hair from her face. "I don't want the whole of Tanunda to know you are here." She switched on the bedside lamp and walked quietly over the carpet to the phone. She was naked and moved gracefully. As she held the receiver to her ear Brockway noticed the subtle shape in the outline of her breasts framed by the light from the bedside lamp. "Hello?" She listened for a moment, then he caught the tension in her reply. "Yes, I am Sharon Langbein." A pause while another question was asked. "Yes, I have seen Mr. Brockway, as a matter of fact." She turned to him and smiled. "He hasn't left yet." Then she mouthed silently, "ABC." Brockway slid out of the bed and put on his underwear. Maybe he was more modest than she, but he knew he would feel better talking to his bosses if he at least had his shorts on. He took the receiver from her. It was his producer.

"Hi, George." He tried not to sound as if he had just got out of bed.

"What are you doing still up there?" the voice snarled. "You should have been back here twenty-four hours ago."

"I had an accident, George—I just got out of the hospital."

"You've got no business having accidents—we're trying

to run a news show down here. . . . Can you handle an assignment?" he added quickly.

"Thanks for your concern," he said pointedly. "What is it?"

"There's going to be a big public demonstration outside the Pine Gap complex in Alice. I want you and your crew to fly up there tonight and cover it for us tomorrow. Can you do that?"

Brockway made a few quick mental calculations. "Yes, that's all right. You organize the flight from Adelaide—will it be the usual flight service?" He heard George flipping through his notes.

"Yes, I am already on to that. PAGAS will fly you, Mike, and Roy up there. What time can you pick it up at the airport?"

"What time is it now?" He heard his producer sigh.

"Jesus, Brockway, don't you even know what time of day it is now?" Then without even waiting for a reply, "It's eight forty-seven."

Brockway was already grabbing for his shirt. "I reckon I can be down there in a couple of hours, say around eleven, okay?"

"Be there," the voice said curtly, then the line went dead.

Brockway put the phone down and began to dress hurriedly. "Look, I'm sorry, Sharon, but can I use your car?"

She was slipping into a silver gray nightdress. "Of course." No trace of resentment in her voice, an instant recognition of what he had to do. "I'll make you some coffee while you are getting ready." She moved past him toward the kitchen and he slid his arm around her waist, pulling her to him. He gazed at her steadily for a moment.

"Listen, Sharon, will you be all right?" She nodded. He continued to hold her. "I'll be back."

She didn't say anything. There was no need; she could

see that he meant it. She kissed him, holding him tightly to her for a moment, then broke away and went into the kitchen. By the time he was dressed the coffee was on the table with a sandwich. He took a bite from it and gulped down some of the coffee.

"I'll get someone at ABC to see about returning your car," he said between mouthfuls. "And try not to worry about anything. I know it's impossible, but try. Will you promise me that?"

She nodded her assent and pulled up the knot on his tie. "I promise," she said. "And keep the car in one piece."

Brockway kissed her lightly on the lips. "Now listen, I'm going to keep a tight check on everything and as soon as I'm back, I'll be up here. Is that okay?"

"Yes," she said a little breathlessly, and added, "please." He held her face between his hands and kissed her. She clung to him for a moment, then picked up the car keys from the table and held them in front of him. "You'll need these," she said. "I won't come out."

He took them from her and smiled, aware of how much it was costing her to remain calm. "Be seeing you," he said. Then he turned and left the room.

She heard the car start up outside, turn around and slowly fade from her hearing. She walked into the bedroom and slid into the space that he had vacated. She held his pillow tightly against her body and gazed sightlessly at the wall.

The first rays of the morning sun were glinting on the wings of the Cherokee 6 as they neared Alice Springs. Brockway heard the engines alter pitch as the pilot put the nose down for his approach, and he rubbed his eyes. He glanced behind him where Mike and Roy were still out. He envied them their slumber. He'd never been able to sleep soundly in an aircraft; it was a knack he hadn't mastered—he didn't like flying very much. The demonstration up here hadn't surprised him—he knew how much popular resentment there was at the prospect of American bases on Australian soil. He viewed this attitude with faint contempt. It seemed to him that Australia, like most democracies around the world, wanted it both ways. The support and protection of the U.S., and none of the responsibilities that went with it.

Australia had been good to him and he intended to use it—make the most of whatever opportunities came his way, but he wouldn't stay. He'd go back one day, on his own terms and in his own time. There were a few people who were gonna eat shit back home and he would enjoy their discomfort. He hadn't forgotten.

He leaned forward toward the pilot. "How much longer?"

"Be down in ten minutes."

Brockway shook the two men behind him. "Come on, wake up. Get your stuff together, we'll be down soon."

Mike grumbled as usual. "What's the hurry—there's plenty of time." But he began to collect his equipment together.

Brockway ignored the obligatory protest. "Mike, have you ever been over this site before?"

"Yeah, once, a year ago, when they brought Whittaker in to have a look at the officers' mess."

"That was all he saw?"

"Yep—and that's more than anybody else. They won't let anyone over the place."

Brockway glanced at his watch; it was nearly 5:00 A.M. "Right, this is what we do. First I want to pick up the car they've got on standby for us. Then we go straight out to the base."

It was Roy's turn to protest. "Aw, c'mon, Harry—we must have something to eat first."

"We'll grab a sandwich and some coffee at the airport and eat it on the way out."

"What's the rush?" Mike complained.

"I want to get there before the protesters do, and try to get some shots of the base. Can I do that?"

Mike looked doubtful. "Well, you can't get near it— there's a security checkpoint a couple of miles from the base."

"What's the terrain like?"

"It's very dry, of course, in a valley—"

Brockway interrupted, "In a valley?"

"Yes, that's right." Mike looked puzzled.

"If it's in a valley there must be some hills nearby, right?"

Mike got it. "Right, and with a telephoto . . ."

They both grinned.

The large red sign read, "WARNING TRAVELLERS. CHECK YOUR FOOD, PETROL AND WATER. THE NEXT PUBLIC STORE IS KULGERA, 168 MILES SOUTH." They ignored the red dusty road that led eventually to Adelaide, and proceeded down the bitumen one that was the link between the base and Alice Springs. According to Mike the security checkpoint was about six miles from their present position, and Brockway was already scrutinizing the area carefully, trying to find a turn-off that would lead him to the hills that rose on two sides of the American base. He saw a signpost indicating a graveled road that led out to the other side of the Macdonnel Ranges through Honeymoon Gap.

They traversed a rough bush track through the valley and passed a couple of farmhouses. Now they could see the two largest radomes, huge white circular structures that contained the antennae. Moments later they were halted by the buffer fence that completely enclosed the base. The radomes were about one thousand yards away.

Brockway got out of the car and stared up at the rocky face of the hill that rose steeply behind them. The other two joined him, waiting for the inevitable question. "Do you think we could get a camera up there?"

Roy and Mike glanced at each other dubiously.

"Do we need sound?" Roy asked.

Brockway shook his head. "No, I just want film of the base. We can link in the presentation somewhere else."

Roy looked at Mike. "Well, in that case, I can help Mike with his stuff."

Mike looked peeved. "What do you mean—stuff!" He turned and started getting the camera from the trunk.

Brockway and Roy smiled at each other, then began to help him with the equipment.

It was a hard slog up the hill. The sun was already burning the rocks, making them hot to the touch, and by the time they reached the top they were exhausted, but the view was worth it. The two largest radomes, mounted on concrete bases, looked incongruously like a couple of giant white tennis balls. There were two smaller radomes, one nestling between them, the other further off to the left. Nearby was a tall steel triangle, one base point-fixed, the other mounted on a track so that it could be rotated in any direction. There must have been more than twelve buildings comprising the installation. The largest was about two hundred feet square.

Surrounding the complex was an outer buffer fence and two inner fences, which even from this distance looked as though they might be electrified.

Brockway urged Mike to be as quick as possible. He was afraid they might be spotted and the film confiscated.

It didn't happen. Mike shot a complete magazine of film, and then they scrambled down the hill like guilty schoolboys stealing apples from an orchard. Mike and Roy were hugely elated on the drive back, but Brockway didn't feel safe until they were on the main road, where they stopped and ate the sandwiches. Seldom had heat-hardened, dry airport sandwiches tasted so delicious.

A sky-blue guardhouse with a sign that read JOINT DEFENCE SPACE RESEARCH FACILITY marked the point which was as close as they could get to the base. A Commonwealth policeman examined their credentials, asked them a few questions, and made some notes.

Some of the early birds had already arrived in their cars. They sat quietly waiting for the protesters to arrive. It was clear the demonstration had been well organized.

Many had flown into Alice Springs from all parts of Australia, and George Greenfield's warning to Roy and Mike about the planning of this operation was justified. They were led by a group of Melbourne ex-students who were committed, almost full-time, to matters that related to the environment. This particular issue had given them the popular support that they had so far lacked, and they obviously intended to make the most of it.

Mike and Roy had got their equipment set up, using the roof of the car as a camera position. It gave them some height, and experience had shown that they were safer if things got out of hand.

Cars began to arrive in ones and twos at first, then it became a continuous stream. The organizers made them park a good five hundred yards from the guardhouse, as they intended to cover the last section on foot. It would do their cause no harm at all if the public thought they had walked all the way out from Alice.

Brockway always gave Mike and Roy a completely free hand in these circumstances. They'd worked together a long time now, and he knew he could trust them to get what he wanted. Brockway simply acted as another pair of eyes for Mike, and would insert his comments later.

He had watched the guardhouse carefully, but it seemed as if there were only two policemen present. The authorities were completely aware of the situation, and Brockway wondered what contingency plans they had made if the demonstration got ugly.

By nine o'clock there were between two hundred and two hundred fifty people present, lining up to march on the guardhouse, and Mike had already filmed their preparations with a telephoto lens. Brockway pointed to a small group of about a dozen men standing slightly to one side. "Get some footage on them, Mike—I think we have got the heavy mob here."

Mike panned across, bringing them sharply into focus. "Uh-huh," he said, his eye glued firmly to the lens. "I think we have the makings of a very interesting situation."

Brockway waited, but Mike didn't enlarge on that. He tugged at his jacket. "For chrissake, Mike, stop being so goddamned cute and tell me what you see."

Mike didn't take his eye off them for a second. "Well, I'll tell you one thing, boss—this ain't gonna be no Sunday school picnic."

Brockway looked upward in supplication. "Okay, Mike, so this is your big moment—who are those guys?"

Mike panned the camera slowly over the rest of the crowd. "We have some of Mr. Smith's favorite Nationalist Socialist friends here today, boss, and any minute now . . ."

"Shit," Brockway said, half to himself. "Do you think we are far enough away?"

Mike didn't budge from the camera. "We'll soon find out."

Brockway shielded his eyes from the glare of the sun. The crowd was starting to move down the road toward the guardhouse. He glanced at his watch—it was five minutes past nine. Brockway saw the policeman who was standing in the road signal his colleague, who promptly picked up the phone and made a call. The demonstrators began to chant slowly, in unison, "Americans out, Americans out," and although Brockway knew it was not directed at him personally, he still felt a small sliver of fear slide down his back. They were about one hundred yards from the guardhouse now, and he heard Mike exclaim, "There they go." Brockway craned his neck to see over the chanting crowd. He saw the Nationalist group start to move into a position about five rows from the front. They were carrying something in their hands now—it looked like truncheons. He yelled at Mike, "Did you see where they got the clubs from?"

Mike continued to adjust the telephoto lens, keeping the leading edge of the protesters in focus. "Yeah, they had them inside their waistbands."

Roy was standing by the front of the car with a long directional microphone, picking up the chants. Brockway yelled down to him, "Get in the car, Roy, and be ready to pull us out of here." Roy looked around surprised, ready to protest. Brockway silenced him. "Do as I say, Roy, and try not to bounce the camera off the car, right." Roy shrugged his shoulders, pulled in the microphone, and clambered carefully into the driver's seat.

Brockway knew that film crews, like actors, were incapable of sensing danger once the camera was turning, and he was taking no chances, not with a group of self-styled Nazis hanging around. They heard the sirens screaming raucously as three truckloads of police came hurtling down the road from the base and pulled up in a cloud of dust behind the buffer fence. Before the trucks had halted, the police, wearing protective helmets and carrying truncheons, were spilling out of the gate and forming a line across the road in front of the guardhouse.

The demonstrators at the head of the column tried to stop, but were pushed forward by those from behind.

Brockway was watching Mike carefully, but he was getting it all. An inspector with a bullhorn standing behind the line of policemen began addressing the demonstrators, warning them that they should not come any closer, that they had made their point and should leave.

However, it was clear that the protesters had not come this far to give up that easily. Those at the front were gradually being pushed forward into the police ranks, who tried to force them back. That was the moment that the infiltrators had been waiting for. They slipped between the leading protesters and, keeping their clubs low and out of sight, began jabbing them ruthlessly into the police. Immediately there was chaos—the police line broke, several of them rolling on the ground in agony. The police began using their riot sticks, trying to protect themselves against the overwhelming numbers. Heads were split, faces covered in blood, people lying on the ground were being trampled upon by those trying to escape from the truncheons.

For a few minutes it was absolute pandemonium and Brockway was glad of their position on top of the car. In that melee it would have been impossible to film anything. The police gradually started to gain the upper hand as more and more demonstrators broke away from the fighting and fled back toward their cars. Mike zoomed in on the two cars where he had first spotted the Nazis. He saw them climbing in, falling over themselves, eager to get away before they were spotted. The two cars roared off down the dusty road. Moments later it was over as the injured were carried away by the two sides. The police did not attempt to make any arrests. It would have been virtually impossible, as the cars were already returning the battered protesters to Alice Springs.

Brockway told Mike to cut and clambered down off the car. He sized up the situation quickly and indicated the position he wanted the camera placed for his piece of commentary.

He stood to one side while they set up. His mind was racing ahead, sizing up the possibilities. He knew that Mike had got some great shots—the film would prove that the neo-Nazis had precipitated the police reaction. But was that what the public wanted to see? They were totally against the bases, and their sympathies would be with the demonstrators. But this hadn't just been a legitimate demonstration—it had turned into an ugly confrontation, and Brockway didn't want to find himself in the position of supporting the police case—not a popular stance in Australia.

Mike and Roy had completed the new set-up in less than three minutes; Brockway spoke directly to the camera. "Today we have seen more than just a demonstration by a few extremists. We have seen a pitched, bloody battle between concerned citizens and the police, who were trying to maintain order, to protect the American military hawks. This base at Pine Gap has been constructed in the heart of Australia, without the consultation or the agreement of the people, and has, by default, made us, all of us, prime targets for nuclear missiles in the event of a third world war. The demonstrators who came here today are not just a few extremists but all sorts of people, who have come from all parts of this continent to register their protest at this American takeover of a part of their country. What even the protesters may not have known, is that while the people of Alice Springs may be eliminated by an intercontinental ballistic missile aimed at this base, the Americans who made it have constructed, in the guise of a school, what is effectively a blastproof nuclear shelter. Furthermore, my investigations indicate that they may also be using a nuclear power source to run the base, as there has been no significant increase in the use of electricity in this area, and it would be impossible to run such a complex plant without such an increase. Finally, may I say as an American, that I am deeply concerned about what I have seen here today, and may I make a plea to the authorities concerned, both here and in the United States, to think again about the need for this base, and the danger to which they now expose Australia. This is Harry Brockway for ABC Television at Pine Gap." Brockway indicated the cut and let out a sigh of relief.

Mike looked at Roy incredulously, then back at Brockway. "For chrissake, Harry, what do you think you're doing? Are you going blind—didn't you see what those guys were up to?"

Brockway held up his arms placatingly. "I saw it, Mike, but I don't want the public to see it—not yet. Let's give them what they want. We generate more impact that way, and we've got something to spare."

Mike spat on the road in disgust. "I don't believe it—what about all the film I shot?"

Brockway grinned. "A little careful editing?"

Mike threw the magazine into the box. "Ah shit, sometimes I don't even know you, Brockway."

The reporter shrugged his shoulders. "What's the problem, Mike—this way we get two films for the price of one, okay?"

14. Nic Bailey

It was a small seedy hotel sandwiched between a massage parlor and a newsstand that fronted onto Darlinghurst Road in the Kings Cross area of Sydney.

Phil Clayton knew the area if not intimately, at least well. It was almost obligatory for tourists to see the whores parading their wares, the drug peddlers and pimps. Tall, leggy women in tight silk shorts and sweatshirts stood outside the parlors encouraging male passers-by to come inside and sample the joys of sauna and massage. But this time Clayton was here on business. Nic Bailey had not been difficult to track down; the Social Security services had led him to Sydney and this seedy hotel. The local police were handling the operation, but Clayton had insisted on being present. The fire escape and stairs were covered, and Clayton and two other policemen went up in the creaky elevator, which smelled of urine, to the fifth floor. Bailey's room was at the end of the passage, and the two policemen were armed just in case. They stood on either side of the door, and after they had indicated they were ready Clayton inserted the key he had got from the clerk at reception into the lock, and then threw the door open.

The double bed was against the far wall next to the window, Bailey sat up at once and visibly paled as he saw the guns. The woman woke up and her eyes widened with fear, too shocked and surprised to even cover her naked breasts. Clayton glanced quickly around the untidy room, then checked the bathroom and tiny kitchenette; there was no sign of the child. Bailey was beginning to get over his surprise and started to ask some questions. Clayton cut him short. "Are you Nic Bailey?"

He nodded. "Yes, but what's this all about?"

The detective picked up a pair of trousers and after checking the pockets, threw them onto the bed.

"We're police. I'm Detective Sergeant Philip Clayton from Adelaide." He showed him his identification. "Are you the father of a child, a girl born to Sharon Langbein almost five years ago?"

Bailey was beginning to recover some of his composure. "Yes, that's right, but it's no secret. Why all this?"

"We're looking for the girl—she's disappeared. As you are the father we thought you might know where she is. Have you seen her?"

Bailey shook his head. "No, no, I've never seen her." He stared at the detective with a mixture of incomprehension and disbelief. "Disappeared," he repeated. "What do you mean?"

Clayton knew then that he could write off this particular lead. It had been reasonable to suppose that a father who has never seen the child might have resorted to taking the girl away unannounced, but instinct told the detective that this man was not responsible. However, he would continue to go through the motions until he was certain.

"Get your clothes on," Clayton said. "We're going down to the station. Maybe you can help us find your daughter."

He glanced at the woman who still hadn't bothered to cover herself. "She can stay here."

The woman smiled at him insolently. "Please yourself— you don't know what you're missing."

The two young policemen exchanged glances, trying to hide their amusement, and put their guns away.

The antique shop was at the top of Elizabeth Street where it joined the main road. In front was a small fountain with a nymph holding a horn through which the water spouted decorously. When she had bought this place with Nic after they had left the university, it had been a junk shop. But they had worked hard on it, foreseeing the possibility that Barossa Valley would develop as a tourist area because of its unique blend of traditional German vineyards and architecture, and its proximity to Adelaide. They had lined the walls with pineboards, which gave it a fresh, gleaming appearance inside. A large mirror down the entire length of one wall made it seem bigger than it was.

The news of her daughter's disappearance had clearly spread through the valley, and a lot of people whom she knew had no intention of buying anything came into the shop just to look at her, curious to see how she was taking it. Some, more generous than others, bought something and tried to express their sympathies. Sharon was surprised by this; few local people had ventured into her shop after Trudie had been born, though it had been nearly five years since her birth. An unmarried mother was still anathema in the valley, and she more so, since she had never tried to hide it or shown any sign of remorse.

Her parents had wanted her to stay with them this morning, to close the shop at least until they knew what had happened to Trudie, but Sharon knew that if she cut herself off from her daily routine she would not be able to bear it. Much better the curious stares of the locals than being alone with her thoughts.

At first she didn't recognize him. He'd grown a beard; he looked older, unkempt, and down at heel. Only when he spoke did she recognize the voice.

"Sharon." He stood before her in front of the counter. His eyes slightly apprehensive. "I heard about Trudie."

She didn't move. She stood rooted to the spot, staring. "Nic?" Her voice, etched with disbelief, echoed hollowly in her ears. She felt weak. It was all rushing back, the memories, the pain she had pushed into the back of her mind, trying to forget. He was speaking. She could see his mouth moving, saying something. She must pull herself together. Behind him, two middle-aged women were watching her intently.

"I'm sorry," he was saying, "I didn't mean to come un-announced, but I just felt I had to get here as soon as I could."

Sharon turned abruptly and walked toward the office at the back. "Would you come this way, please?" she said, trying to sound businesslike. She sat down behind the desk, her legs shaking. He came in and stood awkwardly just inside the door. "Close the door," she said, her voice tight, unnatural.

He did so. "Sorry about that"—he nodded toward the women in the shop—"I'd forgotten what they were like around here." His eyes were red-rimmed from lack of sleep—he looked exhausted.

"Sit down, Nic." She indicated a chair. As he was doing so, Sharon studied him carefully, shocked to see how much he had changed. All the arrogance knocked out of him, he seemed indecisive, unsure of himself. "How did you find out?"

He chewed his lip, then decided to tell her the truth.

"The police—they, er"—he paused, wondering how to phrase it—"they traced me to Sydney." Then a touch of anger. "Christ, Sharon, they seemed to think I had taken her."

"That's hard to believe," she said coldly. "Since you have never even bothered to see her."

He shook his head and looked at the floor. "Yeah, well, I expect I deserved that." Then a flash of the old spirit. "But I would never do a thing like that, and you know it."

She acknowledged that. It had been a cheap crack, but she wanted to hurt him; she could feel it deep down inside her, and the virulence of the emotion surprised her. "I'm sorry," she said quietly. "Would you like some coffee —it's only instant."

He nodded. "Yeah, please, that would be fine."

She filled the electric kettle at the sink in the corner and switched it on, putting some coffee into a couple of mugs. "Why did you come?" she said, her back to him.

He didn't answer immediately, then, "I don't know, really. I wondered how it had happened."

"Didn't the police tell you?"

Again he paused. "Yes, they told me."

She turned and looked at him inquiringly. "Why then?"

He averted his gaze from her. "I suppose I wanted to see you, know how you were."

She looked at him silently for a moment. "And you thought I might need you?"

He looked at her directly for the first time and in his eyes Sharon caught a glimpse of the young student she had fallen in love with nearly seven years before. Now there was nothing. "Yes," he said quietly, "I thought you might." He swallowed hard, finding it difficult to say what he wanted, then almost in a whisper he added, "I need you, Sharon."

The room was still, quiet, just the sound of the clock

ticking in the corner, then the whistle on the kettle began to blow, and Sharon turned and switched it off, pouring the boiling water into the two mugs. She put sugar and milk into one and handed it to him, then picked up hers, and sat down again.

He misinterpreted her silence. "Maybe we could try again, Sharon. Maybe I could help you through this."

She stopped him. "No!" Her voice was shrill, emphatic. "Don't even say that! Don't use her to try and manipulate me." Her eyes were blazing, angry. All the bottled-up emotions of the last five years surfaced.

"I don't want you here, Nic. You're no longer a part of my life or Trudie's. You decided you couldn't stand this valley—the people—and you went, knowing I was pregnant, knowing what I would have to face if I stayed." She was trembling with emotion but not prepared to let him see her cry. "Well, I did stay—I didn't come running after you. I faced these people—my father—and it's all right now, it's working, so I. . . ." She shook her head, finding it hard to articulate her deepest feelings. Then she composed herself and said simply, "I don't need you, Nic. I've got one child to mother; I don't need another."

He sat in the chair for a moment, unmoving. Then he stood up and placed the half-empty mug on the desk between them, staring down at her. "I'm sorry, I shouldn't have come, I. . . ." He stopped and didn't complete the sentence.

They looked at each other, aware that something had changed. Indefinable, a sense of loss, but an acceptance of reality, of truth.

"I guess there's no point in staying." He looked into her eyes, hoping to see some love, some regret, but there was none. He wanted to say something about Trudie, but he didn't feel he had the right.

He nodded. "Okay, I'll go."

A lump surged into her throat, and she drew in her breath sharply, controlling herself. "Good-bye, Nic, take care."

"Sure." He turned and walked to the door of the office, then glanced back. "Thanks for the coffee."

The door closed quietly behind him, and he was gone.

She sat down abruptly behind the desk, gazing at the door, her emotions confused, thoughts tumbling through her head. All the things she had consciously forced to the back of her mind as though they had never happened. She'd had to do that in order to survive, to get through each day, one foot in front of the other. But now they were back, as though something had snapped, releasing a flood of memories.

The clock ticked loudly in the empty room, reminding her of another, much larger and elegant, equally silent, yet full of people—students reading. She could see the high, beautifully-made ceiling, the inscription on the wall. Tom Elder Barr-Smith, then something in Latin that eluded her. They had often sat there, at the long wooden tables, comparing notes, sometimes forgetting to keep their voices low. Then hushed disapproving shushing from the other students. In front of the red brick library and reading room were some lawns bordered by a low wall on which the students would sit, read, and chat. On the other side of the lawn was Union Hall, where films were shown during lunch hours; it also doubled as a theater for students of drama. But Sharon's favorite spot had been the iron footbridge that crossed the River Torrens and led to the park beyond, just in front of the main entrance to the university.

They'd often stood on the bridge and watched *Popeye* pass below. *Popeye* was a small passenger cruiser painted white, with a green trim, that plied up and down the river between the zoo and the downtown area of Adelaide.

It was there in the park, one night, beside the river, that Nic had first made love to her, and she had loved him, her first man. After that they had been inseparable, sharing a house in North Adelaide with several other students, splitting the rent among them.

She had driven Nic to the valley once to meet her parents, and it had been his idea to open the shop. She remembered how they had sweated to make that junk shop presentable, then Nic's gradual disenchantment with the valley and its German descendants. She felt he was altering, or maybe she was just getting to know him better. But the final realization came when she told him she was pregnant.

She had seen the fear in his eyes. He'd tried to make her have an abortion, but she had refused; at least some of the morality of the valley still clung to her. She wanted the child. Instinctively he had been unable to contemplate the thought of marriage, of settling down within a community he found repressive.

In the end he had fled back to Adelaide and left her a note telling her that if she would come with him he would look after her—but no more.

She knew what he meant, that she would have to lose the baby and leave the valley forever. It was at that moment, perhaps, that she first saw him for what he was. A romantic, a drifter. A man who would always evade responsibility, going everywhere, going nowhere. . . .

Sharon decided to stay. It had been hard, but she had not regretted it. Her baby had been beautiful, beautiful. . . . She felt the tears running down her face and turned away from the window. They would not see her misery, no tears for Tanunda, just grief for her child.

She sat down, leaned across the desk, and buried her head in her arms.

15. Trudie

He quietly opened the door and entered the small, sparsely furnished room. A white bedside cabinet, a chair, and a simple bed with a medical chart at its foot was all that it contained. He sat down on the chair and looked at the child lying on the bed; she was sedated. She was wearing a white hospital smock and her face was pale under her suntan, her fair hair pulled back into a neat bun behind her head.

He glanced again at the photograph in the local newspaper he had brought in with him and compared it with the little girl in the bed. They were the same. Her name was Trudie Langbein and her mother lived in the valley. It was an extraordinary coincidence that Spengler should have picked up a local child, and it could complicate matters. He had made good progress with his medical experiments over the last three years, trying to find a way to halt the effects of radiation on the human body. The previous four children had been invaluable and had contributed enormously to his understanding of a possible cure. He needed this one last girl to effect a possible breakthrough that would suspend the breakdown of human cells caused by radiation. He knew that he could die within a year if he did not find a cure. His work on the nuclear pile had not been without its dangers, particularly here in Barossa where the sometimes primitive conditions had exposed him to hazards that would be unacceptable elsewhere, but he had accepted the dangers willingly. He was all that was left apart from Heissler. They were the only ones still making a positive contribution to the ideals of Nazi Germany. The others in South America and elsewhere merely hid—afraid of Wiesenthal and the other Nazi head-hunters. He was contemptuous of their desperate drive toward self-preservation—what was the purpose of surviving if they could serve no cause larger than themselves? Their pitiful lives had no meaning.

His work was vital and without him it could not continue, but Vaas could not contemplate the thought of carrying out the final experiments on this little girl. She was a local child; and he knew her mother. He certainly knew the grandfather, a fine man who had contributed along with many others to the Vatican Connection that had enabled him to reach this valley via the Middle East and South Africa at the end of the war. He'd achieved a great deal since then.

He remembered his arrival by sea at a tiny inlet near Port Broughton on the Spencer Gulf, then his long journey overland in a battered Ford V-8. It had been hot and dry; the flat, wide, Australian landscapes with English road names had seemed menacing and alien. Barossa Valley had been a revelation to him, and he still marveled at how well those early German settlers had continued the Aryan traditions in this tiny fertile valley. It was very much like one of the smaller valleys in southern Germany, warmer perhaps in summer, but still with ample rainfall to keep it verdant and green. Almost at once he had felt his fears begin to vanish and confidence return. Connections were made and opportunities provided for him to practice. He melted into the heart of the community, and disappeared from the eyes of the world.

Spengler had come to work for him quite soon afterward, tending his garden, cutting the grass for pocket money, and Vaas paid him well. The boy interested him. He was shy, introspective, apparently not liked a great deal by his schoolmates, and Vaas began to win his confidence by teaching him German, which the boy welcomed. He did not seem particularly at ease with the more typically Australian children, and eventually Vaas learned from another source of his father's internment during the war. Immediately Vaas realized that this could be turned to his own advantage, and gradually he began to win the trust of the boy's parents, who came to regard him as something of a mentor for Erich, though Vaas made sure they were never fully aware of his beliefs. The boy's father, though bitter and unforgiving toward Australia, was no Nazi, and Vaas knew it. However, young Spengler was more malleable, and when he'd had to leave school early to boost the family income, Vaas immediately stepped in and employed him full-time. In taking the boy under his wing, and helping the family, he had also increased his stature within the community, which was helpful in those early postwar years when he was trying to build up his research facilities. It had been difficult initially, not so much because of money—funds had been made available to him both here and in Geneva—but because of a lack of know-how and hardware: the basic resources that he needed to continue his work on a nuclear program.

Now the final achievement was almost within his grasp, and all he needed was a little time.

Vaas sat slumped in his chair, staring at the sleeping child, weighing the odds. He had to survive, but this child was young—she had her whole life in front of her. It was a consideration that would have counted for nothing against the importance of his work except for one thing: The girl was German.

Vaas made up his mind. He folded the newspaper and stood up. There was an alternative. Spengler could return this Langbein child to a safe place and find another girl. Vaas felt better having made the decision. It was logical, concise, and satisfied all his options; the delay would be minimal. Soon he felt sure he would find a cure for his condition and when he did so, it would have far-reaching effects. Never mind his methods; his results might save the lives of thousands. The thought rekindled enthusiasm and gave him a deep feeling of satisfaction.

Spengler was uneasy. He didn't like the idea of having to return the child, even if she was local. He paced his room, then threw himself down on the bed. How bloody ironic that the doctor should have seen the child's photograph in his father's newspaper. It was bad luck; there had been no way of knowing that the girl on the beach was from Barossa—the odds against that must have been enormous. What the hell was she doing down there anyway?

Sharon Langbein was not unknown to him, nor to anyone else in the valley. Her fight to keep the antique shop in Tanunda and to bring up her bastard child was common knowledge, though he had never met her. Not that it would have made any difference. He had not been watching the mother on the beach, just the little girl. Now he had to take her back and he didn't like it. It doubled the risk and was a break in the pattern. The police were stirred up now and looking; he'd have to be careful.

He stood up, pacing the room again, wondering where he was going to take her. It had to be far away from this valley, but not too far. He could not afford to travel long distances with a child in the back of his car; she might be spotted.

Gerda, his mother, glanced up at the ceiling of the kitchen. She could hear him walking back and forth. The floorboards in his bedroom had worked loose; he always exercised morning and evening, and she was fearful the ceiling would crack. She wondered what was wrong—he didn't usually get agitated. She called out through the open door to her husband, who was sitting in front of the empty fire, dozing, waiting for his dinner.

"You'll have to do something about those boards in Erich's room."

He sat up, startled, waking. "What?"

"The floorboards in Erich's room. I told you about that before—they'll have to be mended."

He relaxed. "Yes, okay, I'll have a look at them over the weekend—how's dinner coming along?"

"Won't be long—you can call Erich if you like."

Gunther groaned, and hauled himself out of the chair. Why hadn't he kept his mouth shut? He could have dozed for a few more minutes. He was tired. It had been a hard day putting the newspaper to bed for the weekend. He walked to the foot of the stairs. "Erich—come on, your dinner's ready."

Spengler stopped pacing, then walked to the door and opened it. "It's all right, dad, I don't want anything. I'm going out tonight."

He heard his father walk away and tell his mother. Faintly he could hear her complaining because he hadn't told her—that had been the last thought on his mind. He put on his leather jacket and ran down the stairs, poking his head around the kitchen door. "Sorry, mum, but I forgot—I've got a date tonight."

She turned from the oven, her hands on her hips, and surveyed him. "You're going out on a date in a jacket like that? No wonder you're not married—who'd want to marry a roughneck like you?"

He grinned. "What do I want with a steady girl when I've got you?"

She flung the dishcloth at him. "Get out of here, before I throw something harder."

He caught the cloth and hung it on the doorknob. "G'night, mum." He glanced at his father. "Make sure she's in bed by nine—I think she's getting old, dad." He ducked out of the room as she threatened him with a saucepan.

The battered old car in the drive was totally inconspicuous. He leaped in and switched on the headlights, then turned on the ignition—she started at once. He drove down past Patterson Hill then right, passing the winery at Seppeltsfield until he came to the main road from Nuriootpa to Tanunda, easing himself carefully into the narrow two-lane highway. He'd put on a good show for his mother. It was important that they never became suspicious of his activities, though he wanted desperately to confide in his father. The humiliation he had suffered at the internment camp must never be allowed to happen again. If the doctor's plan succeeded, it never would. Spengler grinned in the dark—Jesus, these fucking Australians were in for a shock. . . .

He pulled in behind the hospital and checked his watch. Just after nine o'clock. He'd have to stay here until later. He'd decided where he would take the child, but he didn't want to leave Tanunda until the roads were deserted. He got out of the car and made his way to an emergency exit on the ground floor. It looked secure, but one side yielded to his push and he found himself facing the single narrow door of an elevator. He pressed the button and the door slid back. Once inside, he pressed "G" four times and the elevator began to descend swiftly.

Later, after the child had been placed in the large duffel bag that he always used, Spengler left Barossa Valley while it was still dark; he wanted to dump the child in a place where she would be found quickly but that would also be deserted at first light.

He drove down through Gawler and Elizabeth on the Main North Road to Geeps Cross. The sky to his left was just beginning to lighten as he drove into North Adelaide on O'Connel and King William Street. Once into the city center he turned left on Pirie Street until he came to Rymill Park. He slowed the car down; the roads were deserted, not even a taxi this early on a Saturday morning. He parked the car on Bartels Road beside the park, and picked up the bag from the back seat. The child was still under sedation and would not stir for at least an hour or so. She had been dressed in the bathing costume she had worn when he picked her up from the beach and was wrapped in a thick warm blanket.

He glanced right and left before crossing the wide expanse of lawn; there was no one. Quickly he walked about one hundred and fifty yards to a wooden seat beneath one of the trees that backed onto Dequetteville Terrace. He was about to remove the child from the bag when he noticed that the bench was swarming with ants; someone had left a candy wrapper which had stuck between the wooden slats. He glanced to his left—there was another bench. This time no ants. He removed the child from the bag and laid her on it, making sure that she was securely wrapped in the blanket, and tied two pieces of string around her and under the bench so that she would not roll off and hurt herself. This whole dangerous exercise would be pointless if the child fell and broke her neck while she was still unconscious. Spengler, as always, was thorough. That done, he checked once more that he had not been seen and strode back to his car.

Trudie was found by a park attendant at eight o'clock that morning. She was still asleep.

Brockway was still asleep when the phone rang; Detective Sergeant Phil Clayton informed him that the child was already on her way to her mother's place in the valley by ambulance, and that she was unharmed.

That was at 8:45 A.M. By 9:00, Brockway had organized Mike and Roy, and fixed a rendezvous with them for 11:00 at the top of Elizabeth Street in Tanunda.

As he drove up to Barossa a number of questions kept repeating themselves in his mind. Why had Trudie been returned? Why was she the exception? Clayton had said she had been found wrapped in a blanket in Rymill Park —nothing else. No note—the child unharmed, but under sedation. But what was so different about Trudie? What distinguished her from the other victims of the kidnapper? As far as Brockway could see, only the fact that she was a girl.

Another, more personal question was buzzing away at the back of his mind. He wondered if this would alter in any way his relationship with Sharon. Would her feelings toward him change now that Trudie was back?

He passed the S-bend in the road prior to the level crossing where he had run the car off the road on his first journey to the valley with Sharon. He realized now that it was the accident that had moved them closer, gotten her to begin to trust him. He grinned to himself—maybe he needed to have another minor crash to reinstate himself. He pushed the thought irritably from his mind—it was bullshit and he knew it. Why was this relationship so important to him anyway? Well, enough brooding. The emotional side of things would sort itself out; meanwhile he had a job to do.

He was in Tanunda by 10:30 A.M. Mike and Roy had

not arrived yet, and he could see a couple of police cars parked outside her house. A small group of children who had been playing in the park opposite had gathered by her gate.

He left his car at the top of the road and walked down. A policeman standing outside checked his identification and then went into the house. A moment or two later Clayton came to the door and beckoned him in. He grabbed Brockway's arm and led him into the front room. "The little girl's fine, so is the mother, but they are both in a pretty emotional state right now."

Brockway held up his hand placatingly. "It's all right, Clayton, you don't have to worry. I can always do some shots of the outside of the house and front it myself."

The detective stared at him astonished. "Do I hear you right, Brockway? Have you suddenly gone legit?" He shook his head. "I don't believe it. I saw that piece you did on Pine Gap last night. That was all wild speculation, exaggeration, and pure Harry Brockway." He looked at him quizzically. "Come on, what's up?"

Brockway tried to look sincere. "Nothing, maestro, absolutely nothing. All I would like to do is have a word with the lady." The detective began to shake his head. "In your presence," Brockway added quickly, "and if she doesn't want to do an interview—fine. I'll go outside and do a quick presentation myself. Fair or unfair?" he asked rhetorically.

Clayton looked at him suspiciously but could see little wrong with the suggestion, and it would do their reputation no harm to have the child's recovery publicized. "Okay, but just a few minutes with the lady. All right?"

Brockway nodded obediently, trying not to smile. The detective went to the door, then glanced back at him distrustfully. "I'll be back in a minute, right!"

"Right," Brockway repeated. When Clayton had gone

in the reporter burst into soundless laughter, which he hastily controlled when the detective came back a mo-ment later. He gave Brockway a hard look and jerked his thumb, indicating that Brockway should follow. He led him to the bedroom.

Sharon was sitting composedly on the chair watching her daughter playing with some toys. She rose and held out her hand as he came in. "Hello, Mr. Brockway, how nice to see you again." There was an unmistakable twinkle of amusement in her eyes which the detective couldn't fathom.

Brockway gripped her hand tightly and indicated the child. "I'm glad for you, Miss Langbein—more than I can say." He held her hand fractionally too long and heard Clayton snort with disbelief.

Sharon spoke first. "I expect you would like to have another interview."

Brockway nodded. "Yes, if that's okay with you. My crew should be here by now—we could set it up in the front room?"

"Fine," Sharon said. "See you in the front room in a few minutes?"

Brockway glanced at Clayton. "Okay?"

The detective shrugged his shoulders. "Sure, sure." He went to leave the room, then remembered. "Just one thing, Brockway. Don't say anything on the air about the injection marks on the child's arms."

Brockway was puzzled. "Drugs?" he asked.

"No," Clayton said, then amended it slightly. "Well, yes, but only mild stuff to keep her sedated." Then firmly, "No comment, understood?"

"Understood," Brockway repeated.

16. Barossa Valley

Spengler drove the dark blue Mercedes slowly through Tanunda, past the police station and local courtroom on the left, then past the post office, approaching the junction with Elizabeth Street. He could see there was an unusual amount of traffic congestion in the normally quiet residential road. On the corner he saw the ABC Toyota Land Cruiser, and parked a little way down the road a couple of police cars. His passenger spoke for the first time since Spengler had greeted him at the airport.

"What's going on, Spengler?"

He continued to drive northward out of Tanunda toward Nuriootpa. "I don't know, sir—never seen anything like that here before," Spengler lied. He glanced quickly in the mirror but he couldn't see the man's face, or gauge his reaction. Spengler was surprised to see how quickly the media had arrived on the scene to cover the return of the child. It made him nervous.

There was something disquieting, too, about the presence of Redston. The doctor had not told him why this stranger was being brought into the program, but Spengler knew he must be vital, otherwise the doctor would not have invited him here. Spengler was aware that the program had reached a point where there was no going back; soon they would all be exposed to risks that they had always carefully avoided in the past. But that was the price of progress, and if they were to succeed they could not be avoided.

They passed beneath another wooden archway that spanned the road out of Tanunda to the north. Like the one on the south side of the town it advertised a local winery. On his right Redston saw a motel called Wiental and he wondered where he would be staying while he was in the valley. Probably not too far away, he thought, and smiled grimly to himself.

Redston was more than curious about his host. The name he had been given by Christian Streicher a week after he had concluded a deal with SSS worth 500 million Deutsche marks meant nothing. He had never heard of Dr. Kauffmann, nor had he been able to derive any further information from his own sources. Streicher's motives were clear enough. Once he knew the resources Redston had at his disposal, the power that he represented, then the financier was in a position to reveal the possibilities of the research being carried out here in the valley by Kauffmann. Streicher was obviously carrying out Bruno Heissler's instructions, and had been very careful not to spell out the precise nature of the research, though he had indicated that it could be used militarily. Hard though he had tried, Redston could not get any closer than that. Streicher had apologized for the secrecy, but Kauffmann would explain everything, and insisted on doing so personally. It was obvious that the financier's ego was badly dented by this procedure, but he had stuck to his guns, insisting that the trip would be worth making.

It was Redston's task to investigate all possible sources

of armament for his employers, but what kind of weapons research could possibly be conducted in this quiet rural valley?

However, one thing was certain; an international whiz kid like Streicher would not send him halfway around the world on a wild-goose chase.

Spengler turned off the main road about three miles north of Tanunda and headed toward the Seppeltsfield Winery. They crossed a single-lane bridge over a creek bed. Like other visitors to Barossa Valley, Redston was surprised at its beauty, the essentially European nature of its vineyards and buildings. As always Redston made careful notes of his route and any possible alternatives.

They passed through a small collection of bluestone cottages and a village school, called Marananga. There was a bandhall, and as they climbed the hill out of the village, on his right he saw a tiny Lutheran church made of sandstone. The number of churches he had seen since they had entered the valley only confirmed the research he had done before making this journey, but the palm trees were completely unexpected. They began lining the road after they had passed the church, following it around the bend to the left. They were obviously well tended and cared for, probably a part of the Seppeltsfield estate.

The paved road turned right but Spengler drove the limousine onto a red graveled track that continued straight ahead. A large copse of woods bounded the hill rising sharply away from the track, then the car began to slow down as the quality of the surface deteriorated. Finally they came to a halt outside of a red-roofed, bluestone single-story house, set well back among the trees.

Spengler got out and opened the door for him. "This way, Mr. Redston." He led him up the pathway to the white front door and pushed a button. Redston heard the bell chime, then footsteps approached the door. It was opened by a gray-haired man who was probably in his sixties. He introduced himself; it was Kauffmann.

"Ah, Redston, come in, how nice to see you. Welcome to Barossa." They shook hands and he led Redston into a wide, spacious room that looked out over the valley toward the hills to the east. Kauffmann made his way to a small bar. "What would you like? I have most spirits and a beautiful red wine made just around the corner."

Redston declined, "Thank you, but no. I never drink during the day. Do you have a mineral water?"

If Kauffmann was surprised he didn't show it. "Yes, of course." He turned to Spengler who was standing in the doorway. "You'll find a bottle in the fridge in the kitchen, bring it in—Spengler."

Spengler obediently left the room and Kauffmann indicated an armchair near the empty hearth. "Do sit down—how was your trip?"

Redston replied automatically, making suitably polite noises, but studying the German closely. There was something irritatingly familiar about this gaunt tall man, but he could not place him. He let it rest—it would come. After Spengler had brought in his drink and left the room, Kauffmann's manner altered abruptly. "Have you any idea why I wanted you to come to this valley?" He looked at him sharply over the top of his glass.

Redston shook his head. "No, but I intend to find out."

Kauffmann smiled, exposing some yellow teeth. "I like your directness. However, there will be no need for you to 'find out,' as you put it. I have asked you here because I intend to show you the results of our program, the years of work I have put into this project." Redston guessed that he probably wanted some financial backup. "Good," he said noncommittally.

Kauffmann studied him for a moment. "And Bruno,

how is he?" He gestured with his hand. "Forgive me asking, but he is an old friend whom I have not seen for a long time."

"He is fine—the last time we spoke he seemed highly elated by the success of the rocket program." Redston threw that in deliberately and awaited the reaction.

The doctor stood up abruptly and began pacing the room. "Yes, I'd heard it had gone particularly well." He stopped, turned, and faced Redston. "Would you be prepared to take a trip with me into the outback—the desert?"

Redston thought about that for a moment, trying to evaluate the purpose for such a trip. "I might, depends on the reason for going."

"A team of our best men are already out there." Kauffmann's eyes glittered behind his glasses and he sat down opposite Redston, staring at him intently. He spoke quietly. "Tomorrow we will reach the culminating point of our work and discover whether we have succeeded or not." Redston could see the tension on his face, a trace of sweat forming on his upper lip. "Will you come with me to see?" Kauffmann asked. He took off his glasses and wiped his face with a handkerchief. It was then Redston noticed his eyes. One blue, one gray.

Redston nodded. "You couldn't keep me away with a gun."

17. The Simpson Desert

Jiggs had drawn a blank at Coober Pedy. No one, not even his Chinese agent, knew of any mining or government interest in the Simpson Desert.

Jiggs had been careful to disguise his interest, but the ancient Chinese knew him too well by now, and he'd warned him not to poke his nose into other people's business. It had only served to sharpen his intense curiosity. Anything in the outback within a one-thousand-mile radius of his base in Freeling Heights he considered "his" patch. It had been so for over thirty years and he was determined to find out what was going on.

He was within about a dozen miles of the expedition's base camp in the desert when he first spotted the helicopter, flying low and parallel to one of the ridges further eastward. Jiggs brought Molly and Bess to a halt, and shielded his eyes from the sun, squinting into the distance.

The helicopter was heading north toward the site and Jiggs remained motionless until he was sure the pilot hadn't spotted him. He saw the helicopter begin to descend vertically in a cloud of sand that was clearly visible even from this distance. Then it disappeared down into the corridor between the ridges and out of sight. Only then did Jiggs prod Molly into continuing. The helicopter had given him a fix on the position of the site, not that he had needed it. He knew this desert as a good secretary knows the contents of a filing cabinet, and within an hour he had the base under surveillance again, lying on his belly in a position on top of the ridge that separated the base camp site from his camels.

He'd been right. It was a temporary operation; the site had been cleared. All the prefabricated structures he had seen under construction had gone, carted away presumably on the heavy transportation that had brought them here. All that remained was the helicopter he had seen earlier, a large four-wheel-drive van from which ran several thick cables, and two Land-Rovers parked beside it. The van seemed to be the center of interest. A number of men were grouped around it in deep discussion. At one point they all consulted their watches and synchronized them. It was clear to Jiggs that the van was some sort of communications center; where the cables led to he could not tell. They snaked up the corridor as far as the eye could see and Jiggs decided that was his next task—he must discover the purpose of those cables. He was about to return to his animals when he saw the group around the van break up. Four men got into a Land-Rover, while the pilot of the helicopter and three other men stayed by the communications van. The Land-Rover drove slowly off up the corridor following the route of the cables. Jiggs realized that this was the best opportunity he would get to discover the purpose of their presence in this barren desert. He snapped the old telescope shut, and half ran, half fell down the side of the ridge to where he had left his camels hobbled.

He knew the Land-Rover would be able to travel faster than Molly or Bess, and once he was sure he was clear of the site he prodded Molly up over the ridge and into the other corridor. The cables snaked northward, endlessly it seemed. He pushed Molly into as much speed as he could, following the cables and the tracks of the Land-Rover. He estimated that they must be about twenty miles from the original site when something flashed across his eyes. It was the sun, reflecting from an object that glinted high above the floor of the corridor a mile or so ahead of him. He reigned Molly to a halt, and Bess stopped automatically behind them. Jiggs had never seen anything like it. He pulled the telescope from under his saddle and slowly brought the object into focus. It was a high wooden tower about fifty feet in height, and at the top was something dazzlingly bright that from Jiggs's position was reflecting the rays of the sun.

He wondered if it was made of glass, or perhaps it was a radar dish of some sort. The Land-Rover was parked at the foot of the wooden tower, and Jiggs decided he was in a vulnerable position if they decided to return. He forced Molly and Bess up over the ridge again after retracing his steps a short distance so that he was not visible to the men at the tower. Once his animals were secured, he trekked along the corridor until he could see the top of the tower poking up over the crest of the ridge. He began to scale the ridge, his feet sinking into the soft sand, sometimes up to his knees. By the time he reached the top he was exhausted and sweating profusely.

He wiped the sweat from his eyes and gradually raised himself above the rim of the ridge. One of the men was climbing up a ladder attached to the side of the tower. Jiggs adjusted the telescope until he could see him more clearly. His sweat was trickling down over the eyepiece and several times he had to wipe it clear. The man was not young, and he paused several times on the ladder before he reached the top. His hair was graying at the tem-

ples. A tall, thin man about sixty years of age. What the
hell was he doing climbing a wooden tower in the middle
of an Australian desert? Jiggs followed the line of the
ladder upward until the telescope was focused on the object that had glittered so brightly earlier. It was made of
metal, cylindrical with rounded ends. Jiggs estimated it
was about six feet long and two feet in diameter. It looked
like a shell, or a bomb. The truth hit him like a physical
blow. Inadvertently he lowered the telescope and stared
uncomprehendingly at the wooden tower. The cables! He
checked the cables through his glass. They ran up the side
of the ladder from the floor of the corridor and stopped
just beneath the bomb.

The man who had been climbing the ladder had just
reached the top and was contemplating the various connecting points. Jiggs had lived for a long time totally removed from a normal civilized environment. But he had
his radio, and as a miner he knew enough about explosives
and the need for uranium to be familiar with the principle
of nuclear weapons, and tests had been held in Australia
before in the fifties. That's what this was all about—they
intended to explode an atomic bomb here in the Simpson
Desert. The implications made his mind reel—but who
were *they*? Not part of a government program or he
would never have been able to get this close. It would
have been sealed off and there would have been warnings,
as at the Woomera Test Range. Jesus, he had to get out, he
had to get as far away from this thing as he could. His
agent had been right; the bloody Chinaman had told him
not to poke his nose into other people's business, but he
hadn't been able to resist it.

He scrambled down the incline as fast as he could and
forced his tired legs to keep running until he reached his
animals. Quickly he undid the ropes that hobbled them
and clambered up onto Molly's back. "C'mon, you old bag

of skin and bone, you've got to get your skates on, otherwise we'll all get baked for dinner." His camel complained bitterly; she wasn't used to anything more than a leisurely pace under these conditions, but under Jiggs's insistent prodding she began to lope southward as fast as she could along the corridor, tugging Bess behind.

Redston shielded his eyes from the sun and watched Kauffmann working at the top of the tower. He knew now why the doctor had looked familiar to him. When he had been checking out Bruno Heissler before making contact with SSS, he had seen a prewar photograph of Heissler with a slightly older man taken when they were at the university in Koblenz. Heinrich Vaas had disappeared before the war ended, and now it was all beginning to add up. Barossa Valley, the hospital at which Vaas now worked under the name of Kauffmann.

It was all so blindingly simple—yet who would have thought that Australia would provide sanctuary for an escaping Nazi? He understood, too, why this was a moment of supreme importance to Vaas. If the device exploded successfully he would have pulled off something quite extraordinary. It had not taken him long to arm the bomb and Vaas had slowly begun to descend from the tower. It was difficult not to feel admiration for his courage. He was not a young man and the tower was high enough to kill him if he slipped, but he had deliberately set this operation up so that no one else could carry out the delicate and vital task of arming the warhead for detonation. Redston was surprised at the proximity of the tower to the firing position in the communications van, but he waited until the old man had recovered from his exertions before putting the question. Vaas smiled reassuringly. "Not too close at all—in fact, much farther away than is strictly necessary for a weapon of this size. Ten kilotons is relatively small—a very low fission yield."

Redston was not convinced. "What about radiation?"

Vaas climbed back into the Land-Rover beside him, sweating but elated. "Yes, it is high in the immediate area of the fireball, but it falls away dramatically after the first mile with a device like this." He wiped his face with a handkerchief and surveyed Redston steadily. "First degree burns, for example, would only occur up to three-tenths of a mile." It sounded authentic and Vaas was not going to risk anything by getting his figures wrong at this stage of the operation. He seemed eager to press the point. "For example, when the British carried out nuclear tests at Maralinga in South Australia in 1956, some of their troops were placed within a few miles of the explosion and they suffered no ill-effects."

The thick, tinted lenses of his glasses glinted in the glaring sunlight. His face beneath them was expressionless, but was he mocking him? Laughing at his fears?

Redston debated whether he should reveal his knowledge of the doctor's true identity, knock some of the shit out of him, but he decided against it. There would be a better place, a better time. "Good," he said, "I'm glad it's a little bomb."

Vaas paused; he seemed to be making up his mind. "It is no accident, Redston. Heissler's concept for a low-cost rocket with a small payload was known to me—I designed this weapon with that in mind. I felt certain that one day this device"—he turned and gazed at the weapon glinting on top of the tower—"and Heissler's rocket would come together."

Redston was impressed by the thoroughness with which this operation had been mounted, but a nuclear weapons test, however sophisticated, would be monitored. The site would be radioactive and soon discovered. He wondered about the repercussions—he underestimated Vaas.

The quickest route Jiggs could follow was straight back along the corridor, the way he had arrived. He figured that the device would be triggered from the communications van back at the site, and the nearer he could get to that, the safer he would be.

Cruelly he forced the two animals to maintain a pace that was too fast considering the heat. Rightly, he feared that the device would be triggered as soon as the Land-Rover returned to the site in order to prevent the heat from the desert sun causing any malfunctions in the system. Over the soft pounding of the hooves of his camels, Jiggs heard the sound of the Land-Rover overtaking him in the other corridor, then slowly die away as it raced back to the site. Just over an hour after he had fled from the area of the tower, the device was detonated. Jiggs had his back to the center of the explosion, but even in the bright hot sunlight of an Australian desert, a white glare surrounded him, and he saw, just for an instant, the silhouette of himself and his two animals etched on the surface of the corridor in front of them.

Moments later the sound began to vibrate in his eardrums in great waves, like a thousand thunderclaps rolled together. The ground beneath Molly's hooves began to shake and she stopped, terrified. Little rivulets of sand on the ridges began to cascade down onto the corridor like a miniature avalanche, and Molly reared up, almost flinging Jiggs from her back. Somehow he managed to stay on, and as the last quiver of sound faded away he got her under control and slid off her back to try and calm them both down.

It was then that the blast wave struck. At this distance from a small tactical weapon of this size, and diffused as it was by the ridges and corridors of the desert, it was still strong enough to snatch Jiggs off his feet, and if he hadn't clung steadfastly to Molly's reins she would have bolted.

Then he saw the white cloud rising behind them, billowing out at the top like a giant silver mushroom. Jiggs was awed by the power and force of the detonation—he had never seen anything like it and it filled him with a basic primitive fear at its potency and omnipotence.

He knew, too, that there were other dangers from radiation, so he concentrated his attention on calming down his two animals as quickly as he could. It was at that moment that he heard the sound of the helicopter threshing toward him.

Redston and the pilot had taken off the moment that the last vestiges of the blast wave had passed over the site. Already the mushroom cloud was dispersing and drifting away toward the west.

He didn't want to get too close, so he asked the pilot to give him some altitude so that he could get some idea of the blast effect. He spotted Jiggs at once, about eight miles north of the base site, in the corridor that ran parallel to the cables, struggling to hold on to his two camels who were extremely nervous and beginning to shy away at the sound of the helicopter's approach.

Redston was assessing all the possibilities coldly and analytically. How this lone man had gotten out here so close to their position meant nothing. The point was, how much did he know? On these two camels it would have been possible for him to spy on them quietly; he may in fact have observed everything. Redston reached his decision at once. He slid back the door on his side and ordered the pilot to circle around them. He pulled the automatic pistol from his pocket and slid back the safety catch.

The two camels were pulling at the reins, wanting to run from the sound of the helicopter circling above them.

Bess broke free and bolted but Jiggs hung on to Molly. She pulled viciously again, almost jerking him off his feet. It saved his life. The shot tugged at the sleeve of his tattered bush jacket, and Jiggs viewed the blood stemming from his nicked arm with incredulity. He heard the sound of the second shot and saw the spurt of sand as it thudded into the ground at his feet. He glanced up at the helicopter. He could see the gunman lining him up for another shot with the automatic, but he had nowhere to go. There was no cover and he would be dead before he could climb onto Molly's back.

He did the only thing he could. He moved quickly into Molly, keeping her between him and the helicopter. If he could get to the rifle in his saddle . . . The next two shots from the heavy automatic pistol thudded into Molly's side, and Jiggs felt the animal quiver with shock and cry out in terror. Another bullet struck Molly in the neck, splattering the old prospector with her blood, and slowly she began to sag to her knees as though fearful she would crush him. The helicopter was beginning to circle around to get a clear shot at him, and Jiggs dragged frantically at the butt of the rifle. Molly was slowly rolling over toward him, and it was jammed between her side and the ground. The saddle pack held her for an instant, and he gave one final pull with all his strength and the rifle was freed.

He slipped the stock into his shoulder and as the helicopter came into view he fired a complete magazine at it, smashing the plexiglass above the pilot's head. Startled by this sudden danger, the pilot jerked back the controls, and the copter veered sharply away, disappearing over the nearby ridge.

Jiggs dug into his saddlebags and pulled out a cardboard box of ammunition and stuffed as many shells from it as he could into his pocket after reloading.

Molly was still alive, spurts of blood pouring from her

neck and side. Jiggs stood up, heedless of any danger to himself, and looked down at the stricken animal. He could see the terror in her eyes. She looked up at him, unable even to complain. He put the rifle to his shoulder and shot her once, ending her misery.

Jiggs turned away and waved his fist at the empty sky. "I'll get you, you bastards!" he screamed. His voice echoed mockingly down the corridor, gradually fading. He stood for a moment listening. There was nothing else. The copter had gone. He dragged his telescope and his radio from his saddlebag, checked his water, and set off following Bess's tracks southward. . . .

18. ABC, Adelaide

Bill Cameron was staring at a blank sheet of paper, trying to collect together a few scattered thoughts about the content of his next program, when the phone rang. It was Lillian Martin, a kind, elderly lady who had operated the switchboard at Broadcast House in Hindmarsh Square for many years. She had, in fact, retired two years earlier but had been brought back as a temporary measure to help relieve the pressure due to a shortage of staff. Jiggs had been lucky; Lillian felt he ought at least to have a word with Cameron. She outlined what she knew. "He sounds genuine, Bill. He's calling us from a phone in Marree which is the closest one he could find."

"That's way up past Leigh Creek, isn't it?"

"Yes, it's the last stop before the Simpson—about the last place he would find a telephone."

Cameron considered it for a moment. He got a lot of crank calls as a result of his program, but Lillian would not have bothered him if she had not felt he was genuine. "Okay, put him on. I don't seem to be able to get any work done today anyway." He heard her chuckle and then a moment of silence before she prompted Jiggs to speak.

"Go ahead, sir, you are through to Mr. Cameron." Still nothing.

"Hello," Cameron said, "can I help at all?"

Jiggs recognized the voice; it sounded exactly the same. "Mr. Cameron, I'm sorry to trouble you like this."

"No trouble at all, what can I do for you?"

Jiggs suddenly felt apprehensive. He had been thinking about this call all through his long trek south after he had found Bess. He'd had five days to consider it. His natural antipathy toward authority had ruled out any contact with the police and the only person he felt he knew was the man on his radio.

Cameron was used to the taciturn, slightly wary approach of many people from the outback. He tried again. "Is it about the program? Is there something that you would like me to play?"

Jiggs shook his head unconsciously. "No, it's not that." He was finding it difficult to broach the subject, keenly aware that he might be starting something he could not contain. "It's just that I thought you might be interested in something that happened in the Simpson."

Cameron glanced at his watch, but maintained his sympathetic approach. "Well, that depends on what it is," he said reasonably. The familiar voice began to loosen Jiggs's tongue.

"I saw a bomb go off!" Jiggs waited.

There was an uncomprehending silence, then, "A bomb? In the Simpson?"

"That's right, I had taken some opal into Coober Pedy, and on my way there I had tracked some heavy transportation into the Simpson. Coming back I went to see what they were up to, then the bomb went off."

Cameron was staggered by the simple straightforwardness of the man. Either he was telling the truth or he was a complete nutcase. More information was required. "You're a prospector, are you?"

"That's right, opal," Jiggs said.

"Do you normally operate in that area, the Simpson?"

"No, there's no opal in the Simpson—I was just crossing it to get to my dealer."

Cameron knew that, so at least his claim to be a prospector could be believed. He started to jot down a few notes. "When you say you tracked the expedition, presumably you followed them on a four-wheel-drive?" It was the only kind of vehicle that could operate in those conditions.

"No," Jiggs replied. He remembered the misery of his animal. "I use camels; the bastards killed one of them."

Christ, Cameron thought, he is a crank. "Killed?" he said.

Jiggs could hear the disbelief in his voice. "That's right," he said. He was angry and bitter; he should have known this was a mistake. His voice hardened. "They tried to kill me—instead they got Molly."

Cameron sensed that he was losing him, but his journalist's instinct refused to let him go yet. "Molly was your camel," he said gently.

"Yes, I had had her for years. They killed her because of what I saw." Jiggs couldn't think why he didn't put down the phone. He could tell that the Cameron man didn't believe him, but somehow it helped just talking, as he had always talked to this familiar voice. He was asking him something else.

"But why would they want to kill you or your camel simply because you had seen a bomb go off?" A thought occurred to Cameron. "Was it an explosion?"

Silence. He tried again.

"I mean, could it have been a test explosion for oil—a mining expedition, perhaps?"

Still no reply. For a moment Cameron thought he might have gone, then—

"It was a nuclear bomb. They were testing a nuclear bomb. That's why they tried to kill me. I thought someone ought to know, that's why I called you."

Jiggs took the receiver from his ear and stared at it. He could hear the tinny disembodied voice pleading with him to repeat what he had said, but there seemed to be no more point to this conversation. What he had said had sounded ridiculous even to his own ears, only he knew it was true. Molly was dead; somehow he intended to make them pay for that. Slowly he replaced the receiver.

The phone rang noisily, drowning out the muffled vibrations of the demolition work on Tregenna House at ABC. Thankfully Brockway grabbed it. "Yes," he said shortly.

"Hello, is that you, Brockway?" He recognized the voice.

"Yes, hello, Bill, how are you?"

Cameron came straight to the point. "You remember that demonstration you covered up at Alice Springs over the American installation at Pine Gap?"

Brockway smiled to himself. "How can I forget—my producer has hardly spoken to me since."

Cameron chose his words carefully. "Look, Brockway, I know you have been covering these bases at Pine Gap and North West Cape for some time. Is there any possibility at all of the Americans carrying out a nuclear bomb test in some remote corner of Australia?"

Brockway considered this for a moment. "Bill, you're gonna have to come clean with me if you want me to answer that question. Why do you want to know?"

Cameron laughed. "You're a bastard, Brockway. I should have known better than to try that on you. Right, here's the situation." He outlined briefly what Jiggs had recounted on the telephone. "I don't know if there's anything to it," he concluded. "He may be just a crank—but somehow I believed him." He waited for Brockway to answer.

"Bill—"

"Yes?"

"First, they don't have to test small nuclear weapons any more. There is no reason for them to try and do that in Australia; and second, if for some reason they wanted to try out a new variation why in the world would they do it in Australia? He's got to be a crank."

Cameron could see the sense in that, but he was not entirely convinced. "Maybe you're right, Brockway, but I think I'll nose around for a while, see if I can turn anything up."

Brockway realized that if he were too negative Cameron would get suspicious. "Okay, you do that. I'll see if I can come up with anything, then I'll get back to you, right."

He put down the receiver and picked it up again almost at once, then dialed a number. When the university answered he asked to be connected to the seismology monitoring section. He knew they had a monitor at Umberatana in the Flinders, but he didn't know if they were connected with government sources or not. A young voice answered; and Brockway phrased the question carefully.

"Good morning, ABC television here. We have had some reports that the 'Arkaroola Rumble,' as it's sometimes called, has been heard again. Could you tell me if any tremors have been monitored in that area?"

The young voice went away for a moment, then returned. "I have checked the sheet from the monitor at Umberatana. Nothing at all on the fault line between Hewindon in Queensland and Spencer Gulf down here.

Certainly nothing at Arkaroola, but we did pick up a size-able disturbance of some kind."

"Where was that?" Brockway held his breath and waited.

"It's funny, really, there's no known fault line in that region, but we definitely picked up something about two hundred and fifty miles north of Marree in the Simpson Desert."

Brockway let his breath out slowly and tried to sound calm and matter-of-fact. "Thank you, that's probably it then, sorry to have troubled you." He put the phone down and sat there silently for a few minutes trying to work things out. If the old prospector was right and it had been a nuclear test, the government must be involved some-how. Even if they were not responsible and the Ameri-cans had carried out some sort of secret test, then the government, like himself, would now know that some-thing odd was going on in the Simpson and would be checking it out. It was possible, however, that he was the only one in the media who knew of it besides Cameron. He picked up the phone again and began to organize his crew. There was only one way to find out. . . .

PAGAS flew them as far as the dirt landing strip at Marree. There they picked up a four-wheel-drive and headed north, passing through the dog-fence that bounded the southern perimeter of the desert and kept the dingos from spreading into sheep and cattle country. The track ended at Muloorina Homestead, the last human habitation before the Simpson, then they struck out across the dry salt bed of Lake Eyre.

Several times that day they heard and saw aircraft heading northward, and Brockway felt more secure know-ing he had brought a geiger counter with him. He checked it from time to time; he didn't want to run into any radiation areas. Not that he expected to get that far. He felt sure their progress had been spotted and reported by some of the aircraft and he expected that they'd be stopped long before they got within the vicinity of the blast area.

They made good progress over the salt bed and reached the northern edge of Lake Eyre just after nightfall. Roy and Mike had both agreed that they should press on as quickly as possible and after a few hours' sleep, while it was still dark, they headed out into the long straight corridors between the sand ridges of the Simpson.

It was late afternoon when their progress was finally halted. A helicopter came whirling in, low, out of the sun, landing about fifty yards in front of them. Brockway stopped the vehicle as six soldiers came tumbling out, fully armed and alert. They surrounded the Land-Rover and stood silently waiting. Brockway, Mike, and Roy didn't make a move. It was a tense situation and the implications were obvious. After they had been thoroughly scrutinized from the helicopter, an army officer emerged and questioned Brockway closely. He showed the officer his identification and after a brief search they and their equipment were bundled into the chopper and flown to the temporary base camp that had been set up near the test site. Their film equipment was confiscated and they were warned not to stray from the base camp. By now heavier transportation was arriving from the south, and Brockway could see teams of men donning heavy protective clothing preparatory to venturing into the danger areas. He felt angry and frustrated; without his camera he was like a soldier without a rifle—helpless, unable to function. He protested forcibly to the interrogation officer, who plainly wished that the ground would open up and remove Brockway from his presence, but nothing he said made the slightest dent in their firm intention to prevent any filming.

He was warned that this was a top secret military area and no comment could be made without official approval. Then he was dismissed and told that he and his crew would shortly be returned to Adelaide.

He left the tent thoroughly disgusted and found Mike and Roy leaning nonchalantly against one of the parked vehicles. Unaccountably, this annoyed him still further, and he strode angrily toward them. "For chrissake, you two, don't just stand there doing nothing, keep your eyes peeled. The least we can do is try and note what sort of equipment they are wheeling in."

Mike and Roy exchanged a glance. "Take it easy, Harry, don't do your block, take a gander at this." Mike gave a surreptitious nod with his head, indicating that Brockway should come closer. Brockway moved in, puzzled. Mike was wearing his usual baggy, comfortable jacket, and from one of its innumerable pockets he half raised a small metal object that glinted brightly in the sun.

"What is it?" Brockway said; for some reason he was whispering.

Mike looked at him, exasperated. "Don't give the game away, boss." He glanced around quickly. The place was alive with activity, but no one seemed to be taking any notice of them. Mike said out of the side of his mouth, "It's my still camera—they didn't get this one—I've just been taking a few snaps, that's all."

Brockway felt better; all sorts of possibilities flashed quickly through his mind. He grinned broadly. "Well, you old bastard, they haven't beaten us yet." He glanced quickly at Roy. "Don't suppose you have got a miniature tape recorder?"

Roy shook his head glumly. "No such luck, boss." Then he smiled. "But I'll bear it in mind."

Before it got dark they managed to shoot two more rolls of film, wandering around as innocently as possible, forming a protective little group whenever Mike wanted to shoot something. By nightfall Brockway was more than satisfied. They flew them out at first light next day and returned their equipment when they landed in Adelaide.

Brockway had the photographs developed and blown up as soon as they got back to ABC. He had to tell his producer, George Greenfield, that they had been unable to film for security reasons, but neglected to inform him of the secrecy warning.

With the blow-ups of the photographs and information gleaned from the seismology center he was able to get together a program for that evening on ABC. If George had some misgivings he did not voice them; this was a scoop of international proportions.

Brockway went on the air unannounced at 7:00 and blew the top on the nuclear test, linking it with the secrecy that surrounded Pine Gap and North West Cape, and citing the Americans as possible perpetrators of this clandestine nuclear explosion in Australia.

Brockway was immediately suspended by ABC, who on the public broadcasting channel felt their responsibility keenly. The repercussions were enormous, almost exactly what Vaas had expected, though he had not anticipated that the news would break this quickly. Thus far, the presence of Jiggs had proved beneficial and the Americans were getting the stick. Vaas felt lucky.

19. Geneva

He noticed that the ceiling was cracked; a shaky line began near the base of the light fixture and slowly wound its way toward the window, like a river on a map. Curiously it reminded him of Korea, and the officer he had killed nineteen years before. He shivered. God, it had been so cold in that barren, empty place. He was grateful for the warm bed, even if this ancient hotel in Geneva did insist on the traditional duvet. He hated duvets; they were either too short and his feet got cold, or too hot and slid off the bed. He smiled; they were certainly useless if there was more than one in a bed.

The woman had left ten minutes before. She was expensive, but good, and he could afford it. Redston had no time for personal involvement, nor did he seek it. He knew it could be dangerous.

Soon he would be meeting his contact, and he had good news to report. The successful launch of Bruno Heissler's rocket in Africa, coupled with his former colleague's personal triumph with the successful detonation of a tactical nuclear bomb, meant that the door was now open for the operation he had meticulously planned. There remained just one more question that had to be answered. Could Heissler's rocket, built to carry a satellite into space, successfully deliver a small nuclear warhead to a preselected target? The location of the nuclear pile in Barossa Valley demanded that the last phase in the operation take place in Australia. Also, outside of the valley, Vaas might run the risk of being identified, and it was a risk that Redston was not prepared to take.

His research had also disclosed disturbing reports in some Australian newspapers about the activities of the ex-Führer of the National Socialist Party of Australia, Arthur Smith. Some of his allegations had made good copy, particularly one quote, "the quiet Barossa being a hot-bed of Nazis." He had gone on to claim he had got the names of four Nazi sympathizers in Barossa from contacts in Germany, and that the NSPA received financial support from the valley. None of this was given much credence in Australia; nevertheless it was disturbing. Redston didn't want any unnecessary attention focused on Barossa Valley. It would have been much simpler to have completed the last phase of this operation in China, but he knew his employers would not accept his plan until the final test was completed in Australia.

He did not share Vaas's euphoria at the public's acceptance of the suggestion that the Americans were responsible for the test in the Simpson. He knew that the U.S. government could prove otherwise. They, possibly more than the Australian government, would want to know who was responsible, and with their "eye in the sky" satellite capability, any further experiments would of necessity have to be heavily disguised—but it could be done. The rocket had been designed for maneuverability. The mobile launch pad could be set up easily and quickly. It was possible to disguise it as an oil rig, and

Redston had already decided on a site for the launch that would not attract any untoward interest.

He glanced at his watch. The meeting with his contact was, as usual, in an anonymous hotel room. He got out of the bed, washed, shaved, and dressed. Slipping the two rolls of film into his pocket, he left the room and walked down the passage. He ignored the elevator and climbed the creaking staircase to the top floor. No one had seen him, and he walked down the corridor until he stood outside the door to the suite whose number he had been given. It was always a different hotel; soon they would be running out of them in Geneva.

He knocked twice quickly, then twice slowly. He heard the floorboards creak and the door was flung open.

Sou Nu Chai beamed at him and crushed him in a bear hug that squeezed all the breath from his body. Sou Nu Chai had not changed a great deal since their first meeting in the monastery on the border of Manchuria nearly twenty years before. The years had treated him kindly; although graying slightly at the temples, the Swiss cuisine seemed to have made him an even more impressive figure. His attachment to the Embassy obviously agreed with him. Nevertheless he still moved with an animal-like grace and the bear hug confirmed the enormous strength of the man.

Redston used his familiar opening ploy, "What's new, Chai?" The big man laughed uproariously; he enjoyed the outrageous pun more every time they met, which was not as often as Redston would have liked. He relished the company of this huge, friendly man, whose bearish appearance and behavior belied the intelligent subtlety of his mind. Sou Nu Chai shook his head. "Not a lot, Redston. Essentially, Geneva never alters. It is beautiful, of course, almost perfect, but like a Swiss watch the pattern is repeated endlessly. Each embassy tries to analyze the true motives of every other embassy. Often ignoring the obvious reason for any given action. Searching always for some hidden meaning which may or may not exist." He lowered himself delicately into an armchair that seemed much too small for him and wagged a finger at Redston. "But I hear you have been very busy in Africa."

Redston walked over to the bar. "May I?"

Sou Nu Chai waved him on. "Of course, but I thought you didn't drink."

Redston poured himself mineral water. "I don't, but I am thirsty." He smiled at Sou Nu Chai. "She was expensive"—he paused deliberately—"but quite delightful." The room echoed to the big man's booming laughter once again. When it stopped Redston asked as innocently as he could, "You heard about the nuclear test in Australia."

Sou Nu Chai looked at him seriously. "Yes, that was a surprise, not least it seems to the Americans." He sat back in the chair, his eyes twinkling. "But why do you ask that question?"

Redston sat down opposite his old friend. "You know that I went to see a weapons test in Australia, through our contacts with SSS in Africa."

Sou Nu Chai said nothing for a moment, then slowly let out a huge sigh. "Ah, my dear Redston, I perceive your drift. Though surely you are not suggesting that some private, or should I say proprietary company, since it is Australia, has set up shop in nuclear weapons?"

"Not quite. Bruno Heissler you knew about. Before World War Two Heissler worked with Heinrich Vaas at Koblenz. Vaas was a fellow student. During the war Vaas worked on the heavy water scheme in Norway and at one point actually helped to construct a nuclear pile at

Hechtingden. Before the war ended he escaped from Germany—"

"And went to Australia!" Sou Nu Chai said incredulously.

Redston nodded his assent. "That's right." He then proceeded to explain to Sou Nu Chai just why he had gone to Australia and how far the ex-Nazi had progressed since then.

Sou Nu Chai immediately realized what the possibilities were, now that both a rocket and a warhead were available, and his gregarious sense of humor evaporated. "But this is tremendous, Redston." He paused. "How certain can you be that the rocket will operate efficiently with the warhead?"

It was Redston's turn to sigh. "I cannot be certain, of course, but I am reasonably sure. The last part of the operation is to test them both together on a preselected target."

Sou Nu Chai protested, "Just a minute, Redston, we don't want anyone hit with a nuclear bomb, private or otherwise."

Redston shook his head. "Of course not. What I anticipate is a small, nuclear, high-altitude test, somewhere over the Indian Ocean, or possibly the Southern Ocean near Antarctica. No one would be close enough to be affected by it. The radiation yield is not high."

He could see that Sou Nu Chai was impressed. He handed him the two rolls of film. "There are photographs of both the rocket and the nuclear test, and here is something I want you to study very carefully." He handed him an envelope.

Sou Nu Chai looked surprised. "What is it?"

Redston took a deep breath. "If the rocket and the warhead operate successfully together, I want your government to take Heissler and Vaas, plus all their back-up teams, and put them in the forefront of your ballistic missile program. First you will give them all the financial and production muscle they need, and at the same time remove them from the stringencies that are imposed on them by such clandestine operations. Now that the Americans are involved, it will only be a matter of time before Vaas is discovered and eliminated, and I want him out of there before that happens. He, too, is aware of the dangers. Heissler will be more difficult to persuade, but if I can tell him that China could make it possible for him to also work on a viable space program, then I think I could manage to convince him. Secondly, it gives you the one thing you lack. Your missile guidance systems are not very sophisticated, but with their know-how and experience you could rapidly improve on that."

Redston sat back in the chair. He was sweating and tense, but this was vital. Sou Nu Chai pursed his lips and looked at him contemplatively. "I can see the possibilities, Redston, but that's all they are at the moment."

Redston stayed cool. "Listen, so far we have had a successful rocket launch"—he ticked them off with his fingers —"and a successful nuclear test. If we can combine these two I want your guarantee that I can proceed with that plan." He indicated the envelope Sou Nu Chai was holding. "I have worked for your government ever since Korea, and I have known you for nearly twenty years, but this is the biggest thing I have ever had an opportunity to handle." Sou Nu Chai looked unconvinced.

"Listen to me—think about the possibilities objectively. So far, in the field of nuclear weapons, all you've been able to do is make the bloody thing explode. A 'dirty' bomb with high fallout levels, useless for tactical situations. Vaas, even with his limited resources, has already exploded a highly sophisticated nuclear weapon that could easily form the warhead of a missile. You don't have that capability at the moment. Furthermore, if Heissler can be persuaded to work for us, you can also utilize his rocket technology to improve your own, as well as using the rockets for their original purpose—satellite surveillance. I'm not going to let it slip by. If I don't get that guarantee—I work for you no more."

Sou Nu Chai smiled resignedly. "I always knew that one day you would find something you truly believed in. I never thought that it might be China." He leaned over and gripped his hand. "Be assured, Redston, I will do my best . . ."

20. Tanunda, Barossa Valley

Brockway's suspension had caused a good deal of flak at ABC. He was not a popular figure among local journalists, but they supported his right to inform the public of the test even if they condemned the sensational nature of his reports. He did have great public support, and that made life difficult for the brass at ABC; his suspension was already under review.

Meanwhile, he was spending his enforced holiday with Sharon and Trudie, though he insisted on having a room at the Wiental Motel. He did not want her submitted to any more gossip—she was getting enough of that already, as well as rapidly becoming a tourist attraction in her own right. It didn't do the shop any harm.

Trudie had been able to reveal nothing helpful to the police. She had been unconscious throughout the abduction, except, it seemed, for one brief moment when she woke up in a small bare room before relapsing into a sedated condition.

The hot weather had broken temporarily and Brockway could hear the thunder rumbling over the hills that presaged a downpour. Trudie was trying to draw some pictures in a book, but the room had gone quite dark; he switched on the lights. Sharon was in her kitchen, and he heard her exclaim with annoyance, "Damn."

"What's wrong?" he called out.

"I've forgotten something," she said. "I'm doing you the pot roast I promised, and I haven't got any onions left."

Brockway offered to go and get them, but she refused. "You start shopping for me and they really will have something to talk about."

The rain began to slam onto the roof, and Brockway protested that it didn't matter about the onions, but she insisted that if she was going to do him a pot roast, it was going to be done properly. Brockway resisted no more. He have already noted her determined character—it was one of the things he liked about her. So if she intended to get herself soaked in order to cook a meal, then so be it. He smiled to himself; it might be fun drying her off.

She slipped into a hooded raincoat and put on some yellow rainshoes. "Shan't be a minute," she said. "The general store is just on the opposite corner of the main road." She flashed him a smile and kissed him passionately, then darted out before he could respond. He watched her from the window as she splashed up the street, looking not unlike the scene from "Singing in the Rain." Something was tugging at his memory; it was the rainshoes. He went back into the living room and pulled the envelope from his briefcase. One by one he went through the photographs Mike had taken at the security base camp after the explosion. He stopped, then grabbed his magnifying glass. He peered closely at one of the photographs—there it was. Some of the men who were donning protective clothing were wearing yellow plastic overshoes. But why was that still ringing a bell? He turned to the window and gazed blankly out at the street, trying to remember.

The rain was still lashing down, running in tiny rivers down the windowpane. The car, the crash near the railway crossing. Then he remembered. It was in the hospital afterward; he'd been staggering around trying to find someone. There was something about an elevator. It was all fuzzy and indistinct—surely that had all been a dream? But somehow he seemed to remember going down in the elevator. The door had finally opened and he had seen a huge white room. That was it! A man, dressed in white, had stopped him from falling to the ground and he had been wearing yellow plastic overshoes.

He continued to gaze out at the wet, empty street, rolling over the images in his mind, trying to figure out what, if anything, it meant. How could what he had seen at the blast site be connected in any way with the hospital? Perhaps there was a perfectly reasonable explanation. Some research that required protective clothing. Then he remembered something else. The room he had woken up in was very much like the one Trudie had said she had seen briefly. He turned and looked at her sitting on the floor still immersed, painstakingly drawing something in her book. He knelt beside her, looking at the drawing. There were one or two scarecrowlike figures with extraordinary long arms and legs.

"Who is that?" he asked.

She glanced up at him. "It's mummy and you and Jesus," she said.

"Which one is Jesus?"

She pointed to one which was slightly higher than the others. "That one, silly . . . see, he is going up to heaven."

Brockway laughed. "Yes, of course, you're right—I should have known." He looked down at the top of her head wondering how he could ask the question. "Trudie?"

She looked up.

"When you were away from mummy and you woke up in that room, what was it like?"

She looked up at him, puzzled, trying to remember. "It was just a room."

"Did you see anything in it?"

"No, it was empty—then I went back to sleep again."

Brockway nodded. There had to be something if it was the hospital—think! Hospitals. . . . He remembered. She was still drawing, apparently unconcerned. "Trudie, can you remember, was there any smell in the room?"

She stared at the ceiling. "Smell?"

"Yes, a nice smell—clean."

She began to draw again. "Yes, that's right, there was, like the stuff mummy uses in the sink."

"Disinfectant?" he said quietly.

"What's that?" She looked puzzled.

He stood up and went into the kitchen. He found a bottle under the sink and unscrewed the cap, holding it some distance from her nose. "Did it smell like that?"

She sniffed once or twice, wrinkling her nose delicately. "Yes, that's the smell."

Slowly he screwed the cap back on, still kneeling on the floor.

The front door burst open and Sharon appeared in a shower of rain, slamming the door shut quickly behind her. She saw him kneeling beside Trudie clutching a bottle of disinfectant. "Don't let her have that, Harry," she said sharply. He stood up as she removed the soaking raincoat and took it quickly into the bathroom, throwing it in the bath.

"No, of course not," he said quietly.

"What's that?" she called.

He didn't reply and she came to the door and stared at him, puzzled. He was staring fixedly at the bottle in his hand. She realized something was wrong.

"What is it?"

He looked at her steadily for a moment, then said almost inaudibly, "I think I know where they took Trudie."

Brockway stood at the bottom of the steps that led into the reception area of the hospital and gazed up at the tall building in front of him. It was the highest, if not the biggest building in the valley. Few structures were more than two stories high; this one rose to five floors. His room had been up there on the third floor somewhere. He walked into reception and the cheerful curvaceous lady was still behind the desk.

"Hello," she said, her eyes twinkling. "How do you feel today?"

"Not so good," he replied. "Any chance of seeing the doctor that looked after me?"

She looked concerned. "Oh, I am sorry, what's the trouble?"

He touched his head. "I keep getting headaches, and sometimes I feel a bit nauseous."

She started to thumb through her files. "Now let me see." She pulled one out. "Brockway, wasn't it?" He nodded. "Yes," she continued, "that's right. Dr. Kauffmann looked after you."

"Dr. Kauffmann," he repeated. "I'd forgotten his name. Is he the one with a slight foreign accent?"

She looked up and smiled. "Yes, that's right. If you'd like to sit down, I'll see if he can attend to you." She picked up the phone.

He thanked her and sat down on one of the chairs. He looked at the elevator. There were two metal doors that slid apart from the center. The one he remembered had only had the single sliding door, and it had been smaller. The receptionist called his name. He stood up and went over to the desk. She smiled, showing her perfect white teeth again. "If you would like to go up to the first floor, Dr. Kauffmann will see you. He's in room one-oh-four—you'll see his name on the door."

"Thanks," he grinned, then leaned across the desk. "If I can't get rid of this headache, would you be willing to have some dinner this evening and give me a little private treatment?"

If she was surprised she didn't show it; the courteous, professional smile didn't slip for an instant. "Thank you, Mr. Brockway, but I have all the practice I need."

Her eyes continued to twinkle. It was the smoothest put down Brockway had suffered in a long time.

"Et tu, Brute," he muttered, and slid quietly away before his ego was shredded any further.

The elevator doors opened noiselessly, and he stepped inside, then turned. She was still smiling brightly. He gave her a weak one in return and pressed the button for the third floor. He was grateful when the doors shut and her icy beam was no longer visible. The elevator began to climb. It stopped at the third floor and he stepped quickly out into the passage. It ran the length of the building, bounded on each side by identical doors. If he remembered rightly, the one that he had been in was to his left and faced the front of the building. More importantly, there was no other elevator at either end of the corridor. Just a blank wall. He strode quickly down the passageway and stopped outside of the fourth door on his right. He listened for a moment, then opened it quietly. It was empty, furnished much the same as the one he had been in, but the picture on the wall was different. He decided to check one more and moved on to the next one. He listened, still nothing. He opened it and found himself gazing into the startled eyes of a lady who was sitting up in the bed and was in the process of examining her left breast carefully. He apologized and shut the door quickly.

The breast he hadn't recognized, but there was no doubt about the picture on the wall. He moved swiftly back down the corridor to the elevator. Dr. Kauffmann might be getting impatient.

He knocked twice on the door, then poked his head around it. The doctor was sitting behind a heavy, old-fashioned desk. "Morning, Doctor."

He stood up. "Good morning, Mr. Brockway." He indicated a chair. "Do sit down."

Brockway accepted the invitation while the doctor sorted through some papers. He studied him unobtrusively. Brockway guessed he was in his early sixties. Steel gray hair cut short, heavily framed, tinted glasses so thick as to be almost opaque. The accent was undoubtedly German, but there was nothing unusual about that in Barossa Valley. Brockway made a mental note to check out some of the immigration records.

The heavy glasses glinted in the sunlight streaming in through the window and Brockway was suddenly, uncomfortably, aware that he, too, was being scrutinized. "The receptionist said that you were still getting headaches?"

"Yes," Brockway said, perhaps too hastily, "and I sometimes feel a little sick."

"Right." He pulled a tiny flashlight from his pocket and walked around the desk toward him. "Probably nothing to worry about, but let's have a look anyway." He leaned over and shone the light into each of Brockway's pupils, then sat down again. "Have you been doing anything strenuous since you left the hospital?"

Brockway gazed at the floor. "Yes, I had to fly up into the Simpson Desert to cover a story on the nuclear test up there." He looked up quickly, but the tinted glasses made it impossible to gauge any response.

The doctor sat immobile for a moment, then began to look through his papers once more. "I cannot see any trace of the concussion in your condition, but it may be that the amount of travel and the stress factor in your work. . . ." He paused for a moment. "You're a television reporter, I believe?" Brockway nodded.

"Yes, well, I suppose that could aggravate your injury." He glanced up at him and smiled. "Perhaps you ought to take a few days off, Mr. Brockway, give yourself a break."

"I can't, Doctor, I've got a lot of work to do on this story. . . ." He let that hang for a moment, then as casually as he could, "Incidentally, why would one of your orderlies be wearing yellow plastic overshoes? Is there an infectious diseases department here, some sort of research, perhaps?"

The doctor continued to shuffle through the papers, then picked up his report and gazed at it steadily. "No, I don't think so, and if there were"—he looked at him unblinkingly—"I'm sure I would have heard about it."

Brockway shrugged his shoulders. "Yes, of course, probably my mistake."

The doctor stood up and handed him a prescription. "Take two of these three times a day when indicated, and if the headaches continue I suggest you consult your own doctor when you return to Adelaide. It may be you simply need a rest." He held out his hand. "Good-bye, Mr. Brockway." They shook hands and Brockway left.

Something smelled, he knew it. . . .

Though Brockway was still suspended, one of the researchers on the production team got him as much information as she could on Dr. Kauffmann. He had, according to records, arrived in 1937 from Germany during a period of intensive emigration. Between 1936 and 1941, seventy-three hundred immigrants had reached Australia from Germany. Most, though not all of them, were Jews fleeing from Nazi persecution. A few were merely Germans joining relatives or friends in the Barossa region, Kauffmann apparently among them.

The local newspaper, the *Tanunda Deutsche Zeitung*, generally maintained a neutral tone between the wars, but the German communities in Australia were not untainted by fascist propaganda in those early, heady years. In 1934 Die Bruecke was founded as an organ of the League of Germans in Australia and this produced a stream of Nazi philosophy, the main theme being the unification of people of German descent on a cultural basis. The Nazis also captured control of German clubs.

It was difficult to determine how persuasive the Nazis had been. From photocopies of local newspapers that the researcher had sent him, Brockway learned that the people of Barossa Valley had indeed suffered a great deal of persecution during World War One. Pastors had been forbidden to hold services, some schools had been closed, hundreds of German place names had been changed, and many families had been badly treated. All this backed up what Sharon had told him, so it would not have been surprising if some of the population in the valley had been susceptible to the Nazi propaganda of the thirties. Curiously there was no record of Dr. Kauffmann's activities until some time after World War Two, when he had become prominent among those pressing for better medical care in the valley. The hospital was the result of this pressure, and Kauffmann had practiced there ever since its completion. He needed to know more about the doctor.

Brockway drove through the village of Marananga, along the palm-lined road that led to the Seppeltsfield Winery, and parked his car after turning off the main road some hundred yards or so along the red gravel track that led to Kauffmann's house. He walked the rest of the way. Sharon's directions had been correct. The single-story, red-roofed house was set well back among the trees up the hill on his right. He studied the terrain carefully. There was only one way to the house, up a graveled driveway to the entrance that was clear of vegetation and offered no cover. He decided to circle around the back and approach the house through the woods at the top of the slope to the rear. He retraced his steps until he reached a low wall that divided the field between the track and the woods. He scrambled through the hedge that bounded the track, then crouching low behind the wall, worked his way up toward the woods. They were mostly conifer and local pine, closely rooted together, and it wasn't easy to make progress. The low branches tore at his clothing, and by the time he had reached a position close to the rear of Kauffmann's house he was bleeding from several scratches. He watched the house closely for several minutes. It appeared to be deserted and no special precautions to protect it were apparent; just a low stone wall separated the back garden from the line of trees marking the edge of the wood.

Brockway emerged slowly, climbed over the wall, then ran for the rear of the house. The back door and windows were all locked, but he had not come this far to be thwarted by that—if the place was burglar alarmed he'd run like hell. He wrapped his jacket around his arm and brought his elbow back sharply into a bottom pane of glass in one of the windows. It still seemed to make enough noise to wake the dead as it shattered, but no alarm went off; just a few birds took flight briefly from the trees behind him. He managed to force the window open and clambered into the room. It was a small bedroom that opened out onto the hallway that led to the front door.

There were two other bedrooms, one probably occupied by the driver, the other by Kauffmann. Brockway didn't know what he was looking for, something— anything—that might tie in the hospital with Trudie's abduction or give him more information about Kauffmann. Sharon had said that she knew the doctor well; apparently he was in charge of the research laboratories in the hospital, working on diagnosis and possible cures.

Brockway searched diligently, always keeping an ear cocked for the possible return of the occupants, but he found nothing. In fact, what was remarkable, was the total lack of any kind of personal document, photograph, or link with the past. Curiouser and curiouser, thought Brockway. He glanced at his watch. He had already spent almost half an hour in the house and it was time to go. He glanced out the front window, which offered a view of the valley. No one was approaching the house, but he decided he would leave the way he had come. He walked back into the hallway and noticed a pad beside the telephone on the stand. He glanced through it quickly; it was a jumble of telephone numbers and doodles. One name stood out clearly in the middle of a page: Redston. There was a date above it. The date was the day before the tests had taken place. Brockway tore it out and stuffed it into his pocket.

He proceeded more carefully through the woods this time, but the densely packed pines still caught the sleeve of his jacket and ripped it. He was glad to reach the low wall that led down to the field to his car. He ducked behind it and half ran down the slope. He heard something and stopped. A car was approaching along the graveled track. He could only see the driver, a gray-haired man; it looked like Kauffmann. Quickly he ducked down behind the wall. The bullet smacked viciously into the stone behind his head and ricocheted away.

Spengler cursed the arrival of the doctor's car at that precise moment, then loaded another bullet into the breach of his rifle and waited.

Brockway stared incredulously at the white crease in

the wall by his head. Jesus, he was being fired at, though he had not heard the sound of the shot. A silencer! Only a professional assassin, someone who set out deliberately to kill him, would use that. Where the hell was he? He might already be lining him up for another shot. The desire to leap up and run for his life was almost overpowering. But he choked that down—he probably wouldn't even get ten yards. He studied the angle of the mark the bullet had left in the stone. The trajectory indicated that the rifleman must be somewhere back in the trees slightly beyond the point where he had emerged to come down beside the wall. Christ, all he had to do was move along the edge of the woods and he would have a clear shot.

Kauffmann's car was parked in the driveway and Brockway was now in full view of the house, but he had no intention of swapping this side of the wall for the other. Keeping his head well down he began to crawl as quickly as he could on his hands and knees toward the hedge that bounded the track where his car was parked.

Spengler had the space between the end of the wall and the hedge in his sights. Brockway would have to cross that to reach his car and Spengler only needed one good shot.

Brockway reached the bottom of the wall and contemplated the gap. . . . He began to sweat with fear. He had no choice, he knew that. He steeled himself and prepared to leap the gap. As he was about to jump he heard someone yelling at him angrily in German—it was Kauffmann. He leaped.

Spengler's eyes flicked momentarily toward Kauffmann. He saw the quiver of movement from the corner of his eye as Brockway jumped and he fired at the same time, but the distraction had been enough. The bullet smacked harmlessly into the bank after nicking Brockway's trousers as he dived through the hedge. Without pausing he scrambled through the front door of the car on the offside, away from the woods, keeping himself well down on the seat beneath the level of the window. The glass shattered as Spengler began firing systematically. Brockway inserted the key and twisted it. The engine turned over once, twice, then started. Brockway slammed his foot onto the clutch, slipped the car into gear and began to move forward. Thank God he had turned the car around before he parked. Bullets were smacking into the body all around him. He risked a quick look to see where he was going and began to accelerate as fast as he dared. The windshield shattered in front of him as a bullet went through it. He punched a hole in the fragmented glass and sat up, pushing the car into top speed as she bucked and lifted along the rutted track. Suddenly the eerie, silent fusillade ended as the car roared onto the main road and sped away between the two rows of palm trees.

21. Brockway

"But what can I do, Sharon? If I go to the police I've got to tell them I was snooping around Kauffmann's house—that's breaking and entering."

She shook her head determinedly. "Of course, you've got to admit that if you want them to investigate the hospital connection, otherwise you must say nothing about any of it." She looked at him directly. "It depends on what you think you ought to do. Give the police the information that might help them find out who abducted Trudie and the other children, or play safe and say nothing." Brockway had realized that from the start, but hadn't wanted to face the uncomfortable choice. His journalist's instinct was to say nothing, dig deeper, and uncover as much as possible on his own. This time he wasn't the only one involved; he had a responsibility to Sharon and her child. That was something new and at this moment he didn't feel as though he liked it very much. She was waiting for an answer.

"Okay, I'll talk to Clayton, maybe he'll have a few ideas."

She smiled slowly with relief. "Good . . . I think that's right."

Brockway walked over to the phone, paused, then reluctantly picked it up and began to dial. He glanced at Sharon and shook his head resignedly. "I sure as hell hope you're right—Clayton's never gonna believe this." The ringing stopped as the receiver was picked up at the other end. He heard the familiar voice say, "Hello?" Brockway took a deep breath and began to explain.

Clayton arrived within the hour. His face was set and he did not look pleased. Brockway offered him some coffee. "No, thanks." He glanced at Sharon. "Would you mind leaving us alone for a while, Miss Langbein?"

Sharon rubbed her hands nervously on her apron. "No, of course not—I've got some cooking to do. I'll be in the kitchen." She smiled at Brockway encouragingly, and left the room.

Brockway indicated a chair. "I'm sorry, Clayton, having to get you all the way up here, but I thought since you were familiar with the case—"

Clayton stopped him. "Cut the crap, Brockway—what happened? You're in trouble, right!"

Brockway nodded resignedly and slumped into a chair. "Yeah, I guess you could say that." He rubbed his forehead, then looked up at Clayton. "I broke into Kauffmann's house."

"Kauffmann?"

"Dr. Kauffmann—he runs the hospital here in Tanunda. He treated me for a concussion when I had the accident in the car."

"I see—why would you want to do a thing like that? Was his fee too high?" he said caustically.

Brockway sighed. "Very funny—now do you want to know what happened, or don't you?"

"Oh, I am listening, Brockway, and it better be good or you will be suspended permanently—in jail."

Brockway came directly to the point. "Okay, I think Trudie was held in the hospital." Before Clayton could exclaim, he continued. "I was in that hospital, Phil. You remember Trudie said she woke up once—that the room was bare apart from a religious picture on the wall? Well, my room was like that, including the picture. I asked Trudie if she had smelled anything funny—a clean smell. She had, and she identified it as disinfectant."

The detective said nothing for a moment, then, "Anything else?"

Brockway stood up. "Yeah. You remember my report on the nuclear test in the desert?"

Clayton raised an eyebrow. "How could I forget?"

"Well, we saw the inspection team putting on protective clothing, and yellow plastic overshoes."

"So?"

"So when I woke up in the hospital I wasn't feeling too good. I tried to find someone. I remember going down a long way in the elevator." He rubbed his forehead. "I still hadn't found anyone—I guess it must have been in the early hours of the morning—then there was a big room, and just before I passed out I saw a guy wearing yellow plastic overshoes." He looked at Clayton for a reaction. Clayton nodded.

"So you decided to break into Kauffmann's house to see if you could find anything?"

"Right."

"And did you?"

Brockway was about to tell him of the name on the pad, but changed his mind. "No, there was nothing, but that in a way was odd, too. No photos, no records—nothing relating to his past at all. I checked him out. He's German, of course, and is supposed to have arrived here in 1937, but there is nothing about him anywhere until just after the war when the hospital was being built."

Clayton turned away from him exasperatedly. "Look, all you've given me so far is supposition. Trudie smelling disinfectant. You *think* you saw someone in the hospital wearing protective overshoes. Nothing in Kauffmann's house that relates to his past. I can't go around arresting people for not collecting bloody snapshots!"

Brockway gripped his arm. "Look, I don't want you to arrest him, Clayton, but I know there is something phony about that hospital. Call it a gut reaction if you like, but if there is a link between what happened in the desert and the hospital, it might also be connected with the disappearance of the children."

Clayton looked at him disbelievingly. "Wonderful. You know, with an imagination like yours you really ought to write . . . not comment."

Brockway got angry. "All right, maybe you know something I don't. Maybe what happened in the Simpson is a government cover-up after all."

The detective turned away from him, disgusted. "Jesus, Brockway, what a fucking pain you are . . ."

Brockway knew he had pushed his luck too far. "Okay —I take that back, but remember this, and these are facts. One, Trudie is the only child to be sent back; the hospital is here in Tanunda—so is her home. Two, I question the doctor about yellow protective overshoes, and when I am leaving his house I am shot at. The car is in pieces, and that's no supposition. Three, the doctor has not reported the break-in. If he had, the local police would have arrested me by now. How do you explain that?" The detective continued to stare out of the window. "Look, Phil, all I am asking is that we search the hospital."

Clayton considered that. The shooting worried him— maybe Brockway was getting up somebody's nose here in Tanunda. The hospital would scream, but he could handle that. Besides, he wanted to ask that doctor a few things himself. "All right, Brockway, we take a look at the hospital, but first we see the local police. Get your coat."

Dr. Kauffmann received Clayton in his office at the hospital. He was polite and deferential, and readily agreed to let them see the room that Brockway had occupied.

"Yes, that's no problem, Sergeant Clayton. Let me just check where he was—on the third floor if memory serves me." He flicked through a file until he found it. "Yes, that's right. He was brought in late at night suffering from slight head injuries after a car accident."

"What sort of injuries?"

"A cut on his forehead and concussion. He passed out shortly after arrival, but he soon recovered—no, wait a minute—I saw him again the other day. He was complaining of headaches. I examined him briefly, but it wasn't serious. I advised him to contact his local doctor if the symptoms continued."

Clayton believed him, as far as it went. "Was there anything else?"

The doctor looked surprised. "In what way?"

"Did he ask you any questions about the hospital?"

"No, I don't think so." He looked puzzled.

Clayton waved an arm. "It's nothing." He would have to check Brockway's claim about overshoes. Clayton stood up and thanked the doctor. "There is one thing—did anyone break in to your house yesterday?"

Kauffmann regarded him silently from behind the thick lenses of his spectacles and Clayton suddenly felt uncomfortable. Then the doctor smiled. "My word, you have done your work well. Yes, I did find a window at the back broken, but nothing had been stolen so I didn't report it. I thought it might have been some children playing in the woods."

Clayton nodded, but made no comment. "The third floor did you say?"

"That's right, I'll take you up there if you like."

"No need—I have to bring Brockway up from reception first."

The doctor smiled again. "Then I'll meet you up there."

Brockway felt silly. They'd examined the room he'd been in; it was exactly like all the others. He stood in the elevator, waiting until Clayton and the doctor joined him. Once inside, the doors closed silently and the detective gave him a quizzical look. "Okay, Brockway, it's your show."

He pressed the button marked "G," and the elevator descended smoothly to the ground floor reception area. The doors opened automatically, and the doctor moved to get out. The detective restrained him. "One moment, doctor." He nodded to Brockway, who pressed the same button again several times. The elevator didn't budge; he tried again, nothing. The doctor smiled apologetically. "I don't know what you hope to achieve, Mr. Brockway—we are already on the ground floor."

"I know that," Brockway snarled at him, "but there's a basement area to this building and I want to get to it."

"I'm afraid you are mistaken, Mr. Brockway," the doctor said quietly. "This is as far down as the elevator goes."

Brockway could feel the eyes of the detective on him, and the two local police in the reception area were looking at him as though he had just lost his marbles. He turned irritably to Clayton. "I know this thing goes further—I know it."

The detective glanced at Kauffmann. "Do you have an engineer—someone who could let us see the shaft under the lift?"

The doctor nodded deferentially. "Of course, I'll arrange it at once." He walked over to the girl behind the reception desk.

Brockway turned to the detective. "I'm sorry, Clayton, I know this sounds crazy, but there is something down there."

"For your sake, Brockway, I hope so."

A small wizened man about sixty years old arrived in response to the doctor's call. He looked up at the detective. "What's up, mate—won't the lift work?"

Clayton tried not to smile. "The lift works fine, old-timer. We just want to look at the shaft underneath, okay?"

The old man shrugged his shoulders in disbelief, then grinned. "You dropped something down there, right?"

Clayton glanced at Brockway and nodded. "Yeah, that's right—I dropped something."

That seemed to satisfy him. "Why didn't you say so in the first place?" He dropped to his knees, pulled back the rubberized carpet, lifted a trapdoor, and handed the detective a flashlight from his toolbox. "Help yourself."

Clayton kneeled down and switched on the flashlight, leaning down through the trapdoor. Brockway couldn't see past him, and waited impatiently for Clayton to finish his inspection. Finally the detective stood up. Brockway looked at him, waiting for him to say something. "Well?"

Clayton handed him the flashlight. "You look."

Brockway took it from him slowly, then bent down to peer through the trapdoor. He flashed the light on. The shaft ended in solid concrete about twelve feet below the floor of the elevator.

Four hours later he was still in the local police station trying to explain, but his story had begun to sound ludicrous even to his own ears, and the disbelief of the police would have been evident to a thick-skinned elephant. He was uncomfortably aware that his reputation for highly-colored news reporting was rebounding on him.

However, there remained the car, riddled with bullets —the one indisputable fact in his story. It was Clayton who finally disclosed their conclusions on that, and ironically got him off the hook with the local police. Clayton had waited until the small back room in the police station was empty, then after a puzzled silence he exclaimed, "What the hell did you think you were up to, Brockway? Breaking into the house like that."

He didn't answer at once, then he grinned. "Maybe I just don't like Germans," he said with some irony.

Clayton's face remained stony, impassive. "Don't even joke about it, Brockway, you're in way over your head."

"But the car," Brockway said, "what about the car? Why would someone want to knock me off?"

Clayton shook his head angrily. "For God's sake, don't you ever use your brain, surely it's obvious!"

Brockway stared at him uncomprehendingly. The detective spelled it out slowly as though he were talking to a three-year-old. "Someone is trying to kill Kauffmann, not you. You came out of the house and got hit."

"But I wasn't anywhere near the house—I told you that. I was by the wall in the field and the doctor was going by in his bloody car—"

The detective interrupted him. "Kauffmann's denied that. He says he never saw anyone by the wall or being shot at, and frankly, Brockway, I don't believe you. I think you came out of the front door, got into your car, and you were fired at because the gunman thought you were Kauffmann."

Brockway held up his hands. "All right, so why would anyone want to kill Kauffmann?"

"God knows, maybe some freak like you who doesn't like Germans—maybe he's upset a relative of a patient that died—how the hell should I know? It could be anything, but whatever it was I don't want you making any more capital out of this on the tube or I'll have you inside for breaking and entering so fast your feet won't touch the ground." He slammed his fist hard onto the table. Brockway had never seen him that angry. "Now get the hell out of here."

Brockway knew better than to argue. He realized that Clayton was sticking his neck out by not booking him. He said nothing, turned quietly, and left.

He lay on his back in the bed, exhausted. Sharon was lying on her side, her left leg across his, pressing her thigh between his legs while she rubbed the sweat gently from his chest with her hand. She felt good, her skin soft against his. A strand of hair was across his face, tickling his nose. He blew it away and kissed the top of her head nestling below his chin. He felt her respond, sliding her hand down between his legs. It was sensual and gave him intense pleasure, but he warned her softly, "Easy now, Sharon, that's about all I've got left after today's events."

She squeezed him gently, and ran her tongue over his nipple. "That's all I need, Yank—that's enough for me."

He smiled to himself. "Christ, Sharon, you do wonders for my morale, you know that? I really should be feeling depressed."

She took his hand and pressed it to her breast. "That's the last thing I want you to be feeling right now, Mr. Brockway."

"Okay, okay," he said lightly, pecking her on the nose, "just give the old man a chance to recover. I'm not eighteen any more."

"I know"—she smiled wickedly, sending him up—"but you use it so much better."

He slapped her bottom; she screamed and broke away.

Brockway rolled on top of her, holding her arms back behind her head. "For a girl with a strong Lutheran background you're a very passionate lady, did you know that?"

She looked up at him astride her, suddenly very serious, knowing how much she loved him. "Yes, I know—but it is nice, isn't it?"

"Oh yes, very nice, but it's more than that." He paused, holding her fingers to his lips. "I think I'm hooked."

She pulled his head down slowly toward her and kissed him, loving the intimacy of their bodies, the feel of his legs astride her, his penis, soft now, nestling on her stomach. As they kissed she sensed instinctively a sudden change in his mood; he rolled away from her onto his back. "You know, every time I think about that bloody hospital I can't decide whether it happened, or whether I dreamed it all."

Sharon had failed. She'd hoped he would go to sleep without thinking about that again. "Don't talk about it, Harry, it won't do you any good, we've been over it a dozen times. You were hurt. In fact, you collapsed as I was taking you into the hospital. It's possible that you might have been suffering from some reaction."

Brockway didn't answer. He was beginning to feel sleepy. She was right, of course; the whole bloody thing could have been a nightmare brought on by the concussion, but those bloody yellow overshoes. Why was his impression of them so strong?

Sharon heard his breathing alter as he fell asleep. She turned over. Maybe he ought to go back to Adelaide for a while; she could afford to take a few days off now. Besides, she'd like to see where he lived.

He was falling, turning over and over, his arms and legs flailing like a scarecrow. He couldn't reach the button. He stretched out his arm again. If only he could press it he would stop. The metal face of the board was in front of him. There were two buttons, first floor and ground floor. If he could press the lower one, then he would slow down before he hit the bottom. His fingers stretched out, inching agonizingly slowly toward the button. Any second he expected his body to be crushed as the elevator hit the bottom of the shaft, but now his sweaty fingers were scrabbling on the face of the doors.

He got his forefinger onto the bottom button and pressed it. The floor of the elevator came up with a sickening thud, smashing his legs against his chest, flattening him against the floor. He saw the red blood seeping through his yellow plastic shoes . . . then his eyes flicked open and he was gazing at the ceiling of the bedroom. He was bathed in perspiration. His legs were drawn up against his chest. He felt sick—then realized he'd had a nightmare. He lay still for a moment or two, feeling his diaphragm tremble as he breathed in deeply.

It was that bloody hospital again. He had been falling down inside the elevator unable to stop it. . . . He lay absolutely still. There was something else before. What was it? Before he'd gotten into the elevator. He thought back. He'd come out of his room and turned right along the corridor toward the end of the building. Turned right! That was it! He hadn't gone toward the elevator that was in the center of the building; he'd turned right toward the end of the passage. Then when he had felt he was about to pass out, he'd gripped something made of metal—a rail? That's right, he'd gone down one flight of steps. The elevator was at the bottom. A single metal door—he'd groped his way toward it, pressed the button, then as the door opened he'd gone inside and begun to fall. . . .

He slipped quietly out of the bed and gazed out of the back window at the white gum tree, its color subtly washed out by the full moon etching the tree's black shadow onto the lawn. He glanced back at the bed. Sharon was still fast asleep, one arm stretched out across her face, her hair spread over the pillow. Brockway began to dress quietly; he didn't want to wake her up. She'd try to stop him, but he had to know.

He left silently by the front door, closing it softly behind him and walking quickly up Elizabeth Street until he came to the main road. Tanunda was deserted. He glanced at his watch, it was 3:50 A.M. He crossed the road to the far sidewalk and walked along it, trying to stay in the long shadows cast by the moon, past the drug store, the small local library, then under the verandah surrounding the first floor of the tiny museum.

He turned left off the main road. The shadows were darker and longer here, the buildings closer together. The hospital was on his right, towering above the single-story houses around it. The reception area was brightly lit, and he could see a male orderly sitting behind a desk sipping a drink and reading a newspaper. He needed to find another entrance. He slipped around the side of the building. At the back were rows of single-story wards fanning out from the rear of the main building. A single open corridor joined them to it, a line of bare electric bulbs lighting it. He waited for a moment or two but it was silent and still. He slid along the back of the main building until he came to the double doors that opened up to the corridor joining the wards and slipped inside. The doors were made of rubber—and made no sound. He judged that he was in the central part of the complex, therefore opposite the reception area. A corridor led directly into the main building, probably linking with it, and a staircase led up to the first floor. He climbed silently up the concrete staircase, which began to wind around the elevator shaft coming up from reception. He stayed on the staircase until he reached the third floor. He had seen no one; plainly this was the private section of the hospital complex, so probably fewer patients would be housed here. He was now on familiar ground; he walked down the corridor to the room on the right that he had occupied, and then looked back. There was the main elevator going down to reception. But he had come out of this door and turned right. He walked further along the dimly lit corridor until he saw something shining dully on his left. There it was; a brass handrail beside a set of narrow concrete stairs going down. He gripped the rail and began to descend. At the bottom of the stairs was the single metal door of the elevator he had stumbled into on the night of his accident. The concrete stairs continued downward and the sign indicated a fire exit. Brockway realized that the floors below the third did not reach the real end of the building; this was separated from it by a solid wall. He stared at the button, then slowly reached out and pressed it. The door slid open just as it had before and he stepped inside. He could see through the round window into the stairwell he had just left. There were two buttons in front of him, one read "1," the other "G." He pressed the latter and began to descend. He saw the stairwell again as they passed through the first floor, and then it jerked to a halt and the door slid open. Opposite the elevator was another door marked Exit; he stepped out of the elevator and tried to open it but it was locked. He heard the elevator door sliding shut behind him and moved back swiftly, pressing the button before it had completely shut. He got inside once more and stared at the panel. Just the two bloody buttons, yet he had only remembered pressing the bottom one marked "G"; that brought him to here, but this wasn't the room he remembered. He pressed it again—nothing—then three more times. The door began to slide shut and he stood immobile as the elevator began to descend more swiftly than before. He lost all track of depth, perhaps fifty feet, perhaps more, then it began to slow down, and finally halted as suddenly as it had before. He could see a small white room through the round window, then the door slid open and he stepped out. There was a heavy door opposite with two lights above it, one red and one green; the green one was glowing at the moment. In the middle of the door was a small window like the one in the elevator. Brockway realized he was in a safety waiting area. He stepped forward, keeping to one side of the window in the door. He glanced through it. The area was vast, white, probably covering nearly all of the base of the hospital. In the center was a huge circular lead structure—but it was the one man standing by a control switchboard that caught his attention. He was wearing yellow plastic overshoes.

22. Redston

Redston's plans were almost complete. Sou Nu Chai had confirmed the acceptance of his plan by the Chinese government in Peking, and now progress was being made at an ever increasing rate. Even so he was not satisfied; speed was crucial. He wanted the last test successfully completed and the brains behind it removed from the dangers of detection in Australia.

The monthly press reports from Ex Oil Australia were indicating that Richard Grenfell Thomas's theory about uranium deposits at Beverley on the Western slopes of the Flinders Ranges were correct. In 1944 he had suggested that rock deposits eroded down from the mountains over millions of years onto the plain would then sink below the surface until they reached the carbonaceous woody material beneath the surface. There the uranium would be precipitated out of the water solution as a yellow uranium ochre, the principle ore of uranium. Since Ex Oil Australia was drilling in this area between the dry salt Lake Frome and the Flinders, Redston had informed SSS to disguise the rocket and mobile launch pad as drilling equipment. This had been done and it was already in the process of being shipped from Africa to Port Adelaide. Heissler and his team would arrive by air in Adelaide, preceding the shipment by twenty-four hours. Redston intended to meet Heissler and then take him north to Barossa, where he would rejoin his former Nazi colleague; the rest of his team would oversee the loading of the shipment and transportation to the launch site.

The convoy, ostensibly for Ex Oil Australia at Beverley, would attract no suspicion on its long journey to the eastern approaches of the Flinders. The launch site Redston had chosen was north of Beverley and west of the dry salt Lake Frome. About seventy miles from the nearest human habitation at North Mulga. Once past that solitary building they were in the clear. North Mulga was a sheep station; it was also the place where Jiggs picked up his monthly supplies.

The sound of the aircraft's engines was soothing, but Bruno Heissler felt no inclination to sleep. He had never been to Australia before and he kept glancing at the map in the magazine Qantas provided to see where they were. They had taken off from their short stopover at Perth, half an hour before, and he estimated they were running parallel with the coastline of South Australia somewhere over the semi-arid country of the Nullabor Plain.

He was not looking forward to seeing Vaas, his former fellow student. Since the war had ended he'd become increasingly aware of the true nature of the experiments Vaas had conducted during the war to measure the effects of nuclear radiation. He'd read on various occasions that Vaas was on the list of missing war criminals wanted for atrocities committed in the name of science on concentration camp inmates. On one occasion he himself had been questioned by colleagues of Simon Wiesenthal—it was an experience that he hadn't welcomed, and he'd said nothing about his last meeting with Vaas in Koblenz. But if, as Redston had indicated, he had perfected a sophisticated nuclear bomb here in Australia, then it was a remarkable achievement. To have done this in complete secrecy was staggering. He was confident that the rocket would be able to thrust the dummy warhead into the stratosphere and detonate it at any preselected target. It would be interesting to discuss these problems with Vaas. For Heissler, it was merely a technical question, getting the equations right.

He relaxed in his seat and wondered what Vaas would look like; he was about eight years older than Heissler and would be in his early sixties by now. He felt sure he would recognize Vaas even after a gap of—how long had it been? God, it was twenty-six years ago. Christmas 1944 at the hotel opposite the university in Koblenz. He wondered what had happened to Albert—he'd never returned to the hotel—the old man must surely be dead by now. Many things had happened since, but that meeting remained clear. Vaas had wanted him to join him and now he knew where his destination had been.

This curious valley that Redston had told him about, "a small Rhineland in the heart of Australia," was how he had described it. He was eager to see it. However bizarre the choice of Australia by an ex-Nazi fleeing from the Allies might have seemed, it had undoubtedly worked. Perhaps by its very nature, its unlikelihood, it had succeeded. A valley of Aryan descent in the heart of a British Commonwealth country—it had a certain irony, a completeness. The nose of the plane began to dip; soon they would be arriving in Adelaide.

Redston and a young man called Spengler met him at the airport. Redston reassured him about the hotel accommodation provided for his team in Adelaide while they waited for the arrival of the shipment from Africa. It was on time—due to dock at Port Adelaide early next morning. They would not require his presence. The transportation and setting up of the launch pad were not his responsibilities. His skills would be required in the course of consultations between himself and Vaas.

Redston studied Heissler carefully; he had always been impressed by this man. It wasn't just his record, although he was undoubtedly one of the most brilliant rocket scientists to have emerged from Germany at the end of the war, and the Americans had been lucky to get him. No, it was as much his personal response to challenge or new ideas that Redston liked. Even now he was animated, enjoying the smell and feel of a new country, studying the terrain, his eyes alight with excitement. It was hard to believe he was in his fifties. He looked younger, his hair only just tinged with gray, his face suntanned from his almost permanent residence in Africa.

Redston wondered if he ought to tell him that he now knew who his former colleague was, but he changed his mind. He would continue to call Vaas Kauffmann—always better to have something up his sleeve. Not that he expected to need it. Heissler had jumped at the opportunity to develop a space program in China. Perhaps he would achieve it, but whatever the outcome, China would have a much more advanced intercontinental ballistic missile. He wanted to keep Heissler cooperative because they needed his brains to give themselves real status among the nuclear superpowers. Vaas had had no choice. If he had refused, Redston would simply have blown the whistle on him and allowed Simon Wiesenthal and the Israelis to deal with him. But the problem hadn't arisen and as soon as this final test was completed, Vaas and his team would join Heissler and any of his colleagues who cared to accompany him to China. An odd alliance—Mao Tse-tung and the ex-Nazis, but one with enormous potential. Heissler would remain unaware of only one factor. It would not be a dummy warhead on the Australian rocket launch. Redston needed the final proof for his Chinese masters.

Brockway watched the Mercedes limousine draw up in front of the hospital. He saw a young man leap out of the driver's seat and open the back door for the two men inside. He studied them carefully but didn't recognize either. He took a quick shot of them with the telephoto still camera he had managed to wheedle out of ABC. They began to ascend the short row of steps to the reception area, then he saw Kauffmann emerge from the elevator and greet both of them warmly—they seemed like old friends. He continued to shoot until they disappeared from view, then he started Sharon's car and drove down toward the main road. He'd have to pay a quick visit to Adelaide to get these developed at once. There was something about the older of the two men who had arrived at the hospital. Brockway felt sure he had seen him somewhere before, but he couldn't place him.

It was getting dark by the time Redston checked in at the Wiental Motel on the outskirts of Tanunda. He was glad to get away from the Germans; their noisy reunion meal in the restaurant had not been to his liking, particularly since he hadn't drunk anything. He seldom did—it was too dangerous to relax completely when he was working.

He had seen Heissler and Vaas safely off to the house near Seppeltsfield where Vaas lived. There at least, when they recovered, they could iron out the final details for the test.

He walked across the courtyard, the last rays of the sun setting behind him, bathing the line of terraced wooden chalets in a golden glow. He carried his single suitcase up the wooden steps to the outside passage that ran the length of the building and inserted the key into number 33. It was standard, but comfortable. A small bathroom immediately off to his right, then the main room, in it two single beds, a television set, a telephone and some wardrobe space, plus a small fridge containing some drinks, mostly alcoholic. He dumped the suitcase on one of the beds and walked over to the window at the back. He always checked the window. Behind the line of chalets was a field full of purple weed. Behind that ran the single-track railway that ran up from Adelaide, alongside it a back road that joined the main road in Tanunda. He drew the curtains, switched on the television, and began to unpack.

An hour later he was lying on the bed watching a rerun of an old Hitchcock movie, "Strangers on a Train," when the phone rang. The young girl at the front desk said there was a Mr. Spengler to see him. Redston told her to send him over, then took the gun from underneath his pillow and stuck it in his waistband. He put on his jacket and switched off the television, then waited.

Spengler climbed the wooden staircase and knocked twice. Redston opened the door almost at once and invited him in. Spengler walked inside and stood awkwardly while Redston closed the door behind him. He eagerly accepted the offer of a drink and sat on the edge of the low armchair as Redston poured a beer from a can.

Redston could see that he was nervous. He'd wondered about Spengler, what motivated him to throw in his lot with Vaas. He seemed naïve, very young for his age.

He would have been a boy during the war and Redston was curious as to what had committed him so completely to the support of an ex-Nazi. Redston half smiled to himself—he could see the irony in that thought. His own motives for joining the Chinese, while initially seeming to be self-preservation, went much deeper than that, and he was only now just beginning to comprehend them. Spengler kept rubbing the corner of his eyebrow and sat stiffly in the chair. He handed him the beer and sat on the edge of the bed facing him. "Well, what can I do for you, Spengler?"

He appeared to become even more tense. "It's . . . it's about the doctor."

"Dr. Kauffmann?"

"Yes." He looked at Redston anxiously. "I don't want you to think I am disloyal, but there is something that you don't know." He paused, trying to gauge a reaction. Redston's face remained impassive. "Well, I think it could be dangerous."

"Dangerous," Redston repeated without inflection.

"Yes, you see, the doctor has been carrying out some experiments that involve small children."

Redston felt a cold chill of anger harden inside him. "What sort of experiments?"

"I am not sure, but they were in connection with radiation levels that would provide a cure eventually for radiation poisoning."

Redston's voice was calm, reassuring. "You said the experiments involved children. In what way?"

"Well, my job was to get the children for the doctor. Of course I had to take them without the knowledge of their parents."

It was said so matter-of-factly, as if he were talking about a shopping list, so that for a moment Redston almost betrayed his feelings. He stared at Spengler, his eyes expressionless, showing none of the shock and seething anger that he felt. He had to know the full extent of this insanity. He feigned benign interest. "I see—how did you choose these children?"

"I usually found them in or around Adelaide somewhere. I used chloroform, of course; they never felt any pain. Then I would take them to a special room at the hospital and hand them over to Kauffmann."

Redston nodded affably. "And what became of them afterward?"

Spengler looked puzzled. "You mean after the experiments?"

"Yes."

"I don't know. The doctor always dealt with that side of things."

Redston sat quietly for a moment. "How many children did you find for the doctor?"

Spengler began to look worried again. "Well, that's the point, really. Five altogether, but"—he paused, then angrily—"you see, he made me take the last one back!"

"Back?"

"Yes, she was a little girl, the first girl I had been asked to get, but she lived here in the valley and the doctor found out that she was of German descent—her name was Langbein, Trudie Langbein, I think. Anyway, he made me take her back and I had to leave her in a park in Adelaide. It may have jeopardized the whole program."

Redston looked at him without expression. "Is that everything?"

Spengler shifted uncomfortably. "No. Someone has been snooping around, a television reporter named Brockway. He did an interview with the girl's mother and later was admitted into the hospital after an accident in her car. He came back a couple of days ago and the doctor got suspicious of him."

"What happened then?" Redston said quietly.

"Yes, well, that's what I wanted to talk about; that's what I meant about him putting us all into danger," he said childishly. "He told me I had to get rid of him."

"And did you?"

"No, well, I tried. I followed him out to the doctor's house that day, then waited in some woods for him to come back." He was beginning to look agitated again; the memory of it plainly made him angry. "I would have got him, too, without any trouble, but the bloody doctor came back to his house just as I was about to hit him."

Redston smiled. "So, he's still alive?"

"Yes," Spengler said miserably.

Redston stood up and buttoned his jacket. "You did absolutely the right thing in coming to me. I think, first of all, you had better show me the place where the incident with Brockway took place. We shall have to eliminate him, and the sooner I know all about his tricks the better."

Spengler obviously approved of this professional approach. "Thank you, Mr. Redston. I've got my car outside —we can go there at once if you like." He appeared relieved to have gotten the matter off his chest.

"Yes, let's do that," said Redston. "No time like the present."

The headlights of the powerful car revealed the outline of the palm trees as they neared Seppeltsfield, then began to bounce erratically as they left the paved road where it swung right and continued on the track that led to Kauffmann's house. Redston had had plenty of time to think about the dangers which he had suddenly been exposed to and made aware of. That moment of blind fury in the motel had almost betrayed him, but now his emotions were well under control and he knew what he had to do. He did not underestimate the police, and the fact that the girl came from the valley was a connecting link, as was the bungled attempt on Brockway's life. He glanced at Spengler, outlined in the driver's seat by the glare of the headlights. Potential informers worried him as did stupidly sentimental old men—but he still needed Vaas, and once he could be established in a controlled situation, his insanity would be harmless. The program would have to be speeded up—it was vital. Every day they stayed in Australia increased the dangers.

There remained Spengler. If the police got their hands on him, he'd crack the whole thing wide open within an hour.

Spengler halted the car short of the driveway and turned off the headlights. He rolled down his window and pointed outside. "The wall is just the other side of that hedge."

"Have you got a flashlight?" Redston asked.

Spengler leaned across and removed a heavy rubber-encased flashlight from the glove compartment. "Here."

Redston got out and shut the back door quickly. "Perhaps you'd like to lead the way."

Spengler clambered through the hedge and indicated the gap between it and the wall. "I'd have got him here, but that's when the doctor began shouting from the house."

"Where were you at the time?"

He pointed into the darkness. "Up there in the trees."

Redston nodded. "I see—well, you'd better show me."

Spengler moved off in front of him carrying the flashlight. Redston pulled the gun from under his waistband, and as Spengler led the way up the hill in the darkness, he began fitting the silencer. Spengler wondered why Redston wanted to see the place where he had ambushed Brockway, but Redston impressed him—he admired his thoroughness. He picked his way carefully up the hill, shining the flashlight on the ground in front of him. Two red eyes stared fixedly at him in the beam, and he stopped dead in his tracks. The huge rat shot into a hole in the wall beside them and disappeared. Spengler swung round. "Christ, did you see . . . ?" The words froze on his lips as he saw the gun in Redston's hand. Suddenly everything was clear. The drive out here in the middle of the night— the request for him to lead the way up the hill. He'd been betrayed, he'd trusted an Englishman. *Owe them nothing, give them nothing, do not trust them or they will surely take you away from those that you love—promise me. . . .* His father's words echoed in his ears, reminding him. Redston was staring at him unmoving, then slowly he screwed on the silencer. Spengler didn't wait—he didn't think. All he wanted was to go home, lock himself in and never leave. He turned his back on Redston and started to run up the hill, forgetting to even switch off the flashlight.

Redston did not pursue him. Quickly he made the final adjustment, and holding the heavy Lüger in both hands, he took careful aim. The flashlight was bobbing up the hill nearing the tree line. Redston fired; the pistol recoiled in his hand making no sound, just the familiar plopping noise. The light still bobbled its way toward the trees, and he fired twice more. He saw the light fall to the ground, glowing palely, diffused in the long grass. He lowered the pistol and made his way slowly up the hill toward it. As he drew closer he became cautious. Spengler, too, was a potential killer.

The flashlight shone up emptily into his face, mocking him. Spengler had escaped. He bent down and picked up the flashlight and shone it on the ground. The blood clung darkly to the damp grass. Good, he'd hit him. He didn't think his aim had been that bad. He began to follow the trail of blood.

Spengler had not known he was being fired at. Rushing blindly up the hill, he'd heard what seemed like a wasp zip by his ear, then two shockingly violent blows—one in his right arm, the other in his back—threw him face down onto the ground. He could feel nothing at first—he was numb. The smell of the dew on the grass pervaded his nostrils, smelling sweetly, reminding him of summer. Then something else, darker, thicker, touched his neck and then his face. His blood, pumping from his chest where the bullet had emerged, running down the side of the hill, pouring his life away.

He had to get home first—warn his father. He staggered to his feet, the starlit sky swinging around in circles above his head. He heard Redston climbing toward him, and he staggered toward the line of trees. They seemed to recede as he approached—dancing in the sky like spindly leprechauns—then they were around him, calling him, mocking him. *Would you like to ride on my horse, sonny?* A huge black stallion galloped toward him, then stood waiting to carry him home—he was about to climb up on his back when he saw the guard astride it, leaning down, offering to help him up. He turned away, running. The hill beginning to descend beneath his feet toward Seppeltsfield and his home just beyond it.

The night was getting darker, black clouds drifting up between him and the stars; he must get home before it rained, he'd get wet. He was wet, his clothes were sticky *inside*. Oh God, no—had he wet himself? His father would be ashamed, but he must warn him—he must. He felt the ground go hard beneath his feet. The sound of his shoes on the paved surface bounced up toward him. He was on the road. Not far now. He felt tired, he wanted to lie down and sleep, lie in his warm bed and wait for his mother to tuck him in. Later his father would come and, thinking he was asleep, kiss him, and whisper in his ear.

There was the door, the light from the kitchen streaming outward, illuminating the gnats caught in its glow. He reached the door and pushed it open. He saw his mother's face, shocked, coming toward him. He tried to tell her not to worry—where was his father? His mother receded behind him. There he was, rising from the chair, reaching out for him—then he was above him staring down, holding his head in his hands. "Be careful, daddy—they're coming back." He could not hear himself, he tried again. "They're coming back for you—to take you away."

His father's face was receding, getting dimmer. He cried out sharply, "Don't let them take him away, mummy." Then he died.

He stopped; the house was set a little way back from the road, solitary, square, sturdy. The bloodstains continued up the short drive. In front of the house he could just distinguish the outline of a car. He stepped onto the grass verge and staying close to the shrubbery made his way quickly toward the building. He could see light reflected from the trees at the side of the house.

He rounded the corner. The door was wide open, the light streaming from it. He could hear a woman screaming, the sound harsh, grief-stricken. Stepping well back into the shadows of the trees bounding the side of the house, he positioned himself opposite the open door. Now he could see the woman, middle-aged, on her knees crying, beside her, lying on the floor, the body of Spengler. A man crossed his eye-level and slumped into a wooden armchair in the kitchen. Redston moved closer, pressing himself to the wall of the house. He waited—there was nothing, just the sobbing of the woman. Then he heard a chair scrape the floor as the man stood up and crossed the room. He heard him say something to the woman, trying to comfort her. Redston strained forward, listening. The woman stopped crying—then loudly, hysterically, "What did he mean, Gunther? Who is coming to take you away? Oh God, what has happened?"

The man's voice was low, distressed. "I don't know—perhaps he thought he was a boy again. That they were taking me away to the camp." Then his voice broke, and he began to cry. The woman's voice, stronger now, "Come, Gunther, we must telephone the police—whoever killed him is out there somewhere, he cannot be far away."

Redston heard her start to cross the floor toward the door. He leaned back in the shadows, then it slammed shut, and he heard something scamper off in the trees, frightened. Probably a mouse or a hedgehog. He moved quietly away from the wall of the house. There was nothing more to do here. Spengler was dead.

The doctor arrived unobtrusively at the motel an hour later, in response to his call. Redston, as arranged, was sitting in the driver's seat of the car Spengler had used. The doctor slid into the passenger seat and eyed him with a mixture of curiosity and barely concealed annoyance. "Was it necessary to call me out at this time of night? Surely it could have waited until morning."

Redston continued to gaze stonily in front of him, ignoring the question. The silence lengthened and Vaas suddenly felt frightened. "What is it, what's wrong?"

"You're what's wrong, Vaas." It was said so quietly that at first the doctor did not perceive its menace. Then the name that Redston had used registered, like a pebble dropping into a pond. He said nothing; he was almost crouching in the seat. Redston turned and looked at him; his eyes were hooded, expressionless. "Spengler is dead. Before he died he told me about the experiments on the children."

Vaas gazed at him, horrified. "You killed Spengler?" His voice was frightened, disbelieving.

Vaas sickened Redston. He gazed at him disgustedly. "I'd kill you too, now, but for the moment I need you."

Vaas gazed sightlessly at the door of the car. He wanted to justify his actions, tell Redston about his own condition —the radiation poisoning eating into his own blood cells —but he feared that if Redston knew the truth, he would have no further use for him. He remained silent.

"Did you order Spengler to eliminate a man called Brockway?" Vaas began to sweat with fear. Redston's eyes never left him. "Now listen carefully. The police will question you about Spengler because of your association; try to react naturally. Now that someone has died, they are bound to question everybody, but stay calm. Can you do that?"

Vaas nodded his assent.

"You have nothing to fear from Brockway—I will deal with him. Now take this car and give me the keys to yours."

The doctor fumbled around in his pocket until he found them and handed them shakily over.

Redston gripped his wrist. "Pull yourself together, Vaas." His voice was calm, authoritative. "You have seen death many times, it should hold no fear for you. Remember that the success of this operation depends upon you and Heissler. Say nothing, behave naturally—do you understand?"

His face was pale, but he seemed to gain strength from Redston's confidence. "Yes, of course, I will try to do exactly as you say."

"You *will* do as I say, Vaas, otherwise we are all dead."
Redston let go of his wrist, took the keys, and got out of
the car. He stood immobile, silent in the deserted parking
lot long after the car had disappeared. There remained
Brockway, who was lethal.

23. North Mulga

Charlie Miller was about thirty. Typical of the sort of man who inhabited Australia's outback, his face lined, suntanned, and leathery. The climate tended to be even harsher on the womenfolk, aging them prematurely, but Charlie's wife, Sybil, was still in her early twenties, and as yet unaffected by it.

Charlie was an outstation manager for the Wooltama Pastoral Company, who ran sheep in this area. The station at North Mulga was a four-room, square building with a galvanized roof, completely encircled by a verandah, supported by wooden posts. It was the last homestead on a rough track that led south to the road at Wilpena Pound and eventually to Adelaide, nearly four hundred miles away.

It was Charlie's six-year-old son Gavin who first spotted Jiggs and his camel emerging from the heat haze of the subdesert that spread out limitlessly around the station, bounded to the west by the Flinders. He ran excitedly into the kitchen, tugging at his mother's dress. "Mummy, mummy, it's the old man with the camels—come and see." Sybil wiped the flour from her hands with a cloth and followed Gavin out onto the verandah. Her husband was lying beneath the station wagon in the tin shed, stripped to the waist, checking out what he suspected was broken spring. He heard his wife calling and slid out from beneath the vehicle. She pointed and he turned, shading his eyes and looking in the direction she had indicated. The heat haze danced and distorted the outline, but he discerned the shape of a camel with a rider. It was undoubtedly Jiggs, but why only one camel? He walked slowly across to his wife, wiping the oil from his hands on a dirty rag.

"Can you see only one camel?"

She continued to gaze into the distance. "Yes, that's right, but it is Jiggs, isn't it?"

"Oh, it's Jiggs, all right." He rubbed his chin thoughtfully. "Have we got any cold beer in the fridge?"

"Yes," she said, turning into the house. "Would you like one as well?"

"Yeah, I'll have a stubby. Might as well join him."

Gavin ran after his mother. "Can I have some pop, mum?"

Jiggs reined the camel to a halt in front of the house, then poked her once with his stick. Bess sank obediently to her knees and Jiggs climbed stiffly down, nodding a greeting to Charlie.

"Wife's gettin' you a beer, Jiggsy." He watched him preparing the saddlebags for his supplies. "What happened to Molly?"

Jiggs continued to work methodically and Charlie waited. He knew enough about this taciturn old prospector not to press him.

"She died," Jiggs said over his shoulder, his back still to Charlie. "She was gettin' on a bit, but we didn't expect her to go just yet, did we, Bess?" He patted the camel's flank, but she ignored him.

Gavin came running out of the house and leaped down off the verandah in a cloud of dust and raced across to the old man. "Hello, Jiggsy," he said, giving his tattered trouser leg a tug. "Where's Molly?"

Jiggs glanced at Charlie, then ruffled the boy's fair hair affectionately. "Left her at home this time—I think she was a bit tired, son."

Sybil called out from behind the protective screen door to the kitchen. "Come inside, you lot. I've got some cold drinks here." The screening was a necessity in these regions, otherwise the bush flies got everywhere, searching for moisture.

Jiggs downed the small bottle of beer in one swallow; it was delicious—so cold it almost gave him a headache. He always accepted a single beer in this household, where he got about as close as he could to the normality of a family life that he had deserted thirty-odd years before. The boy reminded him of his own son—he'd be grown up by now, but Jiggs never thought past that point. It was too painful.

Gavin was sitting on Jiggs's knee chattering excitedly, filling in the awkward gaps in this unsurprisingly stilted conversation between the adults. Jiggs found it far easier to converse with his camel or the radio than with real people. Gavin was looking forward to his usual ride on the camel but something he said caught Jiggs's attention.

"They were big ones, Jiggsy, I've never seen lorries that big before—the dust went everywhere. Mummy was annoyed—she'd just finished polishing the furniture."

Jiggs looked at Charlie curiously. "What were they doin' up here, do you know?"

Charlie shook his head. "I'm not sure—I think they must have been doing some uranium exploring the other side of Lake Frome. They were the same bunch as that lot down at Beverley." He turned to his wife. "What are they called, Sybil?"

"Ex Oil Australia," she said. "Least that's what it said on the trailer."

"Trailer?" Jiggs repeated.

"Yeah," Charlie said. "There was a big long trailer in addition to the rest of them. I suppose it could have been a rig of some kind."

"How long ago, Charlie?"

" 'Bout three days, I guess."

Jiggs thought about it for a moment, but he wasn't convinced. All sorts of alarm signals were telling him something was wrong. This was the second truck convoy that had trekked north and disappeared into the desert areas, first to the west of the Flinders, now to the east.

"You reckon they went eastward?"

Charlie opened another bottle of beer, but he didn't offer Jiggs one; he never had more than a single. "Yeah, that's right. They continued northward until they were well out of sight, but then we saw the dust cloud swing eastward. I reckon they must have gone between Lake Callabonna and Lake Frome."

The boy was trying to pull Jiggs to his feet. "Can we ride the camel now, Jiggsy?"

His mother scolded him. "Leave Jiggs alone, Gavin—he probably wants a rest."

Jiggs smiled. "No, that's all right, Mrs. Miller." He stood up. "C'mon, son, we'll see if Bess can manage the both of us." He picked the boy up and carried him outside, setting him astride Bess's back in front of him. Then, as Charlie and Sybil watched from the verandah, he prodded Bess who rose complainingly to her feet, and walked twice around the homestead much to Gavin's huge delight.

Later, after Jiggs had packed his supplies and made

sure he had batteries for the radio, he bid them a brief good-bye, slightly embarrassed when both Sybil and Gavin kissed him before he could get away. He waved once and slowly began to disappear the way he had come, into the heat haze toward the Flinders. As soon as he knew he was well out of their vision, he circled northward and headed in the opposite direction, looking for the tracks of the convoy.

24. ABC Television, Collinswood, Adelaide

It was George Greenfield who recognized the blow-up. He stabbed it with his forefinger. "His name's Heissler—he used to work for the American space agency—NASA—in Houston. He came out of Germany the same time as Werner Von Braun. Rocket scientist, one of the best, they say. Worked on the first V-2s during the war. . . ." He stopped, looked up at Brockway. "What do you want to know for?"

Brockway felt a huge sense of elation and excitement, but at the moment he was not sure why. There were a lot of pieces lying around all over the place, and somehow they were all beginning to fit into a pattern. He ignored the question. "What's he doing now, George?"

"I don't know." He paused, rubbing his forehead. "There was something I heard about, around a year ago—wait a minute"—he wrinkled his eyes, trying to remember —"yes, he wanted to develop, privately, some sort of rocket that could help the Third World powers to acquire satellites. The Russians and the Americans have always refused to provide them with that capability."

"Did he succeed?"

"I don't know. Ask our science correspondent—he

might have some information on it. Now you had better get out of here. I'm busy and you're supposed to be on suspension."

"Thanks anyway, George."

His producer slipped his glasses back on and immersed himself in the chaotic pile of paperwork on his desk. "No trouble, Brockway. Glad to see you're still at it, and I don't mean screwing every available female in Adelaide. Let me know if you get anything worth sticking in the program." He looked up and smiled wickedly. "I can always get one of the other boys to cover it."

Brockway made for the door. "Thanks, George—up yours, too!"

Redston had done some checking on Harry Brockway. He knew of his reputation, and of his recent activities—how he had been discredited after the fruitless search of the hospital by the police. Nevertheless he did not underestimate the man; that would be too easy. Plainly he knew something, how little or how much was academic. He was not the sort who would go away. He was a reporter, and he was ambitious. Redston knew the type; Brockway would be back and he had to be stopped—now.

In a week—maybe less—they would be in the clear and he did not intend to be thwarted at this late stage. There was one inconsistency in Brockway's behavior: he had not exploited the interview with Sharon Langbein. It would have been easy to do so—everyone in the valley was aware of the fact that she was unmarried. He had also apparently been picked up by her when he had left the hospital. She might be his weak point—a weak spot Redston could exploit.

After driving back into the valley overnight, Brockway had established that Heissler was not staying at the small hotel in Tanunda, nor had he checked in at the only motel, but a quick look at the register when the young receptionist's back was turned to deal with some calls on the switchboard had disclosed the name of a visitor in room 33 named Redston. Somehow that name seemed familiar to Brockway. Uh huh! The name on the pad at Kauffmann's house! He glanced quickly at the keyboard; number 33 was not there. Brockway concealed his excitement and strolled casually around the courtyard until he spotted the door to room 33 on the first floor of the terraced chalets facing onto the open wooden corridor that traversed the length of the building. He walked back to where he had left his car in the motel parking lot. He sat quietly watching the door, trying to put it all together. Heissler wasn't here; he was probably staying with Kauffmann at the house near Seppeltsfield, but where did Redston fit in? And what was the significance of the experimental complex beneath the hospital? Clearly the protective clothing indicated radiation hazards of some sort and perhaps was a link to the mysterious nuclear test in the Simpson. Was it part of some secret government research that had led to the test? That might explain the reluctance of the police here in Tanunda to believe him— but where did Trudie's abduction and subsequent return fit into that?

He sat trying to figure out what all the events had in common. Trudie lived here in the valley where the hospital was, and Heissler and Kauffmann were of German origin. Heissler had worked for the American space program. Was it possible that Kauffmann was doing the same for Australia? There was something else, too, niggling away at the back of his mind. German origin . . . yes, that was another link. Trudie and Sharon were of German descent, but how in God's name did that fit in? He shook his head angrily. He had a feeling it was all staring him in the face, but for the life of him he couldn't see it at the moment; he was more confused than ever.

The door opened and Redston emerged. He was about five-eleven, lean and clearly very fit. His hair was short and parted at the side. Brockway took two quick shots of him with the camera as he came down the wooden steps, then watched him go to the reception desk and emerge a moment or two later after leaving his keys. He started to walk toward the parking lot, and Brockway fiddled with a map as though he were checking his route.

Redston got into a car and drove slowly past him, turning left on the main road toward the center of town; Brockway followed, keeping as far behind as he dared. He recognized the car; it belonged to Kauffmann, but Redston was a stranger. He'd never seen that face before. His age was difficult to determine; he could have been anything between twenty-eight and forty. As Brockway had expected, he drove to the hospital, leaving the car outside. He saw the receptionist wave him straight through to the elevator; he had been expected.

Brockway sat in the car beneath the trees where he could keep an eye on the main entrance. He did not know what to expect, but maybe if he kept tabs on them for a while a pattern might begin to emerge.

Within an hour he had all the windows wide open. Although protected by the leafy shade of the trees the car was still oppressively hot inside. Worse, he had nothing to drink. He was ill-prepared for a stake-out and he wondered what private eyes did when they needed to take a leak. He'd noticed the black Mercedes that they had been driven around in earlier parked in the hospital driveway, but when the two Germans emerged, accompanied by Redston, he saw no sign of their driver.

They all walked casually over to the car and Heissler got in behind the wheel, while Kauffmann sat beside him.

Redston shook hands with both of them, then turned and walked smartly back to the reception area as the car drove slowly away. Brockway decided to follow the majority since this was clearly a departure of some kind. He waited until Redston had entered the elevator, then drove down toward the main street. He was just in time to see the Mercedes turn left toward the southern approaches of the town.

Redston had been aware of Brockway's presence from the moment he had stepped from his room in the motel. He had said nothing to Vaas or Heissler since he did not wish to alarm them in any way. They were leaving the valley this morning for the launch site, and one way or another the Germans would never be coming back—it was now too risky, and he didn't like loose ends.

He watched Brockway unobtrusively from the window as he slowly sweated it out in the car, and as soon as the last details had been decided upon he had deliberately emphasized their departure in full view of Brockway, anticipating that he would follow them. He wanted the reporter out of the way.

He studied the house carefully. It faced north on Elizabeth Street: a front entrance, two main front rooms, the usual verandah, and a path at the side leading to another entrance at the rear, probably opening onto the garden. No one had come in or gone out, but he had seen movement behind the curtains.

He got out of the car and walked slowly across the road to the front door and pressed the doorbell. It chimed twice. He heard her approaching the door and slipped the pistol from his waistband, shielding it so that only a person standing in the entrance could see it.

Sharon opened the door, saw the stranger's smiling face then the gun in his hand. She froze.

"No need to say anything, Mrs. Langbein, just step back and invite me in as if I were not holding this gun." Sharon moved back automatically and Redston stepped inside, shutting the door quickly behind him. There was a small hallway opening out onto a living room that ran the entire length of the house, connecting to a kitchen area at the back. The bedroom was on the right.

He gestured her into the living room with the Lüger. "Do sit down, Mrs. Langbein, no need to be unduly alarmed. I promise it won't go off unless I want it to and that really depends on you."

Sharon didn't doubt him for an instant. Beneath the civilized exterior of this man she sensed a steely implacability, a strength and power that was unmistakable.

"Your daughter, Trudie, where is she?"

Trudie was asleep in the bedroom. Sharon reacted instinctively. "She is out playing at a friend's—I don't expect her back for an hour or so."

"She will not come back by herself, though, will she— not at four years of age."

He wanted her to be aware of how much he knew about her.

Sharon shook her head. "No, of course not, her friend's mother will bring her back. . . ." She stopped. The thought struck her sickeningly, like a blow to the stomach. "You've not come to take her away again?"

Her eyes were frightened—he could see she was beginning to panic. Good, he'd got the fear he'd wanted, now she would do as he ordered. "No, I do not want your daughter, Mrs. Langbein, nor did I take her in the first place. It's someone else I am waiting for." He smiled reassuringly, but Sharon felt the cold sweat trickle down inside her arms.

"Who, then? What is it you want?" she said, knowing the answer.

Redston walked over to the kitchen area, keeping the pistol trained on the woman. He glanced into the back garden—nothing. He came back and sat down facing Sharon. "It's Brockway I want, Mrs. Langbein, and he'll be back eventually"—he smiled mockingly—"won't he?"

Brockway followed the black Mercedes out of Tanunda, under the wooden arch that read "Orlando Wines Welcome You to Barossa Valley," down the hill and around the S-bend at the bottom. He almost lost them there; he'd hung back cautiously, and because of the bend he did not see them turn off the main road to the right and head toward Gomersal. Luckily they had to traverse a long straight stretch of road and he spotted them before he passed the turnoff. They crossed the creek that ran to the west of Tanunda, then the paved surface disappeared and became a wide gravel track. The Mercedes began to throw up a lot of dust and Brockway dropped as far back as he dared; the road was empty and he hoped the dust would obscure his presence.

The road proceeded straight in front of him, winding up and down long rolling hills, and through wide flat fields with crops growing on either side. There was something vaguely unreal about it, yet familiar. At first Brockway couldn't place it, then, as they came to an intersection and the Mercedes turned left, he remembered. It was like the yellow brick road that led to Oz, except that he didn't need a scarecrow to point him the way.

In front there was nothing at all; they seemed to be totally alone on the wide undulating fields of the valley, the emptiness emphasized by the great bowl of blue sky above them stretching down to the horizon where the gravel road disappeared over the top of a hill. He came to a crossroads. On the corner was a mean, low, granite building that seemed to be abandoned, and Brockway waited a moment or two before he continued to tail the Mercedes.

Five minutes later he saw it take another left turn and as he neared the turnoff he saw a few scattered buildings and homesteads nestling in a hollow just off the main track about a mile to his left. It was Gomersal, and Brockway waited by the junction to see if that was their destination. He saw the car pull off the track and ascend a slight rise to a single-story granite house. The sun bounced off the metal roof as though it were made of glass. Unlike the others, the roof hadn't been painted red; perhaps it served to keep it cooler inside. It was one of the few features of the Australian landscape that Brockway had never quite gotten used to. He liked his houses to be higher, and once outside of the city, one seldom saw it, which was why the hospital in Tanunda was unique. *Shit*, he thought to himself; that explained it. The whole bloody building had been made with that lead structure beneath it in mind. The only practical way down to such a depth was by an elevator and you could only have elevators in tall buildings—neat, bloody neat.

The two men had left the car and gone inside the house. Brockway picked up his camera and fixed a telephoto lens to the frame. He peered through it, adjusting it slightly. He heard the sound of an engine and he thought at first it was a tractor, then from behind the house taxied a twin-engine light aircraft painted blue. He focused the camera on it. He could see two figures in the plane; one of them was certainly the gray-haired Dr. Kauffmann and the other must have been his colleague Heissler, who was piloting the aircraft. He shot some of the film, then watched the plane roll across the wide flat field behind the house and start to ascend.

Brockway slipped his car into gear and proceeded past the turnoff; he didn't want them to realize they had been followed. He glanced out of his side window and saw the light aircraft bank around and start to head north. Once they were out of sight, he turned the car around and headed back the way he had come. He parked about a quarter of a mile from the house and went the rest of the way on foot, sticking close to the side of the road and trying to stay out of sight. He slipped through the main gates and circled around behind the house, using the shrubbery as cover. It wasn't until he reached the top of the rise at the back that he saw the single strip of dirt landing track, neatly cut between the crops, making it virtually impossible to see, except from his position.

There was another single-engine Cessna parked beneath a sideless lean-to that backed onto the house. There had been no sign of movement from that direction, but Brockway stayed careful. The back door was unlocked and he sidled into the room which smelled damp and unused. He searched the house, but there was nothing, just a few odd sticks of furniture—it was obvious the house had been unoccupied for some time. So why was one plane still waiting? It must be for Redston, but why hadn't he left with the others? Brockway suddenly felt uneasy. He left the house and made his way as quickly as he could back to the car.

He opened the back door and found himself staring into the round black hole of the silencer on the pistol which was pointing directly between his eyes.

"Come in," Redston said affably.

Brockway hesitated for a second, debating. . . .

"Don't do it," the voice said pleasantly. "I'm a much better shot than Spengler and I don't miss from this range."

Brockway moved into the kitchen.

"Shut the door, please," Redston said.

He kicked it shut behind him and glanced over to Sharon who was sitting unnaturally still on the sofa beneath the front window. He heard Redston move around behind him and for a moment he thought he might be about to use the gun immediately.

"Over there, in the chair facing the woman, Brockway."

He did as he was ordered, glancing around the room, wondering where Trudie was. He sat down opposite Sharon, trying to look confident; she smiled wanly but it never reached her eyes. She looked frightened, distressed —the spirit knocked out of her. He wasn't surprised. Once was more than enough. She had relaxed when Trudie had come home unharmed, and now this. He leaned forward to grasp her hand.

"Don't touch her, Brockway." The voice was quiet, menacing. "Just sit still, please."

Brockway turned angrily. "What the hell is this all about, Redston?" As soon as he had said it he could have bitten off his tongue. Unknowingly, however, he had lengthened his life—for as long as it took Redston to find out how he knew his name.

Redston smiled. "How was the car this morning, Brockway? You appeared to be frying nicely outside the hospital."

Brockway stared at him, chewing his lip, trying not to look as surprised as he felt. Jesus, how dumb could you get? Whatever made him think he could do the private eye bit? "Yeah," he admitted, "it was hot."

"And presumably," Redston continued, "you followed Kauffmann and his companion and saw them take off from Gomersal."

Redston had carefully not mentioned Heissler's name.

Brockway could not deny it. He said nothing. Somehow

he had to get out of here; he might not make a good private eye, but he knew enough to realize that they were in mortal danger. Redston was no government agent. Not with a gun in his hand, and he would not be talking so openly unless he felt Brockway was no further threat. Someone had tried to kill him up by Kauffmann's house; presumably that had been Spengler. What had happened to him? He didn't need two guesses to know the answer to that one. Which meant that he and Sharon would meet the same fate. Time, he needed time, anything that might distract this man just long enough for him to make a break for it. He also needed to let Sharon know just how dangerous their position was. "Yeah, I saw your German colleagues take off out of the valley. One of them was Bruno Heissler, an ex-Nazi rocket scientist who worked for NASA in America with Werner Von Braun. What's he doing up here, Redston? Anything to do with that heavily protected radiation zone beneath the hospital?"

Redston surveyed him calmly. The time for subtlety had passed. Brockway knew too much and his own future might now be in jeopardy. "How do you know my name, Brockway?"

So that was it; that's what he needed to know—he tried to stall. "When I was out at the motel I saw the register."

Redston sighed. "So why were you looking for it in the first place?"

Brockway grinned. "That's a secret."

The shot made no noise, but the bullet shattered the leg of the wooden chair beneath him and sent him sprawling on the floor.

Sharon jumped to her feet, terrified, her hand flying to her mouth. The pistol swung in her direction. "Don't scream!" The words came out like bullets, hard, commanding. Sharon didn't make a sound. Brockway crouched, about to jump him, but the gun was between his eyes again, the blue steel silencer not six inches from his head.

Trudie emerged from the door behind Redston, rubbing the sleep from her eyes. "Mummy," she said.

Brockway saw the gun swing around instinctively and he jerked up his arm, his fist catching Redston just below the elbow. The gun flew out of his hand, falling onto the carpet near the kitchen. Brockway tried to continue the forward momentum by butting him in the stomach, but he was no match for Redston whose reflexes seemed twice as fast. As Brockway thrust forward, Redston crossed both hands, bringing them sharply up beneath Brockway's chin, straightening him out, and in the same movement he brought his right elbow across, smashing into his jaw, crashing him onto the floor beneath the window.

Brockway saw him turn and make for the gun; he knew he was a dead man once Redston had that in his hands. His face was numb from the blow on the jaw and his legs refused to coordinate properly. There was no way he could reach that gun first. God, he was going to die, sprawled on the floor helpless. The fear, the panic, poured the adrenaline into his veins. He took one leap onto the sofa and threw himself out of the window, crashing onto the verandah and rolling at the same time off the edge onto the lawn below it. He crouched and ran, trying to keep the verandah between himself and the gaping window. He saw splinters ripped off by the soundless detonations of the pistol, but he felt nothing and crashed through the hedge separating Sharon's front lawn from the next. He lay flat on his stomach, waiting.

He heard the front door smash open and from a small gap between the roots he saw Sharon emerge, Redston's arm tight around her waist. He thrust her savagely forward, half walking, half running down the pathway that led to the road. "Don't go to the police, Brockway," he shouted. "Not if you want to see her alive again. They'll never believe you."

Trudie came out of the front door. She was crying and screaming at the top of her voice. "Mummy, please, don't go without me, wait, wait!"

He saw Redston turn and fire two shots at the child and for one horrifying moment Brockway thought he had killed her. The bullets splintered the verandah around the child and she stopped—frozen dumb with fear. He heard Sharon scream, then a door slam shut as she was thrust into the car. He risked a quick glance over the hedge and saw Redston slip into the driver's seat and accelerate up the road toward the main street.

Brockway stood up and walked across to Trudie. She was still standing rooted to the verandah. He picked her up; she was trembling with shock, her eyes wide and frightened, but there were no tears.

He saw some neighbors starting to emerge, staring at the broken window, but he ignored them and walked inside the house, cradling the little girl in his arms, trying to soothe her. Eventually she began to cry, clinging to him tightly, and he wondered what the hell he was going to do. Any minute now one of those neighbors would report what had happened to the police. Redston was bloody right; they would never believe what he said after the fiasco at the hospital. He needed some time to think this out, but first he had to get back to Adelaide—this valley was giving him the creeps. He got some pillows from the bedroom and put them in the car, then sat Trudie down beside him, strapping her in.

He drove slowly up the street onto the main road and turned right past the police station. He saw a police car parked outside and he wondered how long he had before they started looking for him. Jesus, he felt so helpless, he needed time to think this out. Once through the town, he took the right turn toward Gomersal. The single-engine plane was no longer beneath the lean-to at the back of the house; Redston had taken it, and presumably Sharon as well. Brockway searched the empty house a second time, but was relieved to find no sign of her. At least she was still alive. He got back into the car and gave Trudie some candy he had taken from the kitchen. He drove along the graveled road out past the Château Rosedale until he came to the creek near the winery at Château Yaldarra. He forded the shallow creek and rejoined the main road to Adelaide west of Lyndoch. That night Trudie slept with him in his bluestone cottage at Norwood.

25. Lake Frome

Jiggs was coming to the dramatic climax of his recitation and Bess was firmly hooked. She moved steadily along, Jiggs on her back swaying gently with her motion, his head sunk forward on his chest, occasionally flinging out an arm to add dramatic effect. He knew that "Mulga Bill's Bicycle" was probably Bess's favorite; her ears were pricked forward and she was listening intently. He'd reached the point where Mulga Bill had ridden the bike for the first time down the hill and, unable to stop, over the precipice into Dead Man's Creek.

> Twas Mulga Bill, from Eaglehawk, that slowly swam
> ashore:
> He said, "I've had some narrer shaves and lucky rides
> before;
> I've rode a wild bull round a yard to win a five pound
> bet,
> But this was sure the darnedest ride that I've encoun-
> tered yet.
> I'll give that two-wheeled outlaw best; it's shaken all
> my nerve

To feel it whistle through the air and plunge and buck
    and swerve.
It's safe at rest in Dead Man's Creek—we'll leave it
    lying still;
A horse's back is good enough henceforth for Mulga
    Bill.

Bess gave a snort of derision at the mention of a horse.
Jiggs leaned forward and patted her long neck. "Bloody
right, Bess, who needs a horse in this country." He was
about sixty miles east of North Mulga and the prevailing
winds from the west had smoothed out the tracks of the
convoy to some extent, but they presented no problems to
Jiggs. Beneath the wide-brimmed hat his eyes scanned the
terrain, but there was nothing as yet. This convoy was
smaller than the last; the tracks indicated about six vehicles in all, one of them a trailer over fifty feet in length.

Jiggs was keeping his eyes open this time; he had no
wish to repeat the previous experience and he found it
difficult to believe that whoever these people were, they
intended to test another bomb—the fewer vehicles in the
convoy would seem to confirm that.

He pulled the rifle from beneath the saddle and
checked it thoroughly, blowing a few sand particles from
the breech, clipping in some rounds until the magazine
was full. He was going to make the bastards pay for the
loss of Molly. The crack of the rifle shot halted Bess dead
in her tracks. Jiggs strained forward trying to place its
source. The last echoes of the sound reverberated along
the corridor from the east; about two miles away, he estimated. Slowly he pushed the bolt home in his rifle, slipping a round into the breech ready to fire. He slid off
Bess's back and led her to a clump of saltbush where she
could graze. After hobbling her, he removed the long tele-

scope from the saddlebag and carrying his rifle and a water bottle he set off on foot.

They had set up camp near Coonie Creek, and the significance of the shot became evident when he saw the dead body of a wild dingo lying on the floor of the corridor where they had dumped some rubbish. The animal must have gotten through a break in the dog fence which traversed this desert region almost twenty miles further east.

The vehicles had been halted among the scattered, twisted gum trees that drew moisture from beneath the dry surface of the creek bed. They were camouflaged by long ochre-colored tarpaulins drawn across them and pegged into the sandy surface. Presumably, Jiggs decided, to avoid detection from the air. Most of the activity seemed to be around the long trailer, which unlike the others was covered by a tentlike canvas structure, open at the sides to allow access for a number of white-overalled technicians who were working beneath it.

Jiggs focused the telescope onto the trailer. The darkness of the shaded area beneath the canvas structure made it extremely difficult to see what was beneath it, but as his eyes adjusted he began to discern a long tubular shape. Technicians in white overalls were working all around it, which made it difficult to see properly. He wiped the sweat from his eyes and squinted into the telescope again, tracking it slowly down the line of men who were clustered around it like bees around a honey pot. At the end he could see something that looked like fins. Fins! He whistled soundlessly under his breath, then adjusted the telescope quickly and looked at the other end. It was pointed, like a projectile, then he realized—Jesus, it was a rocket of some kind, a bloody rocket! Jiggs was no expert, but its significance coupled with the nuclear test was obvious, even to him.

Jiggs was torn between a desire for revenge and inform-
ing his contact at ABC. He decided he would accomplish
both. The tires of the light vehicles first, then the heavier
stuff. That should slow the buggers down for a while; it
was unlikely that they had spares for all the wheels. He
would have to hit as many as he could. He slid the rifle
from his back, tucking the stock into his shoulder, and
focused the sights on the Land-Rover parked nearest to his
position. He moved the sights of the rifle down the side of
the vehicle until he had the front offside tire neatly between the two hairlines, then he slowly started to squeeze
the trigger.

The low hum of the generator truck seemed to have
changed, and Jiggs paused. He listened; it wasn't the generator at all, he could hear something else. Then he saw a
blue, twin-engine aircraft sweeping slowly around into a
landing position between the ridges. The technicians
working on the rocket had heard it too and had stopped,
watching the aircraft on its final approach. The plane
made a perfect landing in the corridor, then taxied slowly
toward the place where the vehicles were parked. Jiggs
recognized one of the two men who clambered out; he
was the man who had climbed the tower and made the
final adjustments before the nuclear test.

Vaas and Heissler had arrived at the launch site, and
now Jiggs had a problem. With the arrival of the plane, he
could easily be overtaken and caught in precisely the
same way that he had before. One change of tires would
not slow them down sufficiently. He toyed with the idea
of trying to put the plane permanently out of action, but it
was too risky.

Jiggs had a good position on top of the ridge where he
could observe everything and his natural curiosity
tempted him to stay longer than he should. The afternoon
slipped away through his silent, hot surveillance. He be-

came aware of it when the ridge shadows began to lengthen, and he reached into his jacket for the watch. Ten past six; he snapped the fob shut and poked it back into the pouch. Time to go. He had already decided he would travel throughout the night and the following day to reach North Mulga. He was about to clamber down the ridge when he heard the approach of the Cessna. It landed and parked beside the other aircraft. He had never seen the girl before, but he recognized Redston instantly —that face above the automatic in the helicopter was imprinted into his memory. Twice he almost pulled the trigger, only the presence of the girl between him and Redston prevented him getting in a shot. Unwittingly Sharon had saved Redston's life.

26. Norwood, Adelaide

Brockway hadn't slept much that night. Trudie had tossed and turned, jerking in her sleep, and he was worried. He wasn't used to children and he didn't know whether he ought to wake her up or not. There was something about nightmares, and not disturbing them, so he left the child and lay there wide awake most of the night.

What the hell should he do? He wasn't certain of anything anymore. Sharon's abduction had shaken him up, and he was finding it difficult to come to terms with his personal involvement. These last ten years, the failure in the States, and his intense desire to return on top and make them pay for his feelings of personal humiliation, had totally occupied his thoughts and actions to the exclusion of everything else. Now this woman had made him wake up to the sterility of his existence, and he was having to pay the price. Love didn't come free of charge, and the long dark night only seemed to increase his fears. He was grateful for the morning. He made Trudie some breakfast, drank some black coffee, and started to make some phone calls.

First, his producer. George listened intently, hardly

making a comment, as Brockway told him everything. For once George completely dropped the hard-nosed act and Brockway was grateful. He suggested that it might be better to inform Detective Clayton of the developments from an office at ABC. The power of the corporation would be more evident and could help his case. Brockway accepted, and arranged to have one of the young women researchers look after Trudie at the studio. Then he rang Bill Cameron, told him what had happened, and asked him to reach him immediately if the old prospector got in contact again.

Brockway figured that the Germans and Redston had left for a purpose, and he had a pretty good idea of what that was. There was only one place they could launch a rocket: the interior. There was just a chance that the opal prospector might get lucky again. Brockway wasn't looking forward to the interview with Clayton, although he realized the police had to be informed and there was a better chance they would believe him in Adelaide than in the valley where he was already regarded with some skepticism, if not suspicion. Indeed, the disappearance of Sharon from Tanunda was probably already under investigation and it would not take them long to connect him with that. Clayton remained his best hope. If he could convince him he was telling the truth, then it might be possible to get the police into that hospital again, and this time he knew exactly where to lead them.

George rang the detective from ABC after obtaining permission for the police to conduct the interview on the premises, and told him that Brockway was there. Clayton needed no urging; he'd arrive within the hour.

He was alone in the office. The demolition men were still audible, slowly pulling the old house apart. The drilling was insistent and he wondered if everything was about to fall apart for him, too. Inside an hour, Clayton had said. Inside an hour he could be behind bars—withholding information, breaking and entering, there were all sorts of unpleasant possibilities.

The phone rang harshly, breaking into his thoughts. It was Bill Cameron. Brockway sat up and listened, then grabbed a pad and pencil. "Right, I've got it, don't worry, I won't lose him. Put him on. Hello?" He could hear him fumbling with the receiver and for one awful moment he thought he was about to put it down. Then the old prospector's voice came through, faint but determined.

"Are you with ABC?"

"Yes, that's right. I did the television reports on the tests in the Simpson."

Jiggs grunted. "Well, I don't see any television, but the other bloke, the one on the radio, said you could talk to the authorities; pass something on."

"Yes, of course, what is it?" He waited impatiently.

"Well, I've seen them again, the bloody crew who caused that test. I know where they are."

Very calmly Brockway said, "You tell me in your own words exactly where that is, and I'll write it down."

"Do you know North Mulga?"

"No, but I can find it."

"No need. It's east of the Flinders—a sheep station about four hundred miles north of Adelaide. They're out in the desert east of that, north of Frome. Just send a few planes over, you'll find them."

Brockway sensed that he was about to hang up. He had to stop him. "Did you see a woman out there?" He waited, the voice came back, he sighed with relief.

"Yes, that's right. She arrived in an airplane. She was with the bastard that killed Molly."

"Molly?"

"My camel—I'd had her for years." He sounded angry,

truculent, and Brockway knew he had to tread carefully.

"The woman that you saw, was she okay?"

"Yeah, she was all right—silly cow stopped me getting a shot at him."

Brockway closed his eyes, shocked but relieved. "Listen to me." He spoke slowly, desperately trying to make the old man aware of the situation and win his support. "That woman you saw is Sharon Langbein; the man is called Redston. I know what you are saying is true—I need your help. That woman is in great danger. He is using her as a hostage."

Jiggs did not answer and Brockway played his last card.

"If I inform the authorities they will go in, but the woman will die. There is no way he will let her off the hook—you've had some experience of him yourself—he will kill her. Now, I have got her daughter here. She is four years old and I don't want to have to tell that child that her mother is dead." He waited; either the old man would hang up and it would be over, or—

"You'd better get up here, Mr. Brockway. There's only one way to get that woman out safely—on foot."

Brockway opened his eyes. Now he had a chance. He talked rapidly to the old prospector, arranging the details, then he put the phone down.

He glanced at his watch, it was 10:40. Phil Clayton would be here by 11:15, possibly sooner—there was no time for explanations. He pulled the pad toward him.

George,

Something's come up—I am going to try and find Sharon Langbein and get her out before it is too late. I know where she is. Trudie is being looked after by a rather glamorous babysitter who works in the studio. You'll hear from me by Monday, one way or the other, and if I fail you'll know where to send the police. Tell Phil I'm sorry, but I have to try. If I don't get back I'll be relying on him to pick up the pieces.

Regards,
Brockway

He stuck it in an envelope and propped it up on the desk, then he left the office and casually made his way to the parking lot. He drove past Tregenna House and out on to the freeway. Driving as fast as he dared he headed toward the airport, arriving twenty minutes later. He was lucky. PAGAS had a Cherokee he could hire, and by 11:30 he was airborne and heading toward North Mulga after putting a letter to George Greenfield in the mail telling him where he was going and what he intended to do.

It was Friday and the letter would not be opened at ABC till Monday—he had thirty-six hours. The plane droned northward and Brockway sat in his seat sweating, wondering what the hell he was doing. Christ, he didn't even have a gun.

The pilot complained, but landed the Cherokee safely on a mud flat some six hundred yards or so from the station. Once Brockway had disembarked from the plane the pilot turned her around and took off again immediately. It was baking hot and Brockway was sweating immediately, brushing away the bush flies who found him at once, looking for moisture.

As the sound of the plane faded Brockway began to walk toward the station. He could see a camel tethered near the tin shed, then a man emerged from the shade of the verandah clutching a telescope—evidently he'd been under surveillance since touchdown. Charlie Miller joined the old prospector, followed a moment later by his wife who was holding tightly onto their son's hand as he tried to squirm loose.

Brockway stopped in front of them and brushed away a fly. He looked at the old man. "Hi, you must be Jiggs, Cameron told me about you. I'm Brockway."

The prospector said nothing. Charlie broke the uncomfortable silence. "Better come inside—would you like a stubby?"

Brockway grinned. "Best offer I've heard today." He climbed the three steps onto the verandah as the woman turned and went inside.

Jiggs watched him silently, then said as he was about to follow Miller inside, "I'll get Bess ready for the journey. She'll be able to carry both of us." He moved off toward the shed before Brockway could reply. Charlie Miller stuck out his hand and introduced himself, his wife, and his son.

Brockway sat at the table gulping down the ice cold beer from the bottle. The boy was questioning him excitedly about television; he answered automatically, his thoughts elsewhere. He waited for a break in the little boy's queries, then asked Miller if he could have a word in private.

They strolled out onto the verandah, watched curiously by his wife.

"What can I do for you?"

Brockway looked at him, trying to size him up. He knew something about people who lived in the outback so he came directly to the point. "Your rifle"—he nodded toward the gun hung on a rack out of the boy's reach—"could you lend it to me until Monday? I'll pay you the full value of the piece as a deposit."

Miller eyed him quizzically. "Sure—you don't have to give me the full price, though—twenty-five dollars will do." He didn't ask the obvious question, and Brockway hesitated a moment before continuing.

"The car"—he looked in the direction of the shed—"can I rent the car also? I just don't see myself riding the camel."

Miller shook his head. "Sorry, mate, I might need that for the job."

Brockway wished he could tell him the truth but knew he couldn't. He tried again. "Look, I realize your position, but it is the weekend and I'll pay you well." He knew at once he had pushed too far.

"Weekends make no difference out here—I need the car; the gun's different."

Brockway gave him the money and slung the rifle over his shoulder. He started to walk toward the shed where Jiggs was waiting when Miller called out after him.

"Better take this as well." He threw a wide-brimmed hat, and Brockway plucked it spinning from the air. "Don't wanna get sunstroke!"

Brockway stuck the hat on his head. "Thanks, Miller, I appreciate your help."

"No problem—see you Monday, I hope."

Brockway turned and walked toward the camel.

27. The Launch Site

Sharon was gradually beginning to realize that she was finished. The purpose of this temporary site was immediately apparent, and no attempt had been made to lock her up or prevent her seeing the scale of the operation, which only served to increase her fears. Redston would never have allowed her to become so aware of the purpose of this expedition if he had felt she was in any way a threat, which meant only one thing—she would not leave this place alive. Her freedom of movement around the site was deceptive; she could get nowhere on foot and if it had been possible to steal a vehicle—which she couldn't, the keys were conspicuous by their absence—she would not have gone far before the aircraft found her. Only at night were restrictions placed upon her. A long prefabricated building, camouflaged to blend with the terrain, had been constructed. One end contained all the complex electronic launch equipment, and the remainder served as eating and sleeping quarters for the personnel. Including the Germans and Redston, Sharon had counted sixteen. At night she was locked into one of the rooms containing a cot, a chair, and a sleeping bag. The toilet arrangements were crude, but the site had not been constructed with a woman in mind.

No one appeared to pay any attention to her, but more than once she had noticed the concealed interest of some of the technicians. Her position became chillingly clear on the second day. Dr. Kauffmann, who had been carefully avoiding her, was in deep discussion with his colleague when Sharon interrupted. "I'm sorry, Doctor, but I must speak with you."

He surveyed her coldly. "Well, Fraulein, what is it?"

She was surprised at how quickly he had resumed his German identity. She followed suit, it might help. "*Herr Doktor*, I do not know or understand why I have been brought here. My only concern is for my daughter. You must talk to this man Redston and allow me to return to her."

The doctor adjusted his glasses, lower on his nose, giving him face a slightly owlish appearance. "Fraulein, you may not realize it, but you are very fortunate. You will be privileged to see the results of our work"—he waved an arm at Heissler—"which began many years ago, before you were born, and will culminate here very soon. I think it is worth some temporary discomfort. Don't you?" It was a rhetorical question, and he turned his back to her, resuming his work.

Sharon paused, wondering how she could appeal to this man's emotions. "But my daughter, I don't know what has happened to her. When can I go back?"

His glasses glinted as he turned to face her; the eyes, no longer owlish, surveyed her coldly as if she were a piece of meat on a butcher's block. "You are lucky to have your daughter at all, Fraulein—it was my decision to send her back to you." The last words were spoken without emphasis, but shivered inside her, chilling her blood. She was repelled and frightened. She turned and left the room without another word. Outside, the sun blazed down on the hive of activity as the final preparations were being made for the launch, but her hands were shaking, cold in spite of the desert heat.

Heissler was puzzled. Why was it necessary to hold this young woman here at the launch site against her will, and what did Vaas mean by saying that she was lucky to have her daughter at all? He'd tried to question him about it, but Vaas had just brushed it aside and busied himself with the technical problems that faced them. For the moment, Heissler, too, buried himself in the work. There were many preparations—soon they would be fitting the dummy warhead—but he intended to find out about the young woman.

His opportunity came during a break for lunch. He saw the woman collect her food and take it into the living quarters she had been allocated at the end of the prefabricated building. Heissler finished his meal quickly and left the dining area, slipping around the back of the building after making sure no one was watching him. He made his way to the end of the structure and peered around the corner. Everyone was inside eating, trying to avoid the heat and the flies. He crossed quickly to the woman's door and, without knocking, opened it and slipped inside.

Sharon was sitting on the cot, her plate perched on her knees. She glanced up, alarmed, almost dropping the food. Heissler leaned against the door and held up his hands. "Please, do not be afraid—I only wish to ask you a few questions."

Sharon stood up, still clutching the plate. "What is it, what do you want?"

Heissler studied her for a moment, wondering how best he could approach this. "Look, I am sorry, I've no idea who you are; I saw you arrive with Redston, but I know that you don't wish to be here. I heard you ask the doctor earlier if you could return to your child. I don't understand. Perhaps you could tell me what's happening?"

Sharon didn't know whether to believe him or not, and it showed on her face. "Why don't you just ask Redston—or is this just some clever trick of his to make me think you are on my side?"

Heissler could see she was suspicious; he decided on a different tack. "What did Kauffmann mean when he said you're lucky to have your daughter at all—that he had sent her back. Was she ill—in the hospital?"

Sharon flung back her head and laughed bitterly. "You're incredible, d'you know that? Look, I don't care what all this is supposed to be about, but that doctor friend of yours is insane."

He gazed at her incredulously.

"All right," she said, making up her mind. She began pacing the room, trying to get it all together in her mind. She turned and faced him. "Doctor Kauffmann had my daughter kidnapped, I don't know why, that isn't clear yet. Then he released her. That's what he meant about sending her back—about me being lucky—and I was lucky, because four other children have disappeared in the same area over the last couple of years and they've never been found."

Heissler felt sick. At the back of his mind he already knew the truth, but as yet he refused to accept it. He understood now why Vaas had not wanted to discuss it. If what this woman had said was true, and he had heard Vaas say himself that he'd sent the daughter back, then he must have been responsible for the other children, too. He sat down at the end of the cot trying not to believe it, gazing at the floor. "Why did Redston bring you here?" His voice was almost inaudible, and for the first time Sharon began to believe him.

"I'm a hostage. He is trying to prevent a reporter from going to the police—he tried to kill him, but he escaped."

Heissler looked up at her. "What does this reporter know? Please, tell me everything."

Sharon began to explain about the kidnappings, how Brockway had become suspicious of the hospital, and finally how he had discovered the nuclear research area in the basement. When she had finished Heissler continued to sit silently at the end of the cot. He knew now that he had been a fool, that a man like Vaas didn't alter. He'd allowed himself to turn a blind eye toward the inhuman nature of the man. How could he have pretended to himself that the stories he'd heard about Vaas's experiments with the victims of the concentration camps were merely the excuses of Jewish Nazi hunters.

Somehow he had to get out, but he would have to be careful. Redston was ruthless, and if he became aware of his knowledge then there would be no way that he could protect this woman. He stood up. "My name is Heissler, Bruno Heissler. I am here because they need my abilities to launch this rocket. I swear to you I know nothing of all this, but I believe what you say is true. I am going to try and get you out of here, but please, say nothing of this to anyone—I have to think of a way. I need a little time— will you trust me?" He gazed at her solemnly. He looked shocked, older. She knew he was telling the truth.

"I promise, I'll say nothing, but please"—she took a step toward him and gripped his hands—"not too long, there may not *be* much time."

He nodded. "I understand. I'll do my best." He turned, opened the door carefully, then slipped out as quietly as he had come in. Sharon stared at the blank door wondering if she were dreaming—was this really happening to her? She turned and looked at her plate—it was covered with flies. She kicked it against the wall and flung herself face down on the cot.

Brockway was aching; every bone and muscle in his body seemed to be protesting at the motion of the camel. The animal did not appreciate a doubling of her load, and he somehow had the feeling that the beast was deliberately making her bones sharper every mile they progressed.

Jiggs was sitting in front of him and after replying monosyllabically to a few questions about the number of men and machines at the site, he had relapsed into silence.

Jiggs risked a fire that night and cooked some damper— a mixture of flour, water, and salt that he had placed in the hot coals and then served with some tinned syrup. That, coffee, and some dried roo meat was their tucker that night, and Brockway found it surprisingly enjoyable —he was hungry. The flies had thankfully disappeared, and Brockway wrapped himself in a couple of blue blankets and lay on the sheet of canvas Jiggs had put down.

But he couldn't sleep; the ground was hard and he didn't take kindly to the great outdoors. Brockway was a city man; that was an environment that he understood and operated in efficiently. Out here, he had no control. The emptiness, the space, defeated him somehow. He shook his head and turned over irritably. Christ, this was no bloody good. Tomorrow he might be facing real life or death, not some studio discussion about the possibility of World War Three. Somehow they had to get Sharon out. He wondered how he would react if they came under fire . . . and shivered.

Jiggs was wide awake, aware of the American's restlessness. He peered through the flames of the campfire. "You cold?"

Brockway pulled the blanket from over his face. The light from the fire cast strange shadows, but he could just see Jiggs's eyes reflected in the glow.

"Yeah, a bit." He tried to keep the shakiness he felt inside, out of his voice. It wasn't just the lack of warmth that had turned his insides to water.

Jiggs stood up and went over to his pack, pulling out a couple of worn blankets, then dropped them on the ground beside Brockway. He squatted down in front of the fire and thrust some more wood into the flames. "Want some tea?"

Brockway sat up, glad to get his mind off what might happen the next day. "Sure, I'll join you."

Jiggs swung the billy over the fire. The water was already warm; it wouldn't take long.

Brockway watched him. The old man did everything so fluently, with a practiced ease born of long years out in the wilderness. He was curious. "Have you always mined opal, Jiggs?"

The prospector continued to prepare the tea, and it seemed he wasn't going to answer, then, "Yes, I suppose so." Another long pause. "Least I have for thirty years or more."

Brockway let that hang there for a while. He eased himself up to the fire beside Jiggs and held out his tin mug while the old man poured the hot tea. "And before that . . . have you always prospected?"

Jiggs eyed him over the top of his steaming mug, aware of the American's probing, yet curiously he didn't seem to mind. Nothing did since Molly had died. Just finding the bastard in the helicopter. He took another spoonful of sweetened milk from the tin and stirred it vigorously into the tea, then handed the tin to Brockway. "No, not always. Came out here in 'thirty-six."

Brockway copied the prospector, stirring in the thick

sweetened milk. The tea was delicious . . . hot and sweet. He warmed his hands on the mug, then looked at Jiggs and smiled. "It's good."

The old man nodded, gazing thoughtfully into the flames. "Came out here to get away from everything. Landed at Adelaide and trekked the rest of the way on foot. Been here ever since."

Brockway nodded, then glanced out into the darkness. "The camel, that's unusual. Where did you get that?"

"Wasn't unusual then—they used them all the time for hauling goods across the desert . . . Afghans mostly. That's why the railway track from Alice down to Port Augusta is called the 'Gan.' Short for Afghan, because it follows the original track they used back in the eighteen-hundreds." Jiggs glanced out toward where the camel was tethered. "I got two of them off an old trader . . . he was packin' it in. I've always had two up till now. . . ." He stopped and glanced sharply up at the American. Even in the darkness Brockway could feel their murderous intensity. Jiggs threw the last dregs of the tea into the fire where it hissed and spluttered for a while. Then he pulled out his pipe and began packing in some tobacco.

Brockway decided to risk another question. "Before Australia, where were you?"

Jiggs lit the pipe, and puffed on it until it was glowing nicely. "England, London mostly . . . left at the beginning of 'thirty-six. I was getting a bit tied down, a wife and a son. Should never have got married, didn't much like it, so I skipped out." He glanced across at Brockway and grinned, his mood changing abruptly. "Besides, 'Old Bill' was after me."

Brockway was puzzled. "Old Bill?"

Jiggs chuckled deep in his throat. "Don't know that one, eh, Yank!" He seemed to be enjoying the joke. "It's cockney for law—the police."

Brockway nodded. "I see, why were they after you?"

Jiggs's face darkened and for a moment Brockway thought he had pushed it too far. Then the smile returned, exposing the yellow teeth.

"Nothing much—car thieving mostly, but they were getting close, so I hopped it. Couldn't decide whether I was running from the wife or the law. Didn't like cars much anyway—that's why I got the camels." The pipe glowed in the darkness. Brockway felt better. His belly was warm from the hot tea, and he'd learned something— exercised his craft on the old man.

"What about you, Yank, what brings you out here?"

The question took Brockway by surprise. He wasn't used to being on the receiving end. He parried. "What do you mean out here? In the outback?"

Jiggs surveyed him coldly. "No, I know why you're sittin' the other side of the fire. What brings you to Australia? It wasn't for nickin' cars, was it?"

Jiggs was not to be trifled with, but was he mocking him? He didn't think so.

Surprisingly, Jiggs had an irreverent sense of humor, which for years he'd had to practice solely on his camels. It was fun to practice it on the Yank. The American was eying him uncertainly. "Come on, boy, speak up. Fair's fair. You know my dark secret, what's yours?"

Brockway started to laugh, quietly at first, then loudly, throwing back his head and collapsing onto his blankets, the tears running down his face. The camel snorted angrily, annoyed at being woken up. Brockway pushed himself upright and stared across at the old prospector who was still contentedly pulling on his pipe, waiting for him to calm down. The laughter subsided into silence and Jiggs pushed a little more tobacco into the bowl. "All right, you can tell me now. What's so funny?"

Brockway sat up. "I just realized what a stupid son-of-a-bitch I am."

Jiggs made no comment.

Brockway shook his head. "You see, I'm supposed to be using this story—the test you saw in the desert and so forth—to set myself up with a return ticket, first class, to New York, and my own slot on an American network. Now I don't expect you to understand that, Jiggs—"

The prospector interrupted him and said quietly, "You mean your own program on television."

Brockway stared at him uncomprehendingly for a moment. "Christ, I'm sorry, Jiggs—I really am a shit."

The old man nodded affirmatively and grinned at him through the smoke. "You are a bit, but go on."

Brockway poked the fire with a stick and glanced up at Jiggs. "The crazy thing is, I'm sitting out here, risking my life for this woman, and I've just realized I don't give a damn now whether I even go back to New York."

Jiggs didn't reply at once, and a comfortable silence fell between them, disturbed only by the friendly crackle of the fire. Jiggs banged his pipe on the heel of his boot, then blew through it until he was sure it was clear. "Doesn't really surprise me at all, Yank. I'll be doing the same myself tomorrow for Molly, and she was just a camel."

Brockway watched him roll into his blanket and bed down for the night. Somehow his last remark didn't seem in the least bit odd or funny. It just made sense. He lay down and wrapped the blankets around him. He felt tired now and he knew he would sleep.

"Goodnight, Yank."

Brockway looked across at the indistinct figure of the prospector lying on the other side of the fire, then closed his eyes. "Goodnight, Jiggs."

*   *   *

Brockway woke stiff and cold. The sky was beginning to brighten, filtering across the sand ridges to the east. They looked like giant sleeping creatures in the half light, crouched on the desert floor, ready to wake when the sun warmed their bodies. It was easy to understand the aborigine legends out here in the desolation of the interior.

Akaroo, the giant serpent of the aboriginal dreamtime, had slithered down from the Gammon Ranges to slake his thirst on this plain. He'd drunk Lakes Frome and Callabon dry and then retreated back to the mountains, forming the ridges that now resembled his shape. The legend recounts that with his belly so full of water it rumbles from time to time as he tries to change his position back in his hideaway, thus explaining the Arkaroola Rumble, minor earth tremors caused by the faultline running through the Flinders.

Jiggs was already up, brewing some coffee and consuming some beans from a can. After some more damper, baked beans, and coffee, Brockway began to feel more human, though it was impossible to wash, and the flies, unsurprisingly, were finding him again. The hat Miller had given him was similar to Jiggs's and the corks attached to the brim by small pieces of string at least kept them off his face.

They set off immediately after breakfast as the sun began to poke itself above the ridges. The shadows across the corridors slowly began to retreat. Jiggs was sitting in front of him again, swaying easily with the rhythm of the camel, and Brockway tried to do the same, but his muscles were still stiff from yesterday, and already the inside of his legs were sore. The old prospector began to pull his radio from beneath the saddlebags. "Might as well have a bit of music before we get there." He switched it on.

"Here am I, sitting in a tin can," emerged, thin and

lonely. Brockway smiled; the irony did not elude him. Bess may not have been a tin can, but she was just as sharp—he had the aches and pains to prove it.

Bowie's record echoed strangely back from the sides of the corridor they were traversing, the doomed spaceman's last lonely voyage reflecting the vast desolation of this place. It was depressing, emphasizing their own vulnerability, and he was grateful when Jiggs farted loudly. It broke the mood as well as the wind—a normal bodily function, if a trifle smelly, especially from Brockway's position. Jiggs did not apologize, but it did seem to loosen his tongue. "We'll get there sometime today, probably late afternoon. You got any plans?"

"Nothing definite. I need to see the place, try to work out where she is being held—" He stopped.

Jiggs had switched off the radio and was listening.

"What is it?"

Jiggs gestured him to be silent. Brockway could hear nothing except the creaking of the saddle, then that stopped as Bess was reined to a halt.

Jiggs was straining forward. "Do you hear it?"

Brockway picked it up at last. The faint but growing sound of an airplane. Jiggs slid off the back of the camel. "Quick, get down—they mustn't see us."

Brockway threw a leg over the back of the camel and jumped down. Jiggs grabbed the reins of the animal and began to run toward the long shadow cast by the ridge. The noise from the plane was much stronger now, coming from the direction in which they had been heading, but it must have been very low because as yet Brockway hadn't spotted it. He ran after Jiggs who, once under the lee of the ridge, brought the camel to her knees, flinging himself down beside her. Brockway did the same, lying as close to Bess as he could. It was scant cover, but at least they were not out in the open, exposed in the bright sunlight.

The plane seemed to be almost upon them before Brockway saw it. The single-engine Cessna roared down between the ridge tops, low and fast. He felt the camel tense and start to rise, but Jiggs had tight hold on the reins and swore loudly into the animal's ear, frightening Bess into submission. Brockway thought he caught a brief glimpse of Redston as the plane flashed by.

Slowly the roar faded as the plane disappeared. They waited. Would it come back? Had they been seen? The desert was silent, just the soft hiss of the sand on the ridges, brushed by the wind. They lay still for another couple of minutes, but the aircraft did not return. Jiggs poked his head up from the other side of the camel. "What do you think?"

"I don't know. I don't think he saw us, otherwise he would have come back."

Jiggs nodded and stood up, urging the camel to its feet. "We go on, then."

"We go on," Brockway affirmed.

The rocket pointed silently up at the blue sky, the sun glinting dully on the dark gray warhead. From their vantage point on the ridge top Jiggs could see, now that the tarpaulin camouflage had been removed, how the ramp on which it rested was a part of the trailer itself. It had been raised hydraulically, giving the rocket mobility as well as a launch platform.

The prefabricated building from which the launching would be controlled was about two hundred yards from the rocket itself, presumably a precaution in case there was a malfunction of some kind. It would be dark within the hour, and all the vehicles had also been divested of their camouflage. The two aircraft were parked a little way further down the corridor ready for take-off, and Brockway felt certain that the launch was imminent, probably scheduled for tomorrow. They had, it appeared, arrived in time, though as yet he had seen no sign of Sharon.

No one appeared to be moving around the site. Through the windows of the temporary structure he could see the technicians sitting at a long table eating, and the smell of roast meat and cooking drifted up toward them. Brockway felt ravenous and heard his stomach rumble in protest. Jiggs seemed unaffected, but pulled a piece of dried meat from his rucksack and tore it in half. "Thanks," Brockway muttered, having trouble chewing his share into a digestible state. Jiggs took a swig from the water bottle and handed it to him after wiping the top with the palm of his hand. He took a swallow, then as he raised the bottle to drink again he saw her.

She was standing by the side door of the building, just staring out at the sunset. For a moment he had an almost irresistible desire to leap up and indicate their position, but it passed. If she ran for it now they'd be lucky to make a couple of miles before they were caught. She stood by the door for a few minutes, then he saw Redston emerge from behind her and lead her around to another door near the end of the building. He pushed her inside, locked it, and went back to his own quarters.

Now they had a chance. If under cover of darkness they could get her away without raising the alarm, then with the old prospector to guide them, they might escape detection.

Brockway was cold; Jiggs had returned with some blankets and hard tack, but still the sudden drop in the temperature chilled him. He kept glancing at the luminous dial of his watch and then at the launch site, trying to judge whether they had bedded down for the night. Thankfully, out here men adjusted quickly to the conditions, working when it was light, sleeping when it was dark. There was little else to do except perhaps read a book by the light of a candle, although the generator on one of the trucks, humming continuously, provided this site with electricity.

No further work was being done on the rocket during the hours of darkness. Brockway admired their efficiency. Floodlighting would have been too much of a risk; American satellites tracking across the southern hemisphere might pick up the position of the launch site—he was quite sure that surveillance of these areas would have been increased since the nuclear test.

The last light in the temporary building flicked off at 10:15. Jiggs insisted that they wait another half-hour, and he spent that time examining and cleaning the two rifles. When he was satisfied he handed one to Brockway, then they began to make their way down the side of the ridge, their feet sinking deeply into the soft blown sand. They reached the floor of the corridor and stayed close to the side of the ridge until they came to the first of the parked vehicles. There was a fifty-yard gap between them and the door of the room Sharon was locked in, and after a quick look between them they began to cross the open space.

The arc lamps flicked on when they were precisely halfway across, each one of them transfixing the two men in its beam. It was impossible to see beyond the circle of light; they were helpless, pinned within the beams of the arc lamps like butterflies stuck to a page.

Redston allowed himself a smile and shone the flashlight onto Sharon's face, his arm around her tightly, the other hand holding the automatic pistol. "Over here, Brockway, can you see her?"

One of the arc lamps swung on to them; Sharon was defenseless. She had been used, and they had been trapped neatly and efficiently. Brockway dropped his rifle to the ground.

"Yours, too, old man," Redston said almost conversationally. He held the gun beneath Sharon's chin and Jiggs didn't doubt that he'd use it. Reluctantly he let the rifle slide from his grasp.

Redston gave a signal and two men carrying automatic rifles emerged from the outer ring of darkness; one covered the other as he reached down for their weapons. Redston called out, "Bring them over here." The arc lamps traced their progress until they were facing Redston.

If Sharon was distressed she showed no sign of weakness. "I'm sorry, but there was nothing I could do—they would have killed you if I had tried to warn you."

Redston grinned. "She's a bright lady, Brockway—she was right, too—worth chasing after, wouldn't you say." He glanced at Jiggs. "How's the camel, old man? I wondered what had happened to you."

Jiggs did not reply, but spat neatly onto one of Redston's shoes. "Sorry," he said, "I don't usually miss the ground."

Redston's expression didn't alter, but the gun swung away from Sharon and pointed directly at the old prospector's face. Everything seemed to stop for an instant, just the soft pounding of the generator breaking the silence. "Get on your knees," Redston said. The request was almost friendly, but Jiggs had seen death and the intent to kill many times in the wild and he recognized it instantly here—he could almost smell it.

He sank slowly to his knees, the sand chillingly cold. Redston pushed Sharon toward one of the men armed with the automatic rifle, his eyes never leaving Jiggs. "Now clean that shoe for me. I dislike silly accidents and it would be a pity if this thing went off in your face—it's very messy." Jiggs had seen a pistol like that test-fired once before, and the hole it had made had caused the target to be unusable afterward. He pulled down the sleeve of his jacket and slowly wiped away the spittle, aware all the time of the gun pointing down onto the back of his neck. Redston stepped back. "Good." He glanced at Brockway. "Get down, the same as him." He gestured with the pistol. Then, to one of the men standing just outside the circle of light, watching, "Tie their hands—the girl, too."

The man came forward carrying some thin cords. Obviously prepared, Brockway realized they had probably been spotted from the plane and had just been waiting for them to turn up. He felt the cords bite deeply into his wrists, then he was manhandled to his feet and pushed with Jiggs and Sharon toward the building. Redston opened the door to the room where they had believed Sharon was imprisoned and switched on the temporary light with the cord hanging down from the ceiling. "We have been saving this for you—after tomorrow you won't need it." The room was windowless, containing just a single bed and a chair. Once they were inside Redston slammed the door shut from the outside, bolted it, and left.

Brockway sat down on the side of the bed and looked at the other two. Jiggs seemed unperturbed, but Sharon's composure was beginning to crack. "Sorry," he said, "I'll have to brush up on my James Bond."

The joke fell flat, not so much as a smile. Sharon knelt down in front of him, tears beginning to run down her face. "Oh, Harry," she said, and rested her head on his lap.

It was Jiggs who heard it: a soft thud, then something sliding down the wall outside. He looked at Brockway who was talking quietly to Sharon, reassuring her of Trudie's safety. "Quiet," he said softly. They turned and stared at him. He indicated the door, then moved silently, his back to the wall beside it. He heard a voice, "Mrs. Langbein." Jiggs glanced at the girl.

Sharon crossed the small room and stood beside him. "I think it's Heissler—shall I answer?" she asked. Jiggs nodded once—she'd told them of his visit. "Who is it?" she whispered through the door.

"Bruno Heissler—can you turn off the light, I want to open the door."

"Wait." Their hands were still tied, but by climbing onto the chair, Brockway was able to grasp the string hanging down from the ceiling between his teeth. He gave it a quick tug and the room was plunged into darkness. They heard the bolts being drawn back slowly, then saw a patch of opaque light framing Heissler as he opened the door and slipped inside, closing it quickly behind him.

"No one knows I am here," he said softly. "I have dealt with the guard."

Brockway grabbed his arm. "How?"

Heissler stepped back, freeing himself. "With this—I have a gun."

Brockway couldn't see it in the darkness, but he made no sudden moves. "What do you want, Heissler?"

"I am prepared to release you, but first you must agree to let me come with you—I do not want to be here when they attempt to launch the rocket in the morning."

"Attempt?" Brockway said.

It was quiet in the darkened room for a moment, just the sound of Heissler's strained breathing.

"Yes, that's right; it will not achieve lift-off successfully —I have removed a small component from the firing mechanism that will cause it to malfunction. It will probably explode when it falls back onto the ramp."

"Jesus Christ," Brockway muttered, half to himself,

then realizing the implications. "What about the warhead, will it cause that to explode?"

"No, that will not happen; it's a dummy warhead. But I want no further part in this operation of Redston's; that is why I must come with you, and be allowed to return to Africa."

It was impossible for Brockway to guarantee that, but he was in no mood to argue the finer points. All that mattered was as quick an exit as possible from this site. "Right, you've got it, and what you do once we get out of here is of no concern to me. Just cut these goddamn ropes."

Heissler first freed Jiggs who moved at once to the door and opened it fractionally, checking that there was no movement outside. The body of the guard was slumped against the side of the building. Jiggs dragged him inside and picked up his rifle. Heissler meanwhile had cut Sharon and Brockway free.

Brockway's hands were numb and he shook his arms loosely by his side, trying to restore the circulation. He began to suffer acutely from pins and needles. He heard Sharon gasp as she, too, began to feel the symptoms, but there was no time for sympathy—they had to get out. He crossed to the door beside Jiggs. "Anything?"

"No, it's clear."

Brockway peered out at the line of vehicles parked about fifty yards away.

"We may need one of those."

"You may, but I don't."

Brockway stared at him in the gloom, remembering the camel. "You mean Bess?"

"That's right, we stay together."

Brockway said nothing, there was no point. He had become aware of how deeply attached Jiggs was to his animals.

Heissler joined them. "I have no keys. Redston collected

them all so that the girl could not escape in one of the vehicles—how will you steal it?"

"I had an underprivileged childhood; cars without keys were my specialty. First we have to put the others out of action as quickly as possible. That also applies to the aircraft—" He stopped. "Wait a minute, you flew Kauffmann up here, didn't you?"

"That's right."

"Could you fly us out now in darkness?"

Heissler considered it briefly. "No, it's impossible—the corridor is unmarked, and with the ridges so close it would only need the smallest deviation. . . ." He shrugged his shoulders.

Brockway stared out at the line of trucks. "What if I were able to line up the Land-Rover and light the corridor with the headlights? Would you chance it then?"

Heissler protested. "Perhaps, but why not use the Land-Rover—there would be less risk."

"Because," Brockway said shortly, "whatever we do to those vehicles out there, and we've not got the time to do a lot, Redston will have them serviceable by morning. We cannot get to North Mulga by then, and he would be able to reach us by using the aircraft. If we can take-off successfully we can be in Adelaide."

Heissler could see the sense in that; it was a risk whichever way they attempted to escape, but he was committed now. "I will do my best," he said simply.

"Okay, listen. Once I start that engine on the Land-Rover someone is going to wake up." He thought for a second. "Jiggs, you take the knife and deal with the tires on the single-engine aircraft—you won't have so far to go to get to your animal." He held out his hand to Heissler who gave him the knife. Brockway stared at the shadowy figure. "You'd better give me the gun, too."

Heissler did not reply. The silence lengthened, then

Jiggs slipped the bolt home in the rifle. The sound seemed deafening in the small confined space of the room. Heissler slowly reached out and handed the pistol to him butt first. It felt sticky and Brockway realized it was the blood from the guard's head.

"It is loaded," Heissler said. Brockway wiped the butt of the weapon on his trousers, then turned to Jiggs and made one last attempt to persuade him. "Come with us in the plane." He glanced at his watch. "It'll be light inside an hour and you'll be out in the open. . . ." He left the rest unsaid.

The memory of his last encounter with Redston was still fresh in Jiggs's mind, but he couldn't abandon Bess. He shook his head. "No. I'll go back the way I came."

There was nothing more to be said. Brockway hadn't really expected the old man to join them. He turned to Heissler. "Which way will you attempt to take-off?"

Heissler had already made some calculations. "There is hardly any air movement. What light wind there is seems to be coming toward us from the west, so I shall take-off directly down the corridor from the position the aircraft are parked in now."

"Right, listen carefully. All three of you get to the planes—I'll deal with the vehicles. Heissler, you get the Cherokee as ready as you can for take-off—but do not switch on the engines until you hear me start the Land-Rover, got that?"

Heissler nodded. Brockway turned to Jiggs. "Okay, you deal with the tires on the other plane, then get the hell out, understood?"

Jiggs acknowledged, "Sure, I'll use the phone at North Mulga—call you at ABC."

Brockway smiled. "I'll make sure you get straight through." He turned to Sharon and gripped the top of her arms tightly. "Get to the plane, be inside it once I start that Land-Rover, and make sure the door is open—I'll be moving fast, okay?"

She wanted to hold him tightly for a moment, but she knew this was not the time to start getting emotional— they needed to be sharp and decisive. She clasped his hand between both of hers and raised it to her lips. "The door will be open and you'd better come through it, or I'll be out to get you."

She saw his teeth in the darkness and knew he was smiling. "Is that an invitation or an order?"

"Both," she replied.

Brockway gazed at her silently in the darkness for a moment, then turned away toward the door, opening it slightly. He stared out into the desert night. As far as he could tell there was no movement. He glanced back into the room. "All right, keep low and move fast." He looked toward Jiggs. "Good luck."

Jiggs grasped his hand. "Ready," he said. Brockway nodded.

Jiggs opened the door quickly, making sure it didn't bang against the wall. Brockway ran crouching toward the parked vehicles. Once Heissler and Sharon had left, Jiggs shut the door behind him, then ran swiftly after them toward the aircraft.

Brockway lifted the bonnet of the Land-Rover. The fusebox was inside the fender panel. He removed one fuse from its clip, then set it back in the box sideways, one end touching the other fuse, the other hard against its own clip, thus by-passing the ignition switch. He kept checking the site area, but nothing stirred, just the generator on the back of the van breaking the silence.

Heissler, Sharon, and Jiggs had disappeared into the darkness of the corridor. Jiggs moved quickly between the lines of vehicles, letting the air from the tires; it would not delay them long, but he needed every second he could get. Brockway slid into the driver's seat of the Land-Rover, then glanced at his watch. Three minutes since he had left the room. They'd be in the aircraft, ready by now. He crossed his fingers and pressed the starter button. The engine turned but did not engage properly. He began to sweat—the noise must have woken somebody. He tried again, keeping his finger hard down on the button. It turned over, whining protestingly—it was cold. Brockway saw a door flung open and a figure emerge—it was Redston.

"Come on, you bastard," he screamed, pounding the dashboard with his fist. It fired, roaring into life. He pushed hard down on the accelerator, slamming her into gear. He released the clutch and spurted clear of the line of trucks, spinning the steering wheel, turning sharply left. Clouds of sand billowed up behind him as he headed down the corridor toward the parked aircraft, switching on the headlights for the first time.

He heard a bullet ricochet off the steel bodywork beside him, then he saw the two planes looming up in his headlights and he skidded the Land-Rover to a halt beside the Cherokee. One engine was already blowing great clouds of sand up behind it, the other was just beginning to engage. Brockway leaped from the Land-Rover and ran toward the plane, shielding his eyes from the sand blowing sharply into his face. Sharon was leaning out of the door, and now the plane was slowly trundling forward as the power was forced into the engines. He could see Sharon screaming soundlessly at him, her voice swallowed up by the roar of the aircraft. He was alongside the tail section now, the sand dragging at his feet, the slipstream from the propellers tugging at his clothing. It was nightmarish, as though he were trying to run through cotton wool. Her hand reached out in front of him, their fingers touched, she grabbed at his hand, pulling him toward the open door, screaming at Heissler to wait.

Brockway leaped for the door, his side crashing sickeningly into the frame as he fell half in, half out of the plane. Sharon dragged him inside, then banged the door shut as the speed of the aircraft increased.

Heissler fed all the power into the Cherokee's two engines, trying to get the plane airborne before the last flicker of light from the Land-Rover disappeared. The tail lifted from the floor of the corridor. Twice the wheels left the ground as he tried to lift off before he had enough speed, and twice they landed heavily again. He was flying blind now, just a black void stretching out in front of him, no time to check the airspeed indicator. He pulled back on the stick for the third time and they were flying. The jolting and the bumping ceased. The opaque starlit sky became visible as they rose from between the ridges. Heissler held the stick back, climbing as swiftly as he dared—then set course south and west for Adelaide.

Redston fired the pistol until it was empty at the diffused retreating glow of the Land-Rover's headlights, but it was impossible. The sand thrown up by the wheels and the darkness gave him little or no chance of hitting anything. Then he heard the sound of the aircraft's engine as it roared off down the corridor. He waited, hoping to hear it crash into one of the ridges, but gradually it faded as it gained altitude and headed south. He ran across to the room where they had been imprisoned but it was empty, the guard, still unconscious, lying just inside the door. Men were beginning to pile out of the doors, woken by the shots, but Redston cut them out of his thoughts, concentrating his attention on the escape. He was certain he had seen only one person in the Land-Rover before the sand had obliterated his view; the others must have been waiting in the plane. He remembered Jiggs and began to run toward the high ridge to his left. Jiggs and Brockway had left the camel there before attempting the abortive rescue. Redston had kept them under surveillance from the moment he had spotted them from the aircraft, but had waited until they were in the open before making his move. Jiggs, he felt sure, would not leave the animal there to die of thirst.

Redston climbed the soft yielding sand until he reached the top of the ridge, then moved slowly and carefully until he reached the floor of the adjoining corridor. The camel had been hobbled about half a mile to the west, and running as silently as he could he made his way toward it, pausing from time to time to listen intently, but there was nothing, no sound or movement. He began to near the spot where the camel had been left and he slowed down, staying close to the soft sand at the bottom of the ridge. He moved silently forward. . . .

Jiggs had checked the saddle girth on Bess and given it a tug to tighten it up. The animal snorted angrily at being disturbed, and Jiggs spoke softly to her, trying to calm her down. He picked up the rifle to slot it under the saddlebags and whirled around, raising the rifle, as he heard a voice behind him say softly, "Old man."

He saw the barrel of the pistol blaze once. The bullet hit him with incredible force, smashing him backward into the side of the camel before he fell onto the floor of the corridor.

Bess was alarmed and tried to move away, but the ropes that still hobbled her restricted her movement.

Jiggs was dying. He could see the black sky above him, the stars shifting in and out of focus, then something loomed over him—it was the outline of a man. "The camel," he said hoarsely, "release the camel."

Redston peered down at the old man. "Don't worry,

Jiggs, I'll see to that." The prospector was staring at him, his eyes wide. He knelt beside him and felt the pulse in his neck. It had stopped—he was dead. He began to search through Jiggs's pockets. He was curious; this persistent, bloody old man had endangered them all—he needed to know more about him. He found the leather pouch, the gold fob watch inside. He pulled it out and snapped it open. The sky behind him in the east was beginning to lighten; the watch said 4:58. There was something inscribed on the inside of the casing, but it still wasn't light enough to read it properly. He lit a match and peered closely at it; the light from the tiny flame burned brightly for a moment, and he saw the beginning of the inscription.

For my darling husband
on our wedding day,
May 3rd, 1931

The flame went out and Redston lit another. Underneath he read the two names:

Helen Jiggs—William Redston

He stood transfixed, staring at the surname—Redston. The flame from the match burned down to his fingers, but he could not feel the pain; inside he was numb. The light extinguished, he continued to stare unseeingly at the watch. Vaguely he remembered the shadowy figure of his father, the screaming voice of his mother when they fought—his head under the pillow, trying to shut it out. The watch was still warm in his hand. He held it up to his ear; it was ticking steadily. He remembered something else now. He could see the watch; his father was swinging it in front of him on a chain, the light reflecting from its shiny surface, making it seem to glow. His father had let him hold it—then he'd shown him how the cover snapped open and he'd seen the inscription . . . the same inscription. He'd asked him why his mother's name was different.

Redston closed the watch, clenching it in his hand, and gazed down at the figure lying at his feet. The camel moved uneasily, smelling the blood. He pushed the gun in his waistband and knelt down beside the animal, pulling the prospector's shovel from the saddle bag, and then releasing the hobbles from around its feet. The camel pulled itself stiffly to its feet, but did not move away. He slapped the side of the animal with the leather hobble, urging it to go. It moved off a few paces, then stopped, staring back toward the old man lying in the sand, as if it were waiting for him. Redston grew impatient. He suddenly felt an unreasoning anger and ran toward it yelling, threatening it with the leather strap. The animal turned haughtily and began to move away at a steady trot. Redston stopped, breathing heavily, gazing after it—watching it until it was out of sight. Then he turned and made his way back to the body. The light from the rising sun was brighter now, suffusing the tops of the ridges in a fiery glow, but it was still cold in the gully. He pushed the watch into his pocket and stood gazing down at the old man. His eyes were still open, staring. He knelt beside him and closed them with his hand. He looked at his face. It was suntanned and deeply lined—a white stubble of beard covering the chin and mouth. He stared at him, hoping to see some trace of a family connection, but he could distinguish nothing. He picked up the hat that had fallen from his head and covered his face, protecting it from the bush flies. Then, using the shovel, he slowly began to dig a grave for his father.

"Can we launch without Heissler?"

Vaas automatically stood up straight, responding to the authority explicit in the demand.

"Yes, there is no reason to delay. His team have launched many similar rockets—this one is only different in that it carries a warhead. All the problems relating to that have already been ironed out. We were ready to launch late yesterday."

Redston paced up and down the control room, evaluating the position. Vaas watched him apprehensively; Heissler's defection had frightened him. Thank God they still had the other plane. He remembered something. "The radio, the radio in the plane, they will warn the authorities."

Redston continued to pace the room. "Not without the microphone. I removed it yesterday."

That was not the problem, but Brockway would reach Adelaide in approximately three hours. It was already getting light outside and Redston had no intention of abandoning the launch; it was still possible.

Brockway could contact nobody until he touched down. If they launched as planned in an hour's time, then they would have the result of the nuclear warhead's detonation over the Southern Ocean soon after. Once that information was obtained then the mission here in Australia would be complete. He and Vaas could fly north to his emergency rendezvous on the deserted coastline of the Gulf of Carpentaria. The launch crew could travel eastward and might escape the net the authorities would fling around this area—he would reassure them of that—but what happened here once he and Vaas had departed did not concern him. His operations in this part of the world were almost over. He turned to Vaas. "Call the men in, I will explain the position—we launch in an hour as planned."

Vaas almost clicked his heels.

28. Ground Control, Adelaide

Adelaide was not an international airport. Nevertheless, it was usually a very busy one, a flight connection point for all the Australian cities, as well as any flights to the interior for the southern part of the continent. However, at first light on the last Sunday before Christmas, it was fairly inactive, and the ground control approach officer saw the light aircraft appear on his radar screen at once. He could get no response on his radio, but the corridors were clear and he took the customary precautions. It was not the first time that radio contact had been lost with private aircraft, and this one was approaching steadily from the seaward end of the runway.

Heissler controlled the aircraft easily—conditions were perfect. He glanced briefly at Brockway who was sitting behind him with Sharon. "When we land, there will be a lot of questions. I don't intend to be there, Brockway." He waited to let that sink in; there was no reaction. "I've only seen the airport once—it seemed fairly relaxed. I'm going to try to get from the plane into the terminal without being seen."

Brockway glanced at Sharon; he owed Heissler something—she nodded imperceptibly. "Okay, if you make it we'll say nothing—but after that you're on your own. When the police get to me they'll want to know where you are—I can't protect you then."

Heissler glanced at his airspeed indicator, throttled back slightly, and pushed the nose of the aircraft down. The coastline was dead ahead, and the runway clear beyond it.

"That's all I need," he said. . . .

29. The Launch Site

The countdown had reached zero minus thirty seconds and once again the German intonation reverberated oddly in Redston's mind. The small control room at the end of the building facing the launch site was already uncomfortably hot in the early morning sun, and Redston fought to control his childhood memories and feelings of claustrophobia; he was sweating and it was stupid.

The rocket stood two hundred yards away, poised on the hydraulic ramps of the trailer, the desert sun reflecting brightly from the white surface. The condensation from the liquid hydrogen inside the fuel tanks was sliding gently down the curved sides of the narrow rocket. The countdown had reached ten. The launch operator sat tense in front of the control deck, his white overalls stained with sweat. The control room almost crackled with tension. It mattered not that these experienced men had handled more than a dozen similar operations in Africa; each launch presented new problems, new hazards. This was a different location, a mobile launch pad, and sitting on top of that rocket for the first time, a nuclear warhead.

Fünf, vier, drei, zwei, eins . . . the operator pressed the fire button. He was immediately aware that there was a malfunction—the rocket did not fire. The clamps had automatically been released, and slowly the rocket was beginning to topple sideways to the desert floor. His hand swept across the panel to where the button that would control the malfunction was normally placed; it would prevent the explosion of the fuels. But this was not a normal condition. The mobile launch panel was less sophisticated than those on the SSS launch pad in Africa; under stress, the operator was reacting automatically. In that split-second, as his finger was about to descend, Vaas, who was standing behind him screamed, *"Nein!"* The operator's hand jerked spasmodically; his finger touched the button that armed the warhead. The rocket struck the surface of the corridor, splitting asunder. There was a fractional pause, a second that seemed to last forever, then it exploded in a mass of red and orange flame as the liquid fuels ignited.

They ducked as the blast caved in the windows. A hot rush of air swept through the temporary structure, forcing the doors from their hinges. The sound of the explosion rolled slowly away, echoing down the corridors and across the desert. Vaas stood up and stared at the launch operator who was still sitting frozen in front of the control panel, blood from a cut on his forehead running unnoticed down his face. Vaas stretched out a shaky hand and pulled the man around. "Did you arm the weapon?"

Redston suddenly felt cold, the sweat icy on his back. The operator didn't answer, his eyes still fixed on the button his finger had touched. Vaas grabbed the young man and shook him hysterically. *"Did you press the button?!"*

Redston moved slowly toward the control panel, scanning the various dials. The finger of the one indicating the radiation level was reading 730 rads.

It was massive, lethal. The warhead was decomposing two hundred yards away. The distance at this range was immaterial; he was a dead man.

30. ABC, Collinswood, Adelaide

Brockway was exhausted; all day he had been under interrogation, not just by the police, but by members of the security forces. They had gone over everything in the minutest detail—the abduction of the children, the hospital at Tanunda and its connection with Redston and Heissler through Kauffmann. He'd told them of Heissler's break from them at the airport, but as far as he knew, he still hadn't been found.

Sharon, too, had been put through the wringer, providing corroboration where she could; they had been interviewed separately and together. Finally Sharon had been allowed to leave to attend to Trudie. They were both now at Brockway's house in Norwood.

It was dark outside and Brockway stood by the window of his office at ABC. They had all gone now except Detective Sergeant Phil Clayton, who was getting some sandwiches and coffee from the canteen. Brockway had suddenly realized how hungry he was. He hadn't had a proper meal since before he had left on Friday for North Mulga—was that only two days ago? The phone rang shrilly, making him jump. He walked over to the desk and picked it up. "Hello?"

There was silence for a moment, then, "Brockway, I want to see you." The voice was husky, strained, but undoubtedly Redston's.

Brockway sat down; his legs felt weak. He tried to keep the edge of nervousness out of his voice. "What for, so that you can deal with me the way you did Spengler?" The police had revealed his death during the interrogation.

"No, not for that." Redston began to cough uncontrollably and Brockway winced; it sounded vile, as if he were vomiting. There was a moment of silence. Brockway was alarmed.

"Redston, hello, are you all right?" He heard him breathing heavily.

"I have to talk to you at once. I haven't got a lot of time . . . are you listening, Brockway?"

"Yes, I'm here."

"The rocket didn't take off, it blew up, igniting the high explosive charge in the warhead. Do you know what that does, Brockway?" Redston was panting, finding it hard to breathe, and Brockway was suddenly, frighteningly aware of the possibilities.

"A nuclear explosion?"

"No, the bomb was not detonated, but it was armed and the nuclear warhead began to decompose."

Brockway could hear him straining for breath. "Radiation?"

Redston did not reply for a moment and the word seemed to vibrate in the silence. "That's right, I'm finished, Brockway. I have got a few hours left, but not long." He stopped, his breathing laborious, as though he were trying desperately to prevent another paroxysm of coughing. "I have to see you, Brockway—I want you to know what this was all about. The government will try a cover-up, but you at least, will know the truth."

Brockway was tempted to believe him. No one could fake that sickness, and he was flattered—the only one to know! Jesus, what a story. But Redston was a ruthless killer; he'd seen him in action, and he couldn't risk walking into another trap like the one at Sharon's house.

Redston spoke again. It was as if he had been reading his thoughts. "Listen, I know there's no reason for you to trust me, but there's something else." He paused, his breathing wracked, trying to control it. "It's about the old man."

Brockway hadn't heard from him. "You mean Jiggs?"

Redston grimaced painfully. "That wasn't his real name, Brockway—there's a lot you don't know. Will you come?"

Brockway was curious. What the hell did he mean—was Jiggs mixed up in this somehow? Maybe the story he'd told wasn't entirely true. What if the government was involved? Jesus Christ, he'd have to risk it; there was no alternative. He couldn't tell the police. If there was a cover-up he'd never get to know the truth. He steeled himself. "Where are you?"

"Don't be stupid, Brockway. I'll meet you outside the railway station on North Terrace. You stand in the open by the entrance where I can see you. I'll contact you . . . and Brockway?"

"Yes."

"If I see anyone else, you'll never get to know what happened, and no one will know the truth."

Brockway smiled to himself. Redston knew how to motivate him. "I'll be alone, don't worry."

"I'm not worrying, Brockway. . . ." He began to cough horribly again.

Brockway waited until the convulsion began to abate. "Is there anything I can bring you?"

"No." The word snapped out under stress. "It's too late for that—but there is one thing."

"What?"

"Bring a tape recorder—I want this on record, otherwise they'll never believe you. How long will you be?"

Brockway glanced at his watch. "I'll be there in twenty minutes."

The line clicked and went dead.

The main entrance to the railway station stood on a corner. It was an old Victorian building with a high arch over the entrance and a newspaper stand just inside, closed now, as was almost everything else in Adelaide late on a Sunday. The line of taxis stood forlornly on North Terrace, facing the Grosvenor Hotel, the Terrace mostly empty of traffic, just the occasional car waiting impatiently at traffic lights.

Brockway positioned himself to one side of the entrance, placing the tape recorder conspicuously on the pavement beside him. He did not have to wait long. Opposite was a narrow, badly lit street connecting Hindley Street and North Terrace. The car's headlights blinked on and off twice. Brockway took a deep breath, picked up the tape deck, and stepped toward the curb. He knew he was taking a chance; there was little reason to trust Redston, but that wracked and tortured coughing could not be faked, and if he had received a fatal dose of radiation, then it was understandable that this vague and menacing figure, whose background was so obscure, should want to get the record straight. Who better to act as an intermediary after death than a television reporter?

It made sense to a man like Brockway, who could not

conceive of anyone wanting to die in a corner, unknown, unmarked, his disappearance forever a question mark.

He looked right, then left, and crossed the road, stopping beside the car that remained silent, deep in shadow. He could just discern the figure of Redston sitting in the front passenger seat. The side window was wound down. The voice seemed weaker, hoarse.

"Get inside, Brockway, I want you to drive."

He moved to cross in front of the car, but as he did so the headlights of a passing vehicle flicked across Redston's face. Brockway stopped, horrified.

It was white, drained of life, his lips stained with the blood of his vomit, in his hand a dark, sodden towel. The headlights disappeared and Brockway saw the barrel of a pistol poke from the window, trained on his stomach. "I can still use this—now get inside!"

He did as he was told, placing the tape recorder on the back seat. The air inside the car was fetid, a putrid smell of sewer and sickness that revolted him. He sat down beside Redston, swallowing down the bile that rose in his own throat. Redston tapped him on the shoulder with the gun.

"You'd better turn that recorder on—I don't know how long I'll be able to talk."

Brockway affixed the tiny microphone to Redston's lapel, poking the battery into his pocket. Then he switched on the recorder. "Okay," he said, "it's all set."

"Drive the car—take me somewhere quiet where we can talk."

Brockway thought for a moment. "There's an old house in front of the studio. It's half demolished—there'll be no one there at this time."

"Sure, that'll do."

Brockway started the car and began to drive slowly

toward Collinswood. Redston talked quietly, explaining how he had been picked up by the Chinese in Korea, constantly having to stop as his body was convulsed by paroxysms of wretched bloody coughing. Slowly, painfully, it emerged. "I didn't mind working for them, at least the Chinese gave me a chance—it didn't seem to matter where I was from as long as I could do the job. Besides, I felt no allegiance to England—it's done nothing for me."

The last words were spat out and Brockway could feel the bitterness behind them. He could understand that; the States had done nothing for him either, but he sensed that there was more. Redston hadn't given him the truth—not yet. "Bullshit—you're not trying to tell me that you defected to the Chinese because England is a class-ridden society. I don't buy that."

Redston stared at him, his skin almost transparent, the veins standing out clearly. There wasn't much time. "No, it's not the real reason why I packed it in in Korea." He paused, staring at the road ahead. How could he explain to this American his reasons? He wasn't even sure of them himself, it was all mixed up—so many things. But gradually, as he'd gotten older, he had begun to understand himself a little better. Patterns of behavior began to emerge—familiar, repeated. He had resisted introspection, contemptuous of homespun psychology. Nevertheless, it was clear, even to him, that his fears, his isolation, began in that air raid shelter—perhaps even before.

His grandfather had died soon after, his bitterness and grief at the way Billy and his mother had been forced into the communal shelter scarcely concealed from the boy. He'd blamed himself for letting them go, but Billy didn't. For him it was clear-cut, blazingly obvious. If they'd been allowed to stay in their makeshift shelter beneath the stairs of their house, if that stupid, ignorant army officer hadn't insisted on forcing them out, then they would not have been buried beneath the mountain of concrete. His mother would still be alive.

He had tried desperately to make his grandfather see that, nursing him through the bitter, freezing winter, but the old man didn't seem to want to live, and it saddened Billy to see the way he allowed his life to slip away from him, unresisting, deaf to the boy's pleas—eager to join his mother. At his grave Billy had stood almost alone—glad of it, not wanting to be comforted, a deep inanimate sense of bitterness consuming him. As yet unfocused, almost unrecognized, but filling him with rage. . . . It had exploded on a remote, rocky hillside in Korea, directed at what he hated most. But how could he make Brockway understand that? He'd only just begun to understand it himself. It was too close, too personal. He didn't want him to know, so he'd give him something he could understand —fear. His own fear. Fear of dying, now soon to be realized. Not crushed between the concrete slabs, but falling to pieces inside, bit by bit. He wiped away the blood trickling from the side of his mouth, not looking at the American.

"The truth is, I packed it in because I was frightened, because I was cold. Christ, that place was freezing. I had no choice, Brockway. If I hadn't cooperated they'd have tortured me. Besides, by cooperating I got what I wanted —a new set-up, some responsibility. They were good to me, trained me. Made me feel useful, a part of something. My job was to help them acquire technical know-how. That's all they lack, Brockway, they've got everything else, the people, the will. That's what I was doing in Barossa. Vaas and Heissler could have given them the breakthrough they needed, but they'll do it anyway eventually." He broke down again, clutching the towel to his mouth. Brockway waited until he stopped.

"What about Jiggs? What did you mean when you said that wasn't his name?"

Redston put the towel down beside him and reached into his pocket, pulling out the leather pouch. Brockway recognized it—he'd seen Jiggs go through the ritual of looking at the watch several times. Redston offered it to him. "Look inside," he said.

"I don't have to. I know it's the old man's watch. What happened?" He saw the flashing red lights of the railroad crossing ahead and stopped the car by the barrier, waiting for the train to cross.

"After you took off in the plane I remembered where he had left his camel. I knew he wouldn't leave without that. I got there as quickly as I could—he was still there."

Brockway thought he knew the rest. "You killed him."

Redston didn't answer for a moment. "He was carrying a rifle—he heard me and turned—it was him or me. But you're right—I would have killed him anyway."

The train rumbled slowly by in front of them, the lights from behind the steamed-up windows flickering across Redston's drained white face, his lips darkened by blood.

Brockway thought about it. "Why? Because he knew something?"

Redston glanced at him briefly. "No, he knew no more than you did."

"Then why?"

Redston stared straight ahead, his face expressionless. "He'd got in my way, that's why." He waited, then, "Look inside the watch, Brockway. There's a torch in the glove compartment."

He fished out the flashlight, then snapped open the cover and read what it said inside. At first it didn't register. "All right, so it's a wedding present from his wife, so what?"

"The names, Brockway—look at the names."

Brockway sat silent, unmoving, trying to absorb the implications. The vibrations from the train had ceased, and the gates in front of him slowly swung open. Automatically he started the car and resumed their journey. "I don't understand it, it says his name was Redston—his wife's maiden name was Jiggs!" He was stunned, incredulous. Redston said nothing, his eyes fixed stonily on the road ahead. Brockway glanced at him, horrified. "Were you related in some way?"

"He was my father." Some blood trickled down from the corner of his mouth and he wiped it with the towel. "I didn't know that until I found the watch." His voice was toneless, unemotional. "He'd left us when I was a kid. He must have come out here before the war started. Begun working as a prospector. I suppose he couldn't face it—being married; so he left—lived alone, out in the bush."

Brockway was stunned; but it all fitted. Everything that Jiggs had said on that last night in the bush, before they reached the launch site. The silence that followed was broken only by the sound of the car tires on the concrete road. Neither of them spoke; there was nothing more to say, each of them alone with his thoughts.

They were nearing the studio entrance now. Brockway slowed down and crossed the two-lane road into the main entrance. Tregenna House, its roof removed, the walls etched sharply by the moonlight, still stood formidably in front of the studio buildings. He was able to drive the car off the graveled path, into the shell of the building itself. He stopped the car in the place where the trucks stood when they were being loaded with rubble from the half-demolished building.

Redston didn't move. He continued to sit stolidly, locked within his thoughts.

Brockway switched off the ignition and turned slightly toward him. "How did you get out?"

"Took the other plane—landed at Barossa, then drove here." It was incredible; he looked grotesque, emaciated, his eyes bloodshot, swollen as the corpuscles in his body began to disintegrate—yet somehow he had piloted the aircraft to Barossa and driven to Adelaide. Redston shivered. "Christ, it's cold, turn the engine on. Stupid bloody country—freeze all night, burn all day."

Brockway switched on the ignition and boosted the heater. Redston was slumped in his seat, his arms clutched across his body.

"Why don't you let me take you to a hospital—there might be something they could do."

Redston laughed, then clapped the towel to his mouth before he could degenerate into another bout of coughing. "It's useless—I got over seven hundred rads; some of the others are probably dead already." He turned and stared distractedly at Brockway. "But I had to see you first."

The reporter shifted uncomfortably. "Is there anyone you want me to contact, a relative?"

Redston actually smiled, his teeth red, bloodstained. "No, there's no one, and you won't be telling anyone anything."

It was at that moment Brockway realized how easily he had been trapped by his own eagerness, believing that Redston needed him to tell the world through the media. Redston didn't need anyone anymore—he could tell them himself.

Redston tapped the tiny microphone on his lapel. "This thing will do all the talking, Brockway, and you will not survive me. But for you"—he paused—"and my father. . . ." He stopped, swallowing hard, was it emotion or blood? At that moment Brockway really didn't care. The gun pointed steadily at his stomach and he would have traded the story—anything—not to be sitting where he was right now.

Redston leaned back in the seat; the moonlight bathed his face starkly white, turning the blood on his lips to black. "You didn't really think I'd let you get away, Brockway."

"I don't know—I was curious."

"That's what I counted on." He grimaced with pain and clutched at his stomach, but the gun didn't quiver. Brockway sat still. If he had blinked at that moment, Redston would have killed him.

The pain seemed to subside; his face was bathed in perspiration, his eyes bulbous, glittering. He licked his lips. "Now I'm going to get out, Brockway. If you want to try anything, feel free—you'll just die quicker."

He reached around with his free hand and opened the door, then slid himself slowly backward off the seat. His feet were now outside the car and as he straightened up, the door, as always, began to slam shut. For a fraction of a second before Redston was fully upright, the door masked the muzzle of the gun. Brockway shoved in the gear, simultaneously pushing his foot hard down on the accelerator. The car shot forward as the gun fired three times in rapid succession, the bullets fragmenting the windshield in front of him. He was driving blind; the windshield caved in on him, small pieces of glass impregnating his face. He had a vague impression of a huge dark shadow looming up in front of him, then the car slammed into the half-demolished wall and came to a shuddering stop. He was flung forward over the wheel, the strength in his arms partially cushioning the blow, then an agonizing pain in his chest as a rib cracked. He bounced back heavily and lay slumped across the front seat. He heard Redston's footsteps crunching on the gravel as he came toward him; there was nothing he could do—the slightest movement wracked him with pain.

He stared up through the broken edges of the windshield. The moon seemed to be moving, bathing him with its light. Something was wrong, and suddenly in that brief moment of comprehension he realized it was the wall that was moving, toppling down toward him, finally shaken from its foundations by the impact of the car.

Redston looked up at the white light of the moon. The great towering mass of the wall seemed suspended, frozen between earth and sky. He heard his mother scream, "Billy, Billy," her arms outstretched toward him, trying to reach him before the roof of the shelter crushed her life away.

Brockway lay between the seats, trying to protect himself from the collapsing structure. Redston had the gun leveled at him; all he had to do was pull the trigger, but his eyes were gazing out past him, curious, inquisitive, but not frightened, then he was engulfed, pulverized by the masonry of the old house as it fell apart, shaking the earth in an avalanche of bricks and mortar. The rumble slowly faded away, the ground ceased to shake.

Detective Sergeant Phil Clayton emerged from the main building with one or two others who were still staffing the station. He stood gazing at the billowing cloud of dust. Tregenna House had disappeared. The dust slowly settled, then the moonlight began to filter through, and the top of Brockway's crushed car gradually became visible.

He felt no pain, both his legs were numb from the knees down, he didn't know if that was because they were crushed, or simply lacking circulation. The back of his legs were pressed hard against the center span of the vehicle. The roof of the car was no more than three inches from his face, crushed and buckled like silver foil wrapped around a Christmas turkey, only this time he was the meat.

He didn't know how long he had been there. He

couldn't move his arm to look at his watch. Probably about an hour, though it seemed much longer. They had gotten an air hose down to him and were delicately clearing the rubble from one side of the car so that the fire brigade could cut him out. They could not use oxyacetylene torches on the roof—it was too close to his face.

A trace of light from the powerful arc lamps filtered through to him, which made the incarceration more bearable. The darkness had terrified him, but now there was a new fear—he could smell the fumes from the ruptured gas tank. One spark and he would fry. He'd screamed a warning to them and they were aware of the danger. Now they would have to use metal cutters—the risk of fire was too great.

He tried to think of the future. He wondered if Sharon was up there. He hoped she would not attempt to come near him; he didn't think he could bear it. He began to sing an old Dean Martin hit to himself, "Money burns a hole in my pocket. . . ." He stopped. Christ, not burn! He started again, "Every street's a boulevard in old New York . . ."

Some of the heavy studio lighting had been wheeled outside to supplement the arc lamps of the rescue squad. A human chain of men passed each piece of carefully removed masonry from one to the other until it had cleared the site of the car. Brockway had been lucky. Each wall had fallen in on itself like a house of cards, but only one had engulfed the car, and enough of it had remained visible for Clayton to discover Brockway's presence. The detective was standing now with Sharon and George Greenfield. A fireman emerged from the frenzy of the rescue operation to inform Clayton why they had to use the cutters. He thanked him and turned to the others. Sharon's face was strained, anxious.

"What is it?" she asked.

"They can't use the torches—there's too much petrol, but they reckon they'll have him out soon with the cutters."

Sharon did not reply. She moved back again to the edge of the rubble, her eyes focused on the fireman near the center of the activity who was holding the air hose. Faintly above the din she could hear the pump pounding, sending the air through to Brockway. While that continued she knew he must still be alive. She didn't think about injuries—just let him be alive!

Mike and Roy had set up the camera as close as they could to the buried car and were shooting everything. It looked like a London bomb site from World War II. The huge mound of rubble, the rescue squad, working as fast as they dared, passing each piece of wreckage from one to the other. The fire engines, the police. Only the outside broadcast camera crews from the rival television stations seemed out of place. The presence of the television media gave this scene so reminiscent of the Blitz a strange, bizarre quality.

Brockway heard the man's voice. It was so close, if he had been able to move an arm he could have touched him. "We're going to start cutting now, you'll be out soon, sport, no trouble."

Brockway grimaced; he was grateful for the Australian's confidence. "Good—don't take too long—someone's cooking dinner for me." He heard the metal shriek as the cutters were applied. The car lurched as some weight was removed. The fumes from the gasoline grew stronger.

"You all right?" the confident voice asked.

"Yeah, I'm fine, just keep cutting—I never did like this make very much."

A chink of light appeared somewhere down by his feet. He heard the voice again.

"We can see your legs now, won't be long."

Brockway stared up at the crushed metal three inches from his nose, frightened to ask the question, but needing to know. "Are they all right, my legs I mean." He waited. "Sure, they're fine. Your trousers are a bit ripped but no one's looking."

Brockway shook his head in amazement—it was about all he could move. "I'm glad you came, mind telling me what your name is?" He heard him laugh.

"What for—you gonna put me on television, Mr. Brockway?"

"You get me out of here, I might."

"It's Arthur Jackson—we'll have you out in a jiffy."

The light was getting stronger. Brockway raised his head as much as he could. He saw the tip of the metal cutter slice through the metal near his chest, then it was ripped aside and he could see faces. He heard Arthur say, "We're gonna pull you out now."

Then hands were grabbing him, pulling him slowly downward and then lifting him up. The pain in his chest flared again, but he didn't cry out—all that mattered was getting him out, he did not want them to stop. His head inched down toward the edge of the hole in the roof— then it was clear and he was lifted tenderly out by strong yet gentle hands. He heard someone cheer; it was picked up and turned into a wave of sound as the tension in the spectators turned to relief. The arc lights were dazzling; he felt no pain anymore. He was carried carefully by the firemen down the hillside of rubble. He saw an arm waving from behind a camera—it was Mike—and then Roy appeared peering at him anxiously. "Hello, boss—you all right?"

Brockway gripped his hand. "Yeah, I'm all right, don't worry." He pulled him close. "Listen, in the car—on the back seat—is a tape recorder—get it—don't let anyone else hear it till I'm there, okay?"

Roy looked bewildered. "In the car?"

"That's right, Roy—in the bloody car—now get it!"

Roy nodded emphatically. "Sure, boss, don't worry. I'll see to it." He disappeared.

The firemen lowered him onto a stretcher and carried him toward the waiting ambulance. He saw Phil Clayton and George Greenfield hovering, looking anxious. He waved. "Don't worry George, I'm not ill, just some car trouble—set up a meeting for tomorrow." Then he was inside the gloom of the ambulance, the doors banged shut, the sea of faces disappeared. He lay back down on the stretcher and closed his eyes. *Thank God*, he thought, *I made it*. He felt someone grasp his hand. He opened his eyes. It was Sharon.

"Hello, Harry," she said. "Didn't think you were going to get away, did you?"

He smiled and held her close.

The ambulance sirened its way into the sleepy, Sunday, Adelaide night.